The

PRIESTS
NUNS AND PENTECOSTALS
STORIES OF PREACHERS AND PREACHING

The Exile Book of
PRIESTS, PASTORS, NUNS AND PENTECOSTALS
STORIES OF PREACHERS AND PREACHING

edited by
Joe Fiorito

Exile Editions

Ꙫ

Publishers of singular
Fiction, Poetry, Translation, Nonfiction and Drama

2010

Library and Archives Canada Cataloguing in Publication

The Exile book of priests, pastors, nuns and Pentecostals : stories of preachers and preaching / edited by Joe Fiorito.

ISBN 978-1-55096-146-1

1. Short stories, Canadian (English). 2. Clergy--Fiction.
I. Fiorito, Joe, 1948- II. Title: Priests, pastors, nuns and Pentecostals : stories of preachers and preaching.

PS8323.C59P75 2010   C813'.0108921248892   C2010-907142-5

Design and Composition by Active Design Haus
Typeset in Garamond and Gill Sans at the Moons of Jupiter Studios
Cover painting by Norval Morriseau; used by permission of the estate
Printed in Canada by Imprimerie Gauvin

The publisher would like to acknowledge the financial assistance of the Canada Council for the Arts and the Ontario Arts Council, which is an agency of the Government of Ontario.

 Conseil des Arts du Canada   Canada Council for the Arts

 ONTARIO ARTS COUNCIL
CONSEIL DES ARTS DE L'ONTARIO

Published by Exile Editions Ltd.
144483 Southgate Road 14 – GD
Holstein, Ontario, N0G 2A0
info@exileeditions.com   www.ExileEditions.com

Canadian Sales Distribution:
McArthur & Company
c/o Harper Collins
1995 Markham Road
Toronto, ON M1B 5M8
toll free: 1 800 387 0117

U.S. Sales Distribution:
Independent Publishers Group
814 North Franklin Street
Chicago, IL 60610
www.ipgbook.com
toll free: 1 800 888 4741

CONTENTS

INTRODUCTION

There were three priests when I was a boy.
The first delivered hellfire and damnation in an Irish accent.
The second was a jolly Italian friar. The third was a timid
Oblate.

The hellfire priest drank hard. I used to marvel, during early
morning mass, at the way his Adam's apple bobbed when he
threw back his head to drain the chalice; he was, at 7:00 a.m.,
eager for the taste of precious blood.

Drink also made him belligerent. I remember his most
famous sermon, when he glared and growled from the pulpit:
"The people of this parish aren't giving enough money. I
don't want to mention any names, but it's you Italians out
there." Some of us Italians stood up and walked out.

My father's dislike for priests was cultural, as was his support
for the institution of the church; a contradiction, perhaps.

He had been in the habit of tossing whatever he could in the
collection plate, a sacrifice, since we were always broke; such
sacrifice ended the day my father saw the old priest buying
two bottles of Johnny Walker Red on a cold day in winter
when all my father could afford was a bottle of cheap port to
warm his bones.

Jesus wept.

From then on, all was optional.

Worship was not always easy. The whiskey priest used to summon us to church once a year to bless our throats, a ritual I have not encountered elsewhere but in our parish.

We ate fish on Fridays then. St. Blaise was an Armenian martyr who saved a boy from choking on a fishbone. And so, on the feast day of the patron saint of the eaters of fish, the whisky priest would beckon us to the altar railing and press a yoke of candles against our throats, whispering a prayer in hope that we would not choke in the coming year.

The smell of tobacco on the old priest's fingers made me gag, and it put me off fish for the rest of my life.

As for the jolly friar, he had been sent to us from Rome so that he could hear confessions in Italian. All the children loved him because of his sunny smile, and because the only sentence he could manage in English was, "Jesus loved the little children."

The little children were too young to understand why the padre was abruptly sent packing back to Italy. The word on the street was that, as penance, the friar had turned some of the old women of the parish into receptacles, not of the Lord's blessing, but of the sins of his fatherly flesh.

My last priest, the timid Oblate, had a hearty laugh which he used whenever he was nervous; other people made him nervous. I guess no one at the seminary told him that the church, in those days, was full of other people. He would have been better off in a cloistered order.

I mention him because I had a crisis of faith when I was 16 years old. I had come to doubt the power of confession. I turned to him for a private word after confession, on a Saturday afternoon. The timid priest laughed and changed the subject; rather than talk about the mystery and the miracle of absolution, he asked who I thought was going to win the Stanley Cup that year. The Habs won, and I did not lose my faith. I tossed it aside, and I never paid much attention to priests after that.

Do not think I am neglecting the nuns. I love the nuns. The Sisters of St. Joseph taught me to type, without which skill I would not have been able to earn a living. Thank you, Sister Ernestine.

Having been raised Catholic, and having been educated by priests and nuns, I was taught that the clergy were among us, but they had been set apart from us, in order that they might be free from the petty concerns of the world.

Celibacy was viewed – by the church, at least – as both a gift and a discipline which conferred moral authority upon priests; and, of course, no nun need fear any man, not if she was the bride of Christ.

If only it were that easy.

We are not meant to live apart. And power corrupts, even if – or perhaps especially when – it is cloaked in alb and chasuble, or comes hurtling down the corridor with a rattle of beads. The strong find a way to prey upon the weak, and the rotten will always infect the meek. And so we have been read-ing about the clergy for a very long time in the press.

You know from the newspapers, and you will be reminded in the pages that follow, that the seven lovely deadlies – avarice, sloth, lust, gluttony, envy, pride and wrath – do not respect the cloth.

But let's be fair and clear.

Those of us who did not seek holy orders have also thirsted for moral guidance, and we have often swallowed such instruction with our eyes closed, and some of us have twisted ourselves into sad or angry knots in pursuit of perfection, if not purity. Those stories are here, as well.

Mea culpa, kiddo.

I knew a man who, much like Willie Heaps in Hugh Garner's marvelous story, was driven to perform the most brutal act of self-harm, not with a knife but with the shard of a broken bottle. I flinch to think of it.

Oh, for the love of...

There have been famous pastors, pentecostals, and priests in lit-erature: I think of Greene's Crompton; Hawthorne's the Rev-erend Mr. Dimmesdale; Chesterton's Brown; Plath's Shawn; Barry's Gaunt; Steinbeck's campfire preacher, Casy; a few oth-ers, here and there. The shock is that they are human. The fact is, they are also rare. You might, therefore, consider this collec-tion a kind of penance.

If anyone you know wonders if there was ever a time when the clergy were of daily value, let them read "A Sick Call." Just as, if anyone you know wonders about the possibility of perfection in the short story, send them there as well.

These yearners and seekers in such a story keep uneasy company on the page with a delightful congregation of hairy thunderers, revivalists, seekers of redemption, wearers of hair shirts, tent preachers and those who speak in tongues, the kind of folks, in other words, who think the movie "Elmer Gantry" was a documentary; which, brothers and sisters and saints and sinners, it surely was.

A confession: I wanted to be a priest for a brief time when I was 12 years old; what Catholic boy does not, at one time or another, want a pulpit? What religiously wrought up boy or girl has not looked at least once for a little blue smoke on the floor. A little holy rolling. If you know any such young person, give them this book, and let them make an informed choice about holy orders.

Joe Fiorito
September 2010

MARY FANCES COADY

PRACTICE OF PERFECTION

"'There lived a woman named Bona who was as good as her name suggested. She suffered a most severe infirmity in her breasts, which were so eaten away by cancer and so full of worms that it would have been an insufferable torment for any other person. Bona, however, suffered it with patience and thanksgiving.'"

Sister Lucy paused, straightened and pressed the fingertips of her left hand along her left temple, shifting the starched white band that stretched across her forehead. She then lowered her head, continuing to read aloud.

"'St. Dominic loved her much because of her suffering and her advanced virtue. One day, having confessed and communicated her, he asked to see her terrible wound. When Bona uncovered herself and the saint saw the putrid mass of the cancer swarming with worms, he was moved to compassion and begged her to give him one of the worms as a relic.'"

A noise sounding like a stifled gasp broke in at Sister Lucy's immediate left. From the corner of her eye she saw that the white veil of the novice sitting next to her was shaking. The novice, Sister Camillus, held a small piece of white linen in one hand and a needle attached to a string of brilliant red embroidery thread in the other. Her body was hunched over the needlework as if in a state of spasm. Sister Lucy again pressed her fingers against her forehead, then shifted the large book against the edge of the table and resumed reading.

"'Bona told him she would not allow him to take a worm from her breast unless he promised to return it; for she had come to such a pitch of joy in seeing herself thus devoured alive that whenever one of the worms fell to the ground, she picked it up and restored it to its place. So on his word of honour she gave St. Dominic a worm that was well grown and had a black head.'"

Sister Camillus had by now lowered her needlework to her lap. Her head was bent into her chest, and her whole body was so convulsed with laughter that Sister Lucy could hear the rattle of the rosary beads hanging from the belt at her waist. Sister Lucy looked down the length of the plain brown table. On either side, facing each other, their backs erect and their white-veiled heads bent over their needlework, sat the eleven other novices, and behind them, the four recently arrived postulants. All seemed composed and serene.

Sister Lucy continued: *"Immediately the worm turned into a most beautiful pearl. As St. Dominic was handing it back to the woman, it became a worm again, and she put it in her breasts, where it had been bred."*

Sister Camillus's suppressed laughter now began to sound like the faint cries of a wild beast. Sister Lucy looked up at Mother Alphonsine, the novice mistress, who sat at the head of the table, directly facing her. Her head, draped in the black veil of the professed nun, was bent over the billowing folds of the altar cloth she was embroidering, her eyes riveted as if in total concentration. The nun's round, wire-rimmed glasses sat halfway down her nose. Her lips were slightly pursed. For a brief second Sister Lucy wondered if she too was tempted to break out into uncontrollable laughter.

On the wall behind Mother Alphonsine hung a large picture of the Sacred Heart. This was a close-up of Jesus, His gaze fixed so far upward that only the whites of His eyes showed. Halfway down the picture the index finger of His right hand pointed to

His exposed heart, which radiated with yellow streams. Encircling it was a crown of thorns from which fell three drops of blood. The heart itself was pink and fleshy.

Sister Lucy pulled her gaze back to the book, shifted slightly in her chair, straightened, and continued reading. *"As St. Dominic was leaving, Bona's cancer-eaten breasts fell off from her, worms and all; and the flesh began to grow—"*

An electric bell sounded in the hall outside the novices' common room. "This ends today's reading, 'On Conformity to the Will of God' from *Practice of Perfection and Christian Virtue,*" Sister Lucy intoned.

"Praise be to Jesus," said Mother Alphonsine, folding up the altar cloth. There was a catch in her voice, and her face twitched before settling into an expression of recollected calm.

"Amen," Sister Lucy responded, closing the book and making the sign of the cross.

Around her, in a silent flurry, the novices packed their sewing into small black bags and rose from their chairs for their visit to chapel. Sister Camillus remained seated, her body looking like a limp rag doll. She turned toward Sister Lucy. Her eyes were watery and red-rimmed, her whole face caught in a look of helpless laughter.

"It h-had a b-black h-head!" she whispered, her voice shaking, the words exploding from her lips in a shower of tiny bubbles. Her body twisted itself once again into a spasmodic convulsion. Sister Lucy looked away, ran the tips of her fingers along her left eyebrow, then got up stiffly from her chair and headed toward the door.

Downstairs, the whole community was converging on the chapel for the evening visit to the Blessed Sacrament, the thirty or so nuns and the twelve novices and four postulants who were in training to make their vows of poverty, chastity and obedience. By the time the clock on the back wall struck six, each one was in her place, kneeling in silent adoration before the tabernacle which sat in the middle of the altar. Locked inside the tabernacle was the Blessed Sacrament.

The nuns and novices all wore the same habit, a long shapeless black dress tied at the waist with a leather belt from which dangled a large rosary with brown beads. On each head was a veil, black or white depending on each one's vowed status, that covered the shoulders and fell to the waist.

Sister Lucy stared at the green curtain hanging in front of the tabernacle door, and then at the gilded lettering etched in the white high altar: "Jesus My Lord My God My All." Hands clasped tightly, she tried forming words in her mind. "Oh God, oh God," she began. Nothing more came. Around her, she heard sounds of rosary beads against pews, soft breathing, quiet coughs. From behind came sniffling and a quick, muffled snort into a handkerchief. Sister Camillus probably. The after-effects of her giggling fit. "Oh God, oh Jesus," she began again. Her mind was dry, blank. She reached into her pocket for her own handkerchief. She didn't need it, but the action gave her something to do. It also made her head tilt a bit, a movement that gave some relief to the stiffness that was beginning to develop in her neck.

·The pockets were the feature she liked best about the cumbersome habit. In fact, they weren't part of the habit at all; they were cloth saddlebags that hung from a waistband. Slits along the sides of the habit skirt allowed access to them. Inside one of Sister Lucy's pockets were her large white handkerchief, a pen and a black sheath that contained a small pair of scissors.

Inside the other pocket was her permissions book, a small booklet made of pages sewn from used envelopes, in which a novice recorded the virtues she was striving to attain and the penances she was currently performing. Within the same pocket was a small string contraption formed from a complicated set of knots and made to resemble a horsewhip. This was called a discipline. The novice was to use the discipline to whip herself once a month in one of the small rooms at the end of the novitiate corridor. Mother Alphonsine had explained its use to the novices. "Men religious use the discipline on their backs and women religious use it—" she had hesitated briefly, "where they sit down."

To Sister Lucy, the discipline seemed a pathetic remnant of hair shirts and chains. She had gone once to one of the rooms, had taken the limp little thing in her hands and had pulled up the voluminous skirts of her habit and blue petticoat. She had pulled down her oversized underpants. It seemed strange and incongruous to be gazing down at the white of her thigh and the taut elastic garter holding up her black stocking. She stood by the window and, holding on to her volume of skirts, gave a half-hearted swat. She looked out at the expanse of lawn where the handyman was pushing the lawnmower. She thought of the whole court of heaven watching her – God the Father on His throne; Jesus; the Holy Ghost; the Blessed Virgin Mary, the Queen of Heaven herself with her retinue of baby angels and wavy-haired virgin martyrs holding palm branches; St. Ignatius and St. Francis Xavier and all the other great saints of the Church who had gone about with fire in their eyes and the cross of Jesus Christ in their hands. These men had been the backbone of the faith down through the ages. She thought of St. Theresa, the Little Flower of Jesus, holding a sensuous splash of roses against her brown Carmelite robe, her pink lips curled into a kewpie-doll smile. Sister Lucy thought of the whole kingdom of heaven crowded into the little room to watch her, and she felt overcome with shame and embarrassment. She quickly hoisted up her underpants, adjusted her skirt and left the room. She had never returned.

Sister Lucy joined her hands again, slowly intertwining her fingers. She felt a twinge between her left shoulder and her neck and slumped back from where she was kneeling, then inched her way onto the seat of the pew, trying to look inconspicuous. She looked up at the altar and the green curtain at its centre, but could think of nothing but the line of pain that reached up through her neck into her left temple. Her neck had been wrenched a couple of years earlier when she'd fallen off her bicycle on the steep hill just behind her family's farmhouse. The hill had always been daunting to her, but she had given it a try in a moment of daring. Halfway down she panicked and lost control. Her legs shot straight ahead and she leaned back, trying in vain to stop. The bicycle rolled over on top of her. When she picked herself up, pain shot up through her head. It never amounted to anything, however, never hurt enough for her to see a doctor. The bruises on her arms and the cuts on her hands healed quickly enough, but from time to time her neck still gave a twinge and the left side of her head throbbed with a dull ache. Sister Lucy wasn't quite sure if it was pain or not. It was perhaps only discomfort.

Her mind went back to the reading in the common room. She could understand Sister Camillus's fit of the giggles. *Practice of Perfection and Christian Virtue* was a book on virtues that people in religious life were meant to practise. Each treatise ended with a chapter called, "What has been said is now confirmed by examples." These chapters were Sister Lucy's personal favourites, because they gave far-fetched examples of medieval monks and crazy people living in the desert. The examples, like the priest who had an inordinate attachment to his mother and was dogged at every step by the devil mocking him with cries of "Mummy, Mummy," often reduced the novices to ridicule and laughter at recreation.

An early evening gloom had come upon the chapel. The red flicker of the sanctuary lamp sent shadows against the white backdrop of the high altar. Sister Lucy thought about the innocent and radiant Bona, the woman who had let her breasts be eaten alive. Had God really wanted her to suffer like that? Was this what it meant to be holy? She looked over at the side altar of the Blessed Virgin Mary, which stood near the wall to the left of the high altar. The head of the statue faced downwards, the arms extended on either side, the hands open. The folds of her tunic fell down over a flat chest and shapeless body. Had worms eaten up *her* breasts too? Sister Lucy looked quickly back at the high altar, shocked at the flippant thought.

Suddenly feeling tired, she closed her eyes and saw herself as Bona, walking about serene and beautiful, a long white shift hugging her body, golden hair streaming down her back. Underneath, her breasts were wasting away, worms crawling in and out, eating the flesh. Occasionally a look of pain crossed her face; otherwise she let no one know of the ravages within. It was a secret between herself and God. Then the sensitive St. Dominic came upon her and praised God for her holy suffering.

She opened her eyes and shifted her body. Should she tell Mother Alphonsine about the throbbing in her left temple? Would this be the holy thing to do? Maybe the novice mistress would tell her she was being soft on herself. "A little sacrifice is necessary for all of us, my dear Sister," she might say. Was this why Bona didn't go to a doctor, why she refused to wash out the putrid mass of poison from her breasts? Did she believe that God was demanding this sacrifice from her?

Their half-hour visit to chapel was now over, and the novices filed downstairs to the refectory for supper. Sister Lucy noticed that by this time Sister Camillus had composed herself and, like the others, walked straight and erect with head slightly bowed. The refectory was a tiny cell of a room with a table shaped like a horseshoe. At the head of the table a single chair indicated the novice mistress's place. Pushed underneath the two sides were fourteen stools.

Standing at the head of the table, Mother Alphonsine led the novices in the grace before meals. Then, moving sideways to avoid bumping into each other, the novices pulled out their stools and sat down. Three, including Sister Lucy, flopped to their knees. Kneeling during a meal was one of the regular penances, and each novice performed it two or three times a week. It was a good penance, to Sister Lucy's way of thinking. When they had first come into the novitiate, Reverend Mother had given them instructions about not enjoying their food too much. Food was to be eaten for the good of one's health, to satisfy bodily needs, not for base pleasure.

Sister Felicity stood holding a book and facing Mother Alphonsine. The novice mistress nodded as the food, in white serving dishes, made its way down both sides of the table.

"In the name of the Father and of the Son and of the Holy Ghost," began Sister Felicity, making the sign of the cross. She opened the book. *"For Greater Things: The Story of St. Stanislaus Kostka."*

Sister Lucy helped herself to mashed potatoes and meatballs swimming in dark brown gravy, and began to eat. From the corner of her eye she noticed plates on the sideboard holding generous slices of chocolate cake.

"'It was a quiet, humble life, full of peace, near to God, hidden away from men,'" Sister Felicity read. *"'In this life the novices had to continue for two years, before they took upon themselves the obligation of vows. During those two years they tested their vocation, making sure that God really called them to that life; and they tested their own wills to see if they were ready to endure what such a life demanded of them.'"*

Another twinge in Sister Lucy's neck caused her to wince, and she shifted her body. Her feet collided with the wall as they often did when she was kneeling at the table, and she put her fork down while she tried to manoeuvre her legs around each other.

"Stanislaus did just what the other novices did, nothing out of the ordinary. Yet, of course, he was different from the others; he was a saint. What was the difference? Just this: they did things more or less well; he did things perfectly. If he prayed, he put his whole mind and soul into his prayer. If he worked, he obeyed orders absolutely, because in doing so he was obeying God."'

When most of them had nearly finished their cake, Mother Alphonsine said, "praise be to Jesus," and Sister Felicity responded, "Amen, in the name of the Father and of the Son and of the Holy Ghost." Sister Felicity put the book on the sideboard, sat down and helped herself to meatballs. Forks scraped against plates as the novices finished the meal in silence.

Later, after the novices and postulants had completed their evening charges, they seated themselves again in the common room, their black sewing bags on their laps. Their faces were animated this time, with looks of expectation. Sister Camillus once again had a grin on her face. The evening's recreation hour was set to begin.

"Well, praise be to Jesus," said Mother Alphonsine, sweeping into the room, her rosary swaying, a wide smile on her face.

"Amen, good evening, Mother," they shouted. Several began to speak at once.

"Mother, Sister Camillus was certainly edified by the reading on conformity to the will of God," said Sister Felicity with a glint in her eyes. The novices never spoke directly to each other at recreation; they always addressed the novice mistress, but in fact their talk formed a sort of third-person dialogue directed at each other. Looking over at her, Sister Lucy wondered if the smile on Sister Felicity's face came from genuine mischief, or if it masked disapproval.

Several novices giggled. Sister Camillus looked around the group, a sly look on her face as if she might be trying to weigh the possibility of getting some fun out of *Practice of Perfection and Christian Virtue.* "Well you know, Mother," she answered slowly, "the woman was a holy conformer after all, and she probably helped poor St. Dominic with his libido."

Sister Lucy stiffened and lowered her head. She didn't know what libido meant, but the look in Sister Camillus's eyes and the collective intake of breath around the group made her feel that the novice had gone too far, that now the axe was going to fall. Sister Lucy hated that feeling.

"Does anyone have some jokes to tell us?" broke in Mother Alphonsine. Sister Lucy relaxed. This was the novice mistress's way of dealing with an embarrassing situation. She always seemed adept at changing the subject whenever the recreation topic became uncomfortable. Sister Lucy suspected that if she were let loose, Mother Alphonsine could tell a few jokes that weren't considered proper for novices' ears. As it was, she had to remain bland for the sake of edification.

Sometimes she tried to be stern, but sternness didn't become Mother Alphonsine, Sister Lucy thought. The sides of her mouth, which trembled when she tried to put on a serious face during a discussion of one of the readings or an instruction on the Holy Rule, gave her away. Sister Lucy thought she must dread the chapters that came at the end of each treatise of *Practice of Perfection and Christian Virtue.* Right now the group was stilled, as if the jokes, which the novices generally told and retold, always laughing as if for the first time, had suddenly dried up.

Sister Lucy spoke into the hush. "What if any of us gets sick, Mother? Is it better not to say anything, and let it get worse and worse, or is it better to ask to see the doctor? I mean, which is the best way of conforming to the will of God?" Sister Lucy could sense boredom on either side of her, a restless desire for someone to say something that would make them all laugh.

"Conformity to the will of God? I'll tell you about conformity to the will of God," came a booming voice from the back of the group. Sister Catarina was a hefty novice with black bushy eyebrows that continually rose and fell beneath the white band across her forehead. Right now she sat at a table tearing pages from a thick telephone directory and folding them neatly in half, then in thirds. Sister Catarina's after-supper charge included placing these papers, along with a supply of sanitary napkins, in the toilet cubicles of the convent washrooms. The purpose of the folded directory pages was to wrap used napkins.

"Conformity to the will of God is this: that the poor old nuns have the supplies they need at all times."

"The poor old nuns don't need them," laughed Sister Pauline. Once again, Sister Lucy stiffened. She herself would never have had the courage to say such a thing, but of course Sister Pauline could get away with a lot because she came from a family upon which God had set a special seal. Her parents had given all of their five children to God – their three sons had become Franciscan priests and another daughter had become a nun. Now Sister Pauline, their beloved baby, had made her parents' sacrifice complete by following in the others' footsteps and offering her life to God. Everyone else stood in wordless awe of her and her family. Fortunately, Sister Pauline didn't take herself as seriously as everyone else did; otherwise, Sister Lucy felt, she would have been too much to bear.

"Let me tell you this," Sister Catarina barged on. "Folding papers may not seem very important, but this is God's will for sure. When you need these things, you really need them." She paused for effect. "When my family asked me what I do all day, I told them I'm doing very important paperwork."

"Mother, is it possible to know at all times whether you are conforming to the will of God?" asked Sister Lucy. She was dying to get off the subject of sanitary napkins.

"Have you not been following the instructions on holy obedience, Sister Lucy?" Mother Alphonsine had kind blue eyes that rested above the rims of her glasses, and that now gazed on Sister Lucy. "Have you not remembered that the least wish of the superior is the command of the good religious?"

"The next section in the life of St. Stanislaus tells about how he was told to carry wood from a woodpile with another novice," said Sister Felicity. "They were told to carry two or three pieces each and the other novice wanted to carry an armload, but St. Stanislaus said, 'No, we were told to carry only two or three pieces, so that's the will of God for us.' I was wondering – do you think maybe he was just lazy and they turned the story around and made it look like he was virtuous?"

The thought of a saint being lazy intrigued Sister Lucy for a moment, but today's earlier reading about Bona and the worms refused to let go. "But Mother, how do you know if God wants your body to be eaten up by worms?"

"They're expecting more snow tonight, and so we'll have to shovel the walks tomorrow," said Mother Alphonsine, her eyes once again fixed on her embroidery. Sister Lucy looked over at Sister Camillus. The other novice's face was blank, her mouth open slightly. Her eyes, meeting Sister Lucy's, began to dance again and she stuck out her tongue, then bowed her head over a long darning needle that she plunged into a black stocking fitted over a mushroom-shaped form.

Later, at night prayers, as the Litany of Our Lady droned around her: "...House of Gold, pray for us, Spiritual Vessel, pray for us, Vessel of Honour, pray for us, Singular Vessel of Devotion, pray for us..." Sister Lucy imagined a beautiful woman going about helping people, her face full of gentleness and quiet joy, while worms ate up her body. When night prayers were over, and the chapel was darkened except for a single light bulb at the back, a nun read the meditation passage for the next morning. "From the book of the Apocalypse, chapter 3. *'Thus says the Amen, the faithful and true witness, who is the beginning of the creation of God: I know thy works; thou art neither cold nor hot. I would that thou wert cold or hot. But because thou art luke-warm, and neither cold nor hot, I am about to vomit thee out of my mouth; because thou sayest, I am rich and have grown wealthy and have need of nothing, and dost not know that thou art the wretched and miserable and poor and blind and naked one...'"*

As soon as the scripture reading ended, Reverend Mother rang a little handbell from the place where she knelt at the back of the chapel. All the nuns and novices bent down and kissed the floor. Sister Lucy's neck gave a twinge of pain as she straightened. She then filed out of chapel with the others, up the staircase, past the novices' common room, to the dormitory.

She pulled the curtains around her cubicle and stood still for a moment. Beside her bed were a chair and a bedstand on which stood a basin and jug. Folded on top of the jug was her pink and white towel, placed there by the novice whose after-supper charge was to fill all the jugs with hot water. Sister Lucy pulled the plain white bedspread from the bed, folded it and placed it over the top of the chair. She unhooked her rosary from her belt, gathered it up in her palm and placed it beside her basin. Then, methodically, she began to take off her clothes, placing each item on the seat of her chair – her veil, dress, pockets and undervest. Covering her small breasts with one arm, she withdrew her nightgown from under the pillow and then pulled it over the top of her head. She began to undress the lower part of her body: her plain blue petticoat, her underpants. She undid the garters of her black stockings, removed them, and then finally unhooked her garter belt. She took off her undercap and smoothed back her short hair with her hand. She then poured the water, still warm, from the jug into the basin. She wet the washcloth, rubbed it with soap and began to wash, first her face and neck, and then, reaching into the top of her nightgown, under her arms and beneath her breasts. The moist thickness of the cloth felt soothing on her skin. After drying herself, she brushed her teeth, rinsing and spitting into the basin. She put her habit dress over her nightgown and carried the basin to the housemaid's sink in the corridor outside the dormitory. She refilled the basin and brought it back to her cubicle. The next morning, long after the water in the basin had grown cold, she would wash in it.

"Cold water is good for a person in the morning," Mother Alphonsine had said when explaining the dormitory proce-dures. "Besides," she added, "washing yourself with cold water is a nice penance to offer Our Lord first thing in the morning."

Sister Lucy wasn't exactly sure, from Mother Alphonsine's explanation, what the real reason was for washing with cold water every morning. Was it for reasons of physical well-being, or was it for penitential reasons? She suspected the real reason was one of expediency. In the scramble to get washed and dressed and to do the various charges that needed to be done in the half hour between rising and six o'clock meditation, it sim-ply saved time for the novices to have water already in their basins.

After she had taken off her habit dress again, Sister Lucy knelt down beside her bed and stretched her arms to either side. This was the final penance of the day. Three times a week she knelt like this, reciting the Litany of Humility, in imitation of Jesus who had died with His arms outstretched on the cross. "That others may be loved more than I, Jesus grant me the grace to desire it; that others may be chosen and I set aside, Jesus grant me the grace to desire it; that others may be preferred to me in everything, Jesus grant me the grace to desire it..."

She pictured again the beautiful Bona, disfigured by her rotting breasts, smiling through her agony, happy to be suffering for the love of God. Her own aches were tiny in comparison. Imagine the festering breasts, the worms crawling in and out of the pus! She cringed at the thought, and with a jerk, her arms fell and fastened themselves in a tight hug around her body. Her own breasts felt firm against the pressure.

Her head twitched as pain shot up into her forehead. She slumped onto her heels, her arms falling limp on the bed. She couldn't do it. She couldn't suffer for the love of God as Bona had. She had given up everything to become a good religious, but what was she? Weak and mediocre, getting by from day to day. She would become more and more selfish, first in small things, then in greater things. She was lukewarm, that's what she was, one of those people whom Jesus, at the last judgment, will vomit out of His mouth.

She looked up through the crack between the dormitory curtains. In a space of about two inches, she saw Sister Pauline beside her own bed, kneeling erect with arms fully outstretched. Sister Lucy knelt upright again, then slumped forward, the crown of her head resting on the bed, her arms hanging limp at her sides. She felt exhausted and defeated. It was useless to try to become holy. She could never manage it, never.

For a moment, she thought of nothing, aware only of the rough comfort of the blanket under her head. Then she realized that her body was beginning to relax, the pain subsiding.

In a whisper she breathed out the final invocation of the litany: "That others may become holier than I, provided that I may become as holy as I should, Jesus grant me the grace to desire it."

The one-minute bell sounded. Sister Lucy stood up, leaning on the bed. She pulled down her bedclothes and climbed in between the sheets. Then she bunched up her pillow under her neck for traction and closed her eyes. Tomorrow, right after breakfast, there would be a chance to speak to Mother Alphonsine.

BARRY CALLAGHAN

DOG DAYS OF LOVE

Father Vernon Wilson was an old priest who led a quiet life. He said Mass every morning at the side altar of his church, read a short detective novel, had a light lunch, and went out walking with his dog. He was retired but he always made a few house calls to talk to old friends who weren't bothered by the dog, and though he had a special devotion to the Blessed Virgin and the Holy Shroud of Turin, he didn't talk much about faith.

Though he was still spry for a man in his early eighties, he gladly let the dog, a three-year-old golden retriever, set a leisurely pace on a loosely held leash, sniffing at curbs and shrub roots and fence posts. He'd had the dog for a year, a local veterinarian having come around to the parish house of an afternoon to leave the dog as a gift, telling the housekeeper, "I've always wanted to give Father Wilson a little dog. I always felt so at ease with myself and the world whenever I'd gone to him to confession."

In all his years as a parish priest, Father Wilson had never imagined that he might want a dog, and he certainly did not know if he could, in accordance with diocesan rules, keep a dog in the parish home. The new young pastor, Father Kukic, had at first said, No, no, he wasn't sure that it was a good idea at all, even if it was possible, but then the diocesan doctor had come by to give the priests their autumn flu shots and to check their blood pressure, and he had said, "No, no, it's a wonderful idea, I urge you, Father Kukic, if it's not usually done, to do it. It's a proven fact, older people who have the constant company of a dog live longer, maybe five years longer, maybe because all a dog asks is that you let him love you, and we all want Father Wilson to live longer, don't we."

"I'm sure we do," Father Wilson said.

"Well," Father Kukic said, trying to be amiably amusing, "there could be two sides to that argument."

"Father Kukic," the old priest said, feigning surprise, "I've never known you to see two sides to an argument." He clapped the young priest on the shoulder. "Good for you, good for you."

"I'm sure, too, that the dog will be good for you," Father Kukic said.

"I'm sure he will," Father Wilson said, but he was not sure of the situation at all. On their first night walk together he kept the dog on a short leash, calling him simply, "You, dog..."

Then, after ten or eleven days, Father Wilson not only let the dog sleep on the floor at the end of the bed in his room, but sometimes up on the end of his bed, and then one morning he announced over breakfast that he had decided to call the dog, Anselm. "After the great old saint," he told Father Kukic, "Saint Anselm, who said the flesh is a dung hill, and this dog, I can tell you, has yet to meet doggy dung on a lawn he doesn't like."

"Oh, really now," Father Kukic said, and before he could add anything more, the old priest said, "But then, look at it this way, nothing is ever what it seems. Most people get Saint Anselm all wrong. He was like the great hermit saints who went out into the desert, they renounced everything that gave off the smell of punishment and revenge, and so they renounced the flesh, but only so they could insist on the primacy of love over everything else in their spiritual lives... over knowledge, solitude, over prayer... love, in which all authoritarian brutality and condescension is absent, love in which nothing is to be hidden in the flesh..."

Father Kukic sat staring at him, breathing through his open mouth.

"You should be keeping up on your spiritual reading, Father, that's Thomas Merton I was giving you there, you should try him."

"Wasn't he something of a mystic?"

"My goodness," the old priest said, "I think Anselm and I should go for a walk, get our morning feet on the ground."

They walked together every morning just before lunch, sometimes in the afternoon if it wasn't too hot or too cold, and always at night, just before *Larry King*. "If you're going to be in touch, if you're going to keep up with your parishioners," he told Father Kukic, "you've got to know what the trash talk is, too."

When he visited homes in the parish, leaving the dog leashed on a porch or sitting in a vestibule, he talked candidly about anything and everything, pleasing the parishioners, but more and more as he and Anselm walked together, and particularly when they stopped to rest for a moment in front of a building like the Robarts Research Library, he leaned down and patted Anselm's neck and said quietly to him, "Good dog, now you look at that, there's real brutalism for you, that's the bunker mentality of a bully." He scowled at the massive slab-grey concrete windowless wall, the cramped doorway under a huge periscope projection of concrete into the sky. "This is the triumph of the architecture of condescension," he said, pleased that he'd found so apt a phrase for his thought, and amused and touched, too, by how Anselm, looking up at him, listened attentively, and how the dog, at the moment he had finished his thought, came up off his haunches and broke into a cantering walk, striding, the old priest thought, like a small blond horse.

"Beautiful," he said, "beautiful."

Parishioners and shopkeepers soon took for granted seeing them together.

The only times that Anselm was not with him, the only time he left the dog alone in his bedroom, was when he said Mass at the side altar early in the morning or when he went to visit a parishioner sick at home.

Once, while he was away on a sick call, Anselm had chewed the instep of a shoe he had left under the bed, and a week later he had swallowed a single black sock.

That had caused an awkward moment, because the dog had not been able to entirely pass the sock and Father Wilson had had to stand out on the parish-house lawn behind a tree and slowly drag the slime and shit-laden sock out of the dog.

"Anselm, my Anselm," he had said, "you sure are a creature of the flesh."

But it was while he was at prayer that he felt closest to Anselm.

It was while he knelt at prayer before going to bed, kneeling under the length of linen cloth that hung on the wall, a replica of the Holy Shroud of Turin, that Anselm had sat down beside him and had nestled his body in under his elbow so that the old priest had embraced Anselm with his right arm as he had said the Apostles Creed, feeling deeply, through the image of the dead face on the Shroud, the Presence of the Living Christ in his life and now, every night, they knelt and sat together for ten minutes, after which Father Wilson would cross himself, get into bed, and Anselm would leap up on to the bed and curl at his feet so that as he went to sleep, the old priest was comforted not just by the heat and weight of the animal in his bed, but the sound of his breathing.

His devotion to the Shroud, however, had not been a comfort to his young pastor, Father Kukic, who had snorted dismissively, saying that when a seminarian in Paris he had travelled through the countryside one summer, and as a believer, about to be ordained, he had been embarrassed to come upon a church near Poitiers that had claimed to house "one of the two known heads of John the Baptist," and another that had said they possessed "a vial of the unsoured milk of the Virgin."

"The unsoured milk... I like that," the old priest had said, laughing.

"Well, I don't, and no one else does either," Father Kukic said. "It's embarrassing."

"Only a little."

"And as for your cloth, no one had ever heard of your Shroud til somewhere back in the 1500s."

"Not mine, Father. Our Lord's."

"Oh please."

"The thing is this, Father, there are certain facts," and Father Wilson had patiently tried to describe the two images on the Shroud – the front and back of a man's wounded body and his bearded face, his staring eyes and skeletal crossed hands – and how all this, after experts had completed a microscopic examination of the linen, had revealed no paint or pigment that anyone knew of, nor did the image relate to any known style... and furthermore, "Somehow, the Shroud is a kind of photographic negative which becomes positive when reversed by a camera, the body of a man somehow embedded in the linen as only a camera can see him, a way of observing what no one could have known how to possibly paint."

"These all may be facts, Father, but they prove nothing."

"Exactly, my dear Father. But you see, I prefer that facts add up to a mystery that is true rather than facts that add up to an explanation that is true."

"Like what?"

"Like the Virgin Birth."

"Nonsense. That's a matter of faith."

"No, it's a matter of temperament, Father."

They had never spoken of the Shroud again.

There were nights through the winter when the old priest, before going to sleep, had felt, as he had told Anselm, "nicely confused." Kneeling under the Shroud, knowing how dark and freezing cold it was outside and staring up into the hollowed dead yet terrorized eyes of the Christ, he had felt only warmth and unconditional love from the dog under his arm, and after saying his prayers he had taken to nestling his face into Anselm's neck fur, laughing quietly and boyishly, as he hadn't heard himself laugh in years, before falling into a very sound sleep.

At the first smell of spring, he opened his bedroom window and aired out his dresser drawers and his closet, breathing in deeply and deeply pleased to be alive. He gave Anselm's head a brisk rubbing and then, having borrowed the housekeeper's feather duster, he took down the linen shroud that had been brought to him as a gift by a friend all the way from Turin, and he dusted it off at the window and then laid it out for airing over the sill, as his mother had done years ago with the family bedsheets.

In the early afternoon, leaving Anselm asleep, he went out alone to visit an elderly couple whose age and infirmness over the long winter had made them cranky and curt and finally cruel to each other, though they still loved each other very much, and he hoped that they would let him, as an old friend, go around their flat and open their windows, too, and bring the feel of the promise of spring air into their lives again.

When he returned to the parish house, to his room, he was exuberant, enormously pleased with himself, because his visit had ended with the elderly couple embracing him, saying, "We're just three old codgers waiting to die," laughing happily.

When he opened his door, he let out a roar of disbelief, "Nooooo, God." Anselm was on his belly on the bed and under him – gathered between his big web-toed paws – was the Shroud. He was thumping his tail as he snuffled and shoved his snout into the torn cloth. The old priest lunged, grabbing for the Shroud, yanking at it, the weight of the startled dog tearing it more, and when he saw, in disbelief, that the face, the Holy face and the Holy eyes of the Presence were all gone, shredded and swallowed by the dog, he raised his fist – hurt and enraged – and Anselm, seeing that rage and that fist, leaped off the bed, hitting the floor, tail between his legs, skidding into a corner wall where, cowering and trembling, trying to tuck his head into his shoulder, he looked up, waiting to be beaten.

"Oh my God, oh my God," the old priest moaned, sitting on the edge of the bed, drawing the ruined Shroud across his knees.

He could not believe the look of terror, and at the same time, the look of complete love in the dog's eyes, and for a moment he thought that that must have been the real look in Christ's eyes as He hung on the cross, His terror felt as a man, and His complete unconditional love as God, but before he could wonder if such a thought was blasphemous, he was struck by a fear that, having seen his rage and his fist, Anselm would always be afraid of him, would always cower and tremble at his coming. As a boy, he had seen dogs like that, dogs who had been beaten.

He fell on to his knees beside the dog in the corner where, night after night, he had prayed – saying the Apostles Creed, affirming his faith – and Anselm had sat there, too, waiting to go on to the bed to sleep. He took Anselm's head in his arms, feeling as he did his trouser leg become warm with an oily wet-ness, the dog, in the confusion of his fear and relief at being held, having peed. The old priest hugged him closer and laughed and Anselm came out of his cower and then stopped trembling. Rocking Anselm in his arms, he was about to tell him he was a good dog and he shouldn't worry, that he loved him, but then he thought how ludicrous it would be for a grown man to talk out loud to a dog about something so serious as love, and so he just sat in their wetness holding Anselm even tighter so that Anselm would understand and never doubt.

LEON ROOKE

THE HEART MUST
FROM ITS BREAKING

1.

This is how it happened that morning at the church. Timmons
was speaking on a topic that had us all giggling, "What You Do
When and If You Get to Heaven and Find It Empty," and we
were all there and saw it. How suddenly before Timmons got
wound up good the wood doors burst open and there in the
sunlight was someone or something, like a fast-spinning wheel
made up of gold, though it couldn't have been gold and was
probably some funny trick of the light. Anyway, there it was,
and beckoning. Must have been beckoning, or calling somehow, because two children got up from their seats at the front
and quiet as you please marched right out to him – to him or it
– and went through the door, and that was the last any of us
ever saw them. Then a second later that other kid – Tiny
Peterson was his name – went out too, but his mama was in
time to save him. Now I'd lie about it if I could or if I knew how,
but it was all so quiet and quick and then over that I wouldn't
know how to improve on the actual happening. Out that door
and then swallowed up, those two kids, and that's all there was
to it.

2.

He can say that's all if he wants to. Roger Deering sees an affair
like this the same way he sees his job, which I would remind you

is delivering mail. He drops it through the box, if he can be troubled to come up the path, and then he's gone. What he's left you with don't matter spit to him. But I live in that house now, my sister's house, and I can tell you the story don't end there. They were my sister's children, Agnes and Cluey. Sister was home in bed sick so I'd taken little Agnes and Cluey to church to hear Timmons give what we hoped would be a good one, and right after the second song, with Timmons hardly begun, Cluey who was on my left stood up and whispered "Excuse me," and brushed by my knees, then Agnes on my right stood up, mumbled "Me too," and they went on down the row, scraping by people, getting funny looks, and then going on down the aisle pretty as you please. I thought Cluey had to go to the bathroom. He was always doing that, never going when you told him to and it embarrassed me. But you do get tired of telling a boy to wait wait wait when he's squirming and crossing his legs, trying to hold it in. I don't mean he was doing it that day, I'm only saying that's what I thought he got up for. He'd been nice as pie the whole time, both of them, both while walking along with me to church and while sitting there waiting for Timmons to get primed. So I was in a good mood and bearing them no malice, though they were a long shot from being my favourite nieces and nephews. Sister had been ailing for some while and they were feeling dopey about that, we all were. That was the day Sister died, in fact the very minute, some said. Some said they'd looked at their watches when that door burst open and Cluey and Agnes went out never to be seen again and that very second three blocks over was the very second Sister passed on. It was close, that's all I'm saying, and my skin shivers saying that much, especially when I remember about the blood. But I'm not saying anything about the blood on Sister's window, being content to leave that to the likes of Clayton Eaves who is still dunning me for that ten dollars. I don't like to think of any of it as the truth, for I'm living in Sister's house now and I know sometimes I hear her and she hears me. Sister dies and her two children disappear the same minute and it does make you think. Though I didn't see any whirling light or gold spinning at the door. I felt a draft, that's all. Like most people with any sense I thought the wind had blown it open, and when people say to me there wasn't any wind that day I just look through them, since any fool knows a gust can come up. Still, it's strange. I can't think what happened to the children. No one wanted them. I couldn't and Sister wasn't able. Their daddy couldn't have come and got them because none of us hardly remembered who their daddy was, or wanted to, because even in his best of days he hadn't been what you'd call a solid citizen. He wasn't right in the head, and not much in the body either, and even Sister knew that. So she had her hard times, raising that pair without a hand from him who hadn't been seen I think in nine years when all this happened. No aunts or uncles would have come for them. We don't have kidnappers around here. No, it defies explanation and I've given up trying. When Sister wakes me calling in the night I sit up in bed and answer back and we go on talking that way until her spirit quietens.

I hope Cluey and Agnes are all right, wherever they are, that's all I hope. I don't agree with those who say they're long-since dead, nor those who say they're in heaven either. Timmons might.

3.

Sure they're dead. I don't know how, or how come, or why, not having the divine intervention on it, but you can't tell me two children dressed for church and without a penny or snotrag between them are going to get out of this town without anyone knowing it. There are just two ways for entering or leaving and that's by the one street that leads off to Scotland Neck at one end and Enfield at the other, and they didn't go either of those ways. Couldn't have, because a hundred people rocking on their porches that fine Sunday when they should have been at Spring Level hearing my sermon on The Empty Hell would have noted their progress and likely turned them around.

So they're dead. Yep, and their bones plucked by now. Dust to dust and the Lord's will abideth.

Somebody picked them up right off the church grounds, I'd say, right there at the door, and spooked them away. Why, I don't know. They are ordinary children, no better or worse than most. Funny things go on in this town the same as they do anyplace else and I figure those two are buried this minute down in somebody's cellar or in a backyard where a thousand things hidden go on day in and day out. I've preached till I'm blue in the face, the same as one or two other ministers have, and it's done no good. Not a lick. You can't stamp out the devil's work for he's like a mad dog once he gets going. That's what it was, of course. The old devil keeping his hand in. If it hadn't been those two children, it would have been something worse.

We searched the woods, every rock, weed, and clover.

Nothing. Not a hint.

About that door. I saw something but *what* is something else. It wasn't gold, though. It was more like a giant black shadow had spun up over the stairs and filled the doorway. I remember remarking to myself at the time: it's got so dark in here so suddenly I'm going to have difficulty reading my text. I was going to ask Minny at the organ to turn more light on, when Cluey and Agnes got up and distracted me. A second later it was light again. If I'd known what was to happen I would have called out. But who knew? That's how you know it's the devil's work, I say, because you don't. You just don't. You never will.

4.

Timmons is right. I was at the organ. I didn't want to be, having a bad cold, but I was. They couldn't get anybody else. My nose was runny, I told them, and I had aches – but so what? "Minnie, now Minnie, you come on down." So I did. Yet it's the same story every time and nobody ever even bothering to keep up. I've heard cows mooing in a meadow had more rhythm and feeling than the people in that church. But I saw nothing. Saw and heard nothing. No light or gold. No shadow. No children either. It takes a lot in that church to make me turn around. Back trouble, leg trouble, I wore a neck brace for ten years. I keep my back to that lot and that's how I like it. One time a curtain caught fire back there when Orson Johnson – the cross-eyed one – was playing with matches. I looked around then. That's about the only time.

5.

My name's Orson, I'm the one she's talking about. What I wished I'd done that day was burn the whole building down. But I didn't and I growed up and I was back there the day those two walked out. Back there whittling on a stick with this Fobisher knife I have. With the wife and hoping it would wind up early, though I knew it wouldn't, so I could go home and have dinner, maybe grab some shuteye. But, yes, I saw them. I felt my neck crawl too, before they ever stood up, because some thing was behind me. Maybe not at the door, but behind me certainly. My skin froze and I remember gripping my wife's wrist I got that scared. I thought it was Death back there, Death calling, and He was going to lay his cold hand over my shoulder and speed me on off. "What date is it?" I asked my wife. "How long we been married?" Now I don't know why I said this, but I know it scared her too, though she just kept shooshing me. I didn't want to die. Hell, it seemed to me I'd only started living. But "shoosh" she says, so I shoosh. I shoosh right up; I couldn't have said another word anyway. I sat there with my knees knocking, waiting for Death's hand to grab me. Then I see the kids coming down the aisle. They got their faces scrubbed and that ramrod aunt of theirs, Gladys, she had slapped some worn duds on them and got their hair combed. Death's hold on me seemed to loosen a bit and I thought how I might slip out and ask them how their mother was doing – whether she was still in her sick bed or out of danger yet, that sort of thing – maybe slip them a quarter because I'd always felt pity for those kids – and I tried to move, to wiggle out the side and sort of slink to the back door, but what it was I found was I couldn't move. I couldn't stir a muscle. And a second later my hair stood out on my head because a voice was hissing in my ear. "Don't go," it said. "Don't go, Orson, it will get you too."

Though I didn't think then that "too" business was including the kids. I might have got up if I'd known that. I might have headed them off, tried to save them. If anyone could have. I don't know. Oh, they're dead, no question of that. I think they were likely dead before nightfall. Maybe within the hour. It's too bad too, especially with their mother going that same day.

6.

I felt Orson stiffen beside me. He looked like death warmed over and he started jabbering beside me, shivering so hard he was rattling the whole row. I put my hand down between his legs and pinched his thigh hard as I could but he didn't even blink. He was trying to get out. So I put my hand up where his man parts were and I squeezed real hard and told him to hush up. "Hush up, Orson, stop playing the fool" – something like that. He was freezing cold. He had sweat beads on his brow an inch thick. I brought my heel down on his foot, trying to get

him quiet, then I heard him say "Death, Death, Death." And
"Don't go, don't go." He didn't know what he was talking. I saw
Aaron Spelling, in front of us, lean over and say to Therma that
Orson Johnson had a briar in his behind. Therma turned and
looked at us. Her mouth popped open. Because Orson was such
a sight. He got his hand away real quick from where it was; I just
clamped my fingernails into his thigh and kept them there the
rest of the service.

Later on we had to get the doctor in, I'd hurt him so and the
infection must have lasted a month.

I didn't notice the kids; I had my hands full with Orson.

It was three whole days in fact before I so much as heard of
the children gone missing or dead and of their mother's death.

7.

I was nursing Tory when she took her final breath. By her bed-
side I was with a teacup in my lap and watching the window because I thought I'd heard something running around out there.
Like a galloping horse it was. But my legs were bothering me,
and my sides, so I didn't take the trouble to go to the window
and see. I sat sipping my tea, listening to the galloping horse.

It was a day like many another one up to that time except
that the house was empty, it being a Sunday, and other than that
horse. A few minutes before, when I got up to get my tea, I'd put
my head down on Tory's chest. I was always doing that, couldn't
help it, because although I've sat with hundreds of sick people I'd
never heard a heart like hers. It was like water sloshing around in
a bowl; she hardly had no regular heartbeat is what I'm saying.
So I'd put my head down over her chest and listen to it slosh like
that.

I couldn't see how a human being could live with a heartbeat
like that. The horse it keeps right on galloping. Now and then
I'd catch a whir at the window, whitish, so I knew it wasn't no

dark horse. Then all at once my blood just stops, because something has caught hold of me. I look down at my wrist and there's
the queerest hand I ever saw. Thin and shrunk and mostly bones.
The hand is all it was in that second, and I shrieked. The china
cup fell to the floor and broke. Saucer too. Tea splashed all over
me, so I afterwards had to go in and soak my dress in cold water.
There were the long red nails though. A vile colour but Gladys
said Tory liked it. That she wouldn't feel comfortable in bed, sick
like that, without her nails painted, because how would you feel
to be in bed like she was and looking like death, in case anybody
came in. So let's keep her civilized, Gladys said, and one or the
other of us kept her nails freshly painted. So after my minute of
fright I knew it was Tory's hand, her who hadn't moved a twitch
in three months, suddenly sitting up with a grip like steel on my
arm. It was practically the first sign of life I'd seen in her in the
whole time I'd been minding her. She was sitting bolt-up, with
her gown straps down at her elbows so her poor little bosom, the
most puckered, shrivelled little breasts I ever hope to see, was
exposed to the full eyes of the world.

She had her eyes locked on the window.

And there went the horse again, gallop, gallop.

I got hold of myself, got her hand off me, and stooped down
over her. I was about to say, "Now little lady, let's get that gown
up over your bosom before you catch your death" – but then
that word caught in my throat so I said nothing. And I'm glad
I didn't or I might of missed what she said. Her eyes were on fire
and she was grabbing at something. At the very air, it seemed to
me. "You'll not get my children!" she said. "No, you'll not get
them!" Well, my skin crawled. I don't know why, don't know to
this day. Just the way she was crying it. "You'll not get them, not
my Cluey and Agnes!" She was screeching that out now, as
frightened – but as brave too – as any soul I hope to see. "You
can't have my children!" On and on like that. And she was twist-

ing around in bed, flailing her arms, striking at something with her poor little fists. *"No, you can't!"* she said. Then this even worse look come over her face and for the longest time she wasn't making human sounds at all. Half-animal, I thought. Like something caught in a trap. I thought she'd finally bit the noose – that her mind had gone. I kept trying to get that gown up over her breast works – you never knew who would come barging into that house without knocking or breathing a word, even her sister has crept in sometimes and scared me out of my wits. And she's fighting me, not letting me get her back down in the bed. She's scratching and yelling and kicking – her whose legs the doctor claimed was paralyzed – and she's moaning and biting. Then she shrieks, *"Run! Run! Oh, children, run!"* And this perfect horror comes over her face, pure agony it is, and torture worse than I've ever known a body to feel. *"No!"* she screams. *"No! Please! Please don't!"* and the next second her breath flies out, her eyes roll up, and she sags down like a broken baby in my arms. I put her head back on the pillow and fluff it some. I pull her straps back up and smooth out her gown over her chest's flatness. I pat the comforter up around her neck. I get her hair looking straight. I close her eyes, first the left then the right just as they say you ought to do, and I root in my purse and get out two pennies. I go in and wash them off and dry them on my dress, and I put them nicely over her eyes. Then I sit watching her, trembling more than I ever have. Wondering what has gone on and thinking how I'm going to have to tell her sister and those poor children when they come in from the church. Not once giving mind to that broken china on the floor. I reckon I never did. I reckon someone else must have come in and cleared that mess up. Maybe Gladys did. Or maybe not. I plumb can't guess, because one second I'm there sitting looking at my hands in my lap and the next second I'm thinking What about that galloping horse? Because I don't hear it any more.

No, it's so quiet you can hear a pin drop. And I hear it too. Pins dropping, that's what I think. This shiver comes over me. I have the funny feeling I'm not alone in the room: that there's me, a dead person, and something else. I look over at the bed and what do I see? Well it's empty. Tory ain't there. I hear more of these pins dropping and they seem to be coming from the window so I look there. And what I see is this: it is Tory, come back to some strange form of life, and sliding up and over, over the sill and out of that window. That's right, just gone. And I guess I fainted then, that being the first of my faints. The next time I open my eyes my sight is on that window again and this time Tory is coming back through it, sliding along, and her little breasts are naked again, she's all cut up, and blood has soaked through her and she's leaving a trail of it every inch she comes. "Help me, Rosie," she says. Well that's what I'm there for. So I get her up easy as kittens – she hardly weighs an ounce – and I get her back into bed. "They're safe," she says. I say, "Good." I say a lot of comforting words like that. "Don't let anyone see me like this," she says. "I'm black and blue from head to toe." It's the truth too, she sure is. "Have Gladys quietly bury me," she says. "Closed coffin. Can you promise that?" I said sure. She patted my hand then, poor thing, as though I was the one to be comforted. Then she slips away. She slips away smiling. So I get the pennies back on. I straighten the covers. Then I sit back in the chair and faint away a second time. I'm just waking up when Gladys comes in from church to tell me that Agnes and Cluey have gone and there's been a mighty mess at the church and some are saying the children are dead or gone up to heaven. I pass out my third time. I can't help it. I fold down to the floor like a limp rag and I don't know what else is going on till there is a policeman or a doctor at my elbow, I don't know which.

8.

It was me, Sam Clive. Clive. C-L-I-V-E. Officer Sam Clive. I
wasn't there in any official capacity. I lived then just two doors
down from Tory and that day I felt in my bones how something
was wrong. I was out in my yard mowing and this funny feeling come over me. I looked up and it seemed to be coming from
her house. It was shut up tight, the house was, but there was this
whirring disc in the sky. A flying whatayacallit I at first thought.
Anyway, it seemed to sink down in the woods just behind her
place. So I strolled over. I saw curtains fluttering at her sick
room window and I was brought up real short by that – because
that window had always been closed. Every day, winter and
summer, on account of Tory was holding on by such a thin
thread. Heart trouble, kidneys, pneumonia – the whole she-
bang. I stepped closer, not wanting to be nosy and more because
of this eerie feeling I had. Well, I saw those curtains were dripping blood. It was pouring right off that cloth and down the
boards, that blood. And I thought I saw something sliding up
over the sill the minute I come up. Flutter, flutter. It was the
curtains I guess. Though I don't recollect it being a windy day.
But that blood, heck, you can still see where it dribbled down
the side of the house, because they never painted it over. They
painted the rest of the house, the sister did after she got it, but
for reasons known only to them they painted up to the blood
and stopped right there. Anyhow, I hurried on over. I looked
through the window and there was this fat nurse down in a heap
on the floor beside this broken china and Tory in the bed with
bright pennies over her eyes.

9.

I done the paint job. I give the old gal a good price and me and
one other, my half-brother who was helping me then, we went
at it. White, of course, that was the only colour she'd have. And

she wanted two coats, one put on vertical and one crossways. I said why. She said her daddy told her when she was a kid that's how you put paint on if you wanted a thing to stand up to the elements more'n a year or two. I said I'd never heard that. I said Tom Earl, Have you ever heard that and he said No, no he hadn't. She said Well that's how she wanted it and if I wouldn't or couldn't do it or didn't think I was able then she reckoned I wasn't the only painter in town and a lot of them cheaper'n me. Ha! I said. I said it's going to cost you extra. She said I don't see why. I said because Miss Gladys it will take me a good sight longer painting this house the fool way you want it. You can't hardly git no speed painting vertical because the natural way is to go crosswise following the lay of the boards. She said it might be natural to a durn fool like me but that weren't how her daddy done it and I could do it and at the price quoted or I could shove off and go out and stick somebody else. So I got the message. Two coats? I said. Two coats, she said, Hank Sparrows can't you do that neither? I shook my head a time or two. There weren't any way I was going to make one red cent out of it. I'd be doing well just covering wages and gitting the paint paid for. But her sister had passed on and neither hide nor hair of her kin had been seen, those two children, so I said well it won't hurt me none to do this woman a favour.

I got Tom Earl and him and me took at it. It went right smooth and we did the same top job we always did. Till we got to the window. I brushed the paint over them dark red streaks and said to Tom Earl Well it'll take a second coat but that ought to do her. But when it dried, even after the third and fourth coat, them blood streaks were still there same as they were when we started. Tom Earl said Well she ain't going to pay, you know that, until we get these streaks covered over. I looked at him and I said You're right there, you done spoke a big mouthful. And I went out to the truck and got me my tools. Got me my ham-

mer and chisels, my blowtorch too: one way or the other I was
going to git that blood removed.

Well she comes running. She has got her head up in a towel,
one shoe off and the other one on, and she's dripping water, but
still she comes running. What are you doing, what are you
doing, she keeps asking, are you going to take hammer to my
house or burn it down? Is this what you call painting, she says.
So I looked at Tom Earl and he's no help, he just shrugs his
shoulders. I look to her and I say I've painted and I've painted
and it's still there. What is? she says. Hank Sparrow are you trying to two-bit me? No'm, I say, but there's something peculiar
going on here. There sure is, she says, and it's you two with no
more sense than a cat has pigeons. Now hold on a minute, I say.
So I take her round the house and I show her how we've put on
a good seven coats minimum. But still that blood where your
sister crawled up over the ledge. You leave my sister out of this,
she says. She says, Hank Sparrow I have known you Sparrows
all my life and there has never been one of you didn't try to
weasel out of work and didn't lie with every breath scored. Now
give me that brush, she says.

Tom Earl and me we give it to her. We coat it up good and
we wrap a little tissue over the handle so she won't get none on
her hand, and we let her to go to it. We stand back picking our
teeth and poking each other, laughing, because one, the way she
held that brush in both hands with her tongue between her
teeth and bent over like she was meaning to pick up dimes, and
two, because we knew it was a lost cause and no way in hell that
paint was going to do it.

See there? she said. See there? Now is that covered or isn't it?

Give it a minute, we said. You give them streaks about two
minutes and your eyes will pop out.

Well she stood right there with us, insulting us up one
side and down the other every inch of the way. But we took

it. We said nothing hard back to her. We knowed she was going to get the surprise of her life and be walking over hot coals to beg our pardon. And in two minutes, sure as rainwater, those streaks were back. They looked fresh brand-new, even brighter.

She went back and stood under the tree studying it, thinking her and distance would make a difference.

It's this paint, she said. This is a shoddy paint you're using.

Well we saw there was no end to it. So we got her in the truck between us, her with her hair still up in this green towel, and we drove down to the hardware. She got Henry Gordon pinned in the corner not knowing which way to turn but no matter how hard she pinned him he kept telling her that the paint we had was the best paint made and there weren't none no better including what went on the mayor's own house. I'll see about this, she said. And danged if she didn't call the distributor, long-distance, charging it to Henry. What is the best paint made? she said. And he said the very one we'd put on her house. She slammed down that phone. All right, she said, but Henry Gordon you have sold these two so-called working men a bad mix. I want another. Help yourself, Henry told her. She marches in his stockroom, says eenymeenyminy-moe over the cans, and comes out with one. All four of us now go back to her house. She has me git the lid off and she dabs over that blood again, so thick it just trickles down to the ground. We wait. She is now fit to be tied. I have lost a dear sister, she says, and lost my precious niece and nephew, and now you are telling me I've got to live with the curse of this blood?

We said it looked like it. Every one of us did, jumping right in with it. Because that blood was coming right back up. It was coming up bright as ever.

Well I never, she says.

So we go inside and stand in her kitchen and she gives each of us a Coca-Cola. It surpasses meaning, she said. I don't understand it. I don't guess I'm meant to.

We said Yesmam.

All right then, she said, I will just have to leave it there. It's meant to be left there. It's meant to be some kind of sign or signal. A symbol.

We didn't argue with her. I didn't even raise a hand when she said she was holding back ten dollars paint money because I never finished the house. There was something spooky about that place. All I wanted was to git shut of it. Me and Tom Earl took her cash and I give him some and me and him went out drinking.

10.

He drank. I didn't because I was only thirteen and the law wouldn't have it. But I knew Cluey, had seen him around, and that Agnes too because she was always at his heels, and I'd hear the stories of how the woman had died and Cluey and Agnes had gone up in thin air. I had beat up some on Cluey, being something of a bully in them days. I had bloodied his nose once and left him sobbing. I remember it and know it was him because he threw a rock at me and got me on the kneecap. And because of what he said. "My daddy will git you," he said. I was nice enough not to say "What daddy?" And I was glad I didn't. Because that night something tripped me as I was walking home along the dye ditch, and I fell off into that ditch and broke my left leg. It was somebody there all right, that's all I'm saying, and it wasn't Cluey or any other thing with two legs. It tripped me up, then it put a hand on my back, and I went tumbling over. I was with Tiny Peterson. He can tell you.

11.

It's every word true. But what I want to get to is that church. Timmons was being his usual assy self, playing up like he was doing a cameo role for *Rin Tin Tin*, yammering on about emptiness this and emptiness that, when the wood doors burst open. I was already turned around, trying to smack at a little girl back there, when Cluey come by me. I had my legs up high and he couldn't get past. So he dropped my legs. I'd just got them back up when his little sister tapped my knee. "Excuse me," she said. "Me and him are going out to see my daddy. That's him at the door."

I raised up high in my seat and looked again at that door. People behind me started hissing but I didn't care. There was something in that door all right, but it wasn't hardly human. It didn't have two arms and two legs and it didn't have a face either. But it was beckoning. I saw Cluey and Agnes walk into the thing, whatever it was, and then they simply were not there anymore. There was nothing. I thought it was a vision. Timmons just then got his smart voice back and was saying something about "Heaven is empty." The empty heaven, something like that. I admit it. Goose bumps rose high on my arm as a kitchen window. I was really scared. Now why I did it I don't know to this day, but I went running out after them. I figured that if maybe their daddy was out there then maybe mine was too and he might save me from my empty heaven. I went flying out. I sped out over everybody's knees and trampled on feet and the next second I was outside in the yard. Cluey and Agnes couldn't have been five seconds in front of me. And what I saw there gave me a chill I can feel to this minute. There was this woman there in a white gown which was down to her waist so I could see her nipples and these real wizened breasts. I reckon to this day it's why I like big-bosomed women. But what she was doing was struggling with this creature. Creature is what he was, make no mistake about that. She had her arms and legs wrapped around him, pulling and tugging and chewing – pure out-and-out screeching – while the creature thing was trying to throw her off and still hold on to poor Cluey and Agnes who by this time were just bawling. The creature was dragging them along and that woman was up on the creature's back, riding him, biting into the thing's neck, punching and clawing. Well it let go of the children. It gave a great howl and tore the woman off itself and practically bent her double. I mean it had her with her back across its knees and it was slamming her down all the while she screamed "Run! Run! Oh children run!" And they streaked off. I've never seen nothing tear away so fast. "Run! Run!" she cried. And they did and it was about this time that I heard this galloping, and a great white horse came out of the woods. The prettiest horse I ever will see. It galloped up to the children and slowed down and Cluey swung on its back, then got Agnes up there with him, and that horse took off full-speed, faster than I'd think a horse could. Then gone, just flying. The creature still had the woman. It slammed her down one last time and from where I was, hiding behind the tree, I could hear it: her back snap. *Snap*, like that, and the creature flung her down. It let out a great roar – of hatred, of pure madness at being thwarted, I don't know which – and then it took off too. But in the wrong way, not after the children. It seemed to me, the longer I looked at it run, that the closer it came to having human form. It had arms and legs and a face, though that face looked a million years old and like it hated everything alive.

That's all I saw. My own momma came out then and fixed her finger over my ear and nearly wrung it off. "Git yourself back in yonder," she said, "and don't you move one muscle lessen I tell you you can. When I git home I mean to put stick to your britches and you are going to wish you'd never been born."

I whimpered some, though not at my ear or at any threats she made. I never told anyone till now. Hell with them.

12.

The horse came by my place. I was out on the porch rocking away when it come by. Mary was in her chair with peas in her lap, shelling them. It was white, that horse was, it had two riders. They were up in the hills though. They were out a good far piece. There was something unnatural about, I thought that. About how fast that horse was running, how it didn't get slowed down none by tree or brush. I said to Mary how I'd never seen no horse like that, not around here. Not anywhere else either, I reckon. My dog was down between my legs and he got up and took off after them. About a quarter hour later he come back whimpering, his tail drawed up under his legs. He went under the house and moaned. It took me two days to git that dog out.

13.

See that horse? He told me. And he pointed. I went on with my shelling.

Wonder why they don't take the road, I said. Wonder whose it is.

I never saw no children. Didn't see what the dog did either. I didn't look that long. I can't sit out on the porch all day like him, watching what goes on. I got my own concerns to look after. Still, it was unusual. In the kitchen washing my hands I found myself staring out at a blue jay in the tree. Was that a horse, I ast myself, or was that a ghost?

14.

I thought when I went out and tweaked his ear that the sobbing Tim was doing wasn't on account of that ear. He was snow-white and trembling and it was all I could do hold him up. If I hadn't been so mad and set in my ways I would have known he'd seen something. It weren't no way for me to behave, whether it's to your own flesh or another's – but my husband had run out on me again and I imagine that had something to do with it.

But I'm sorry for it. I think it was the last time I wrung that boy's ear.

15.

You are all looking at me. Keep looking, then. You've always come to me with your aches and pains, now you're coming to me with this – is that it? I've told you my end before. I've never held anything back, and I won't now. Yes, I signed the certificate. She'd been slipping a long time and we'd all expected her death. I spent more time than most worrying about her. I said to her one day, "Tory," I said, "my medicines are doing you no good. I know you are in terrible pain all day and we both know you haven't got long. If you've a mind to, and want me to, and realize I am only raising this issue because I am aware of your misery, then I could give you something to help you go out easy and gentle and without the smallest pain."

She always told me she'd think on it. She'd let me know, she said. Then one day, after I'd given her every painkiller I could and none of it was helping her the slightest bit, I raised the question again.

"I'd like to go off, Doctor," she said, "in a nice and swoony dream just as you describe. But I can't go yet. I've got to hold on for my children's sake because I know one day he is coming back. I've got to stay and save them from him, if I can."

I knew, of course, who she was talking about. You can't live here as long as I have without knowing that. But I said: "Tory, if he does come back, we will take care of his hide. You don't have to worry about his harming your kids."

"You don't understand," she said. "There will not be a single thing a living soul can do. No," she said, "I will have to take care of this myself, if I'm able. But I thank you."

I didn't mean to divulge this. Though I don't see how it alters anything. It tells us something of the spirit she had, I suppose, and confirms the love and concern she had for that boy and girl. The rest of it I'd discount. I never saw evidence of anything to the contrary while I was in medical school. Nor since, either. Yes, I signed the death certificate. You know as I do that it was a natural death. The heart couldn't any longer do its job. Yes, she was black and blue all over. Yes, there was blood on the curtains, and not merely her own blood either. I ran a test. The report came back to me and an idiot at the laboratory had scribbled on it, "Please provide more information."

Well, I didn't. I wasn't about to let myself be made a fool of up there.

I'm done. Let Tory and her children rest in peace, I say. Let these stories stop right here.

ROCH CARRIER

THE WEDDING

Translated by Scheila Fischman

Martine would have scorned a thousand castles, and all the balls that might be held there, for a single little daisy from Didier. She never looked out her window without wishing to see him and her wish often came true: a great part of Didier's life was spent trying to be as close as possible to Martine. No one in the village was as happy as they were and no one envied them.

How many farmers went through their fields in search of a lost cow, how many fishermen fell asleep listening to the song of the river without knowing that close by, behind a curtain of rushes there was being performed the simple liturgy of two people who refuse to be two?

It was astonishing, then, when the word spread that Martine was expecting a child. Martine was dumfounded. Didier was confused. He went away, going off towards the city in search of money. Obviously, he did not return.

The child was born. Waiting for the child and waiting for Didier were mixed up together to a certain extent. The birth of the child was a little like Didier's return.

Although she grew accustomed to the child's presence Martine began once again to hope for her lover's arrival. She knew that he would consent to return only when he had made his fortune. Then he would shelter his family in a house that Martine would decorate with little daisies to prolong their youth.

Alas! she had to become reconciled not to wait any longer for Didier.

A very large stone building stood nearby, inhabited by women whose faces disappeared beneath intricate white head-dresses. Martine entrusted her child to them.

The old nun who received her took the child and clasped it tightly to her bosom, which was not completely flattened by the black fabric. Then she opened a screened door and disappeared. Martine could hear nothing but the sound of doors that creaked, one after the other and each one farther away. Finally everything was quiet except for several muffled steps that slid along the length of the corridor, silent as a viper. Martine suddenly had the impression that she had not experienced her love or her long wait or her heavy months of solitude. That road – painful, but happy as well – was erased like a chalk mark.

Martine left the building light-hearted, as though she were going to meet Didier under some musical tree, in a field where their love would add its light to the wheat. Had Didier really left her? Had he not arranged a rendezvous in one of their usual retreats? No. Martine was dreaming. An old, bent nun, the eldest of the community, approached silently and asked, "Are you ready?"

Martine was ready for anything. She followed the nun. Behind them older nuns in their complicated black robes formed a cortege. Martine, infinitely sad, listened to their hymns. The old nun walked rapidly. Martine could hear her panting. The cortege followed the road for a long way, then turned off towards a flat grey field at the end of which the sky was slanting. Now Martine saw nothing but the grass bending evenly beneath the wind that had risen with a voice like that of the nuns. She would have sworn that heaven was covered with the same grass. The wind twisted the robes and made them blacker. This atmosphere was prolonged for several minutes, several hours perhaps. As the cortege advanced the grass became higher. It reached the nuns' knees, then their thighs; it came up

to their waists, touched their faces and finally covered them
entirely. Then the leader made a gesture indicating that they
were to stop.

They had arrived at a river of black water. The nuns, who
had walked in two parallel rows, separated and lined up along
the river, thereby giving Martine two great black wings. On the
order of the eldest, the women in black brought their left hands
to their belts and with their right, in a single gesture, they broke
their rosaries. The old nun gathered them up and tied them,
and then Martine let them bind her arms, hands, legs and feet.

During all this time the nuns had been singing their hymns.
The eldest ordered them to be silent and said, "Look carefully
at this water that's cast a veil over the truth."

The sibylline phrase appeared very simple to Martine and it
did not cause her any anguish. She merely looked at the place
the old nun was indicating. She was not astonished to see
Didier in a black suit, rising to the surface, his limbs tied like
her own. He smiled at her. The old nun gave Martine a motherly push and the current carried her gently along. One by one
the nuns let themselves fall into the river after her. Their gowns
were indistinguishable from the black water. They were smiling.
The cortege formed perfectly parallel lines. Carried along the
water and the silence they passed through the shadow without
disturbing it, slid beneath the leafy arches without frightening
the birds and went towards – what?

The ceremony had taken place far away, very far. However,
the child of Martine and Didier had followed it with a troubled
eye. She saw her mother pass below her window and she recognized her even though the water had brought her hair down
over her face. She recognized her father whom she had never
seen. She remembered kisses she had never received from him
and rides on his back that she had never taken. She repeated
words he had never taught her. Her father and mother smiled

at her, she answered them and they were illuminated by an extraordinary happiness. She watched them go farther away with the water, followed by eighty old women who reflected an identical happiness.

When she could no longer see them, a key turned in her door.

"My daughter," said a soft voice, "life is waiting for you."

The child of Martine and Didier left her dungeon. She was a young girl, pretty, and her body had borrowed its movements from a flame. She wanted to smile. But her lips were dead.

JACQUES FERRON

MÉLIE AND THE BULL

Translated by Betty Bednarski

Mélie Caron had only thirteen children. She expected to have more, one a year until she died; but after the thirteenth, Jean-Baptiste Caron, her husband, said to her, "Stop, Mélie!"

So the poor woman stopped, not yet fifty years old. She remained unsatisfied, deprived of her due, all warm and trembling like an animal checked in full career. However, her trouble was not without remedy: did she not have her thirteen children? Thirteen children is not much; but it is a family. Alas! the consolation was short-lived. One by one her children left her. She had fed them too well: full of ardour were the boys, ripe and tender the girls; once fully grown there was no holding them back. In the end Mélie lost them all. She remained alone with her old man.

He, like a prisoner whose sentence is served, now found his freedom. He was no longer to be found at home, but spent most of his time with the other freedmen of the village, old eccentrics of the same breed as himself, parleying and laying down the law, drinking whenever the opportunity arose, and then pissing, drop by drop, the burning fire of his repentance. Mélie would take advantage of this to offer herself: "Let me help you, old man."

The suggestion was enough to make the waters flow again. Forty years of married life had taught the old man much; he knew that at the slightest sign of weakness his wife would get him into her clutches and not let go till she had mollycoddled him into senility. He remained on his guard.

"Thank you, Mélie. I'm all right now."

Now it came to pass that the old lady, deprived of children and husband, her corpulence notwithstanding, began to feel confined, loath to be restricted to her own company. Humours began to rise to her brain. At first this made her head swim, then she felt unsteady. It was the end of August. Alone in her kitchen, with her fly-swatter in her hand, she listened: not a fly in the house. The silence astounded her. In the absence of flies she was prepared for much worse: for the appearance of snakes, of preposterous frogs, of demons armed with scapularies, against which her fly-swatter would have been useless; prepared for an attack of raving madness. She was on the point of screaming when she heard a moo which saved her. Fleeing her monsters, she rushed out.

Outside, giving shade to the door, there rose a cherry tree, with flashes of sunlight and the redness of cherries moving among its leaves: beyond that there stretched a garden, then, as far as the river, a field. Mélie crossed the garden. The calf in the field saw her; with his tail in the air he came up towards her with faltering little leaps. The fence that separated the field from the garden brought them both to a stop. The old lady leant down; the calf raised a round, wet muzzle: they looked at each other. And suddenly Mélie Caron was moved by a feeling worthy of her heart. This muzzle, this trust had overwhelmed her; tears came to her eyes; had she been able to cry tears of milk she would have wept buckets to satisfy the appetite of the poor animal.

That evening when Jean-Baptiste Caron came home, she announced to him: "In future I shall look after the calf."

The soup was steaming on the table.

"Fine," said the old man, sitting down. Discussions have never been known to keep soup hot. Better polish it off now and talk later. When he had eaten his fill: "Why look after the calf, Mélie?" he asked.

She replied: "Because I want to."

"Have I by any chance not taken good care of him?"

"Good or bad, you'll not take care of him any more."

"Fine," said the old man, who in actual fact was not particularly concerned about the calf.

He was nevertheless surprised a few days later to see his old lady in the field, sitting under a huge, black umbrella, which protected her from the sun and whose light shade, far from hiding her from view, made her most conspicuous.

"What are you doing there, Mélie?"

"Knitting."

And so she was.

"Perhaps you'd be more comfortable knitting in the house."

"No, old man, I'm more comfortable here." And she added: "Besides, I can't leave him now."

He asked anxiously: "Leave who?"

"Come now, old man, the calf, of course!"

The animal was lying at Mélie's feet. The picture was not lacking in charm. But to Jean-Baptiste it gave not the slightest pleasure.

"Shall I tell you something, Mélie? Shall I?"

She made no objection.

"Well," he said, "you look like an escaped lunatic, and that's a fact."

"Old fool, yourself," she replied.

You cannot reason with a woman when she is in full possession of her faculties, much less when she loses them. Reason attacks front on; such bluntness is a drawback; with the weaker sex you have to use some stratagem, or simply take them from behind.

"If Mélie were twenty years younger," the old man said to himself, "a few little pats on the behind would bring her to her senses."

In fact he could have done with shedding a few years himself: he had long since lost the art of those little pats. So how was he to bring about a recovery? What could he do to stop the old lady's madness becoming the talk of the village?

"It'll be quite simple," thought Jean-Baptiste Caron. "Since she's mad over a calf, I'll sell the calf."

In this way he hoped to cure her. The remedy was simple indeed. He went off at once and made the necessary arrangements with the butcher. The next morning at daybreak along came his man, paunch bulging beneath a white apron. He had donned for the occasion a bowler hat. He took away the calf. Soon afterwards old Mélie, still heavy with sleep, came out of the house suspecting nothing. The cherry tree, branches held high, for it had not yet lowered its panoply, revealed a strangely slender trunk. The sun was coming up. Dazzled, the old lady stopped a moment to blink her eyes, and then set off along the garden path, calling: "Littl'un! Littl'un!"

She reached the fence; there was still no sign of the calf. Again she called him, but with no better luck. Then she made a thorough search: she searched high and she searched low, but, from the garden to the river, the field was empty.

"Ah, mercy me!" she cried.

And back she rushed, the sight of the water having convinced her that the animal had drowned. Is it Christian to put rivers at the bottoms of fields? This arrangement of Nature's filled her with indignation. In her haste she bumped into the cherry tree, who, preoccupied himself, had not seen her coming, absorbed as he was in the foliage, distributing his fruit to the birds. The birds flew away, cherries fell to the ground, and the wicked servant was caught in the act at his very roots. Much to his surprise the old lady continued on her way. So he signalled to the birds to come back.

Mélie Caron went back into the house.

"Old man, old man, the most terrible thing has happened."

This most terrible thing roused no interest.

"Can you hear me, old man?"

He could not hear her, and for a very simple reason: he was not there. The old lady ran to his room: she searched high and she searched low, but the bed of Jean-Baptiste Caron was empty.

"Ah, mercy me!"

But at the sight of the chamber-pot she was not alarmed. No old fellow who had trouble pissing is ever swept away by the flood. Besides, the pot was empty. However, this incapacity of her husband's for drowning did not altogether lessen the mystery of his disappearance. Mélie Caron remained as in a dream. At first her dream revealed nothing; on the contrary it masked her view; the veil was coloured, for she was dreaming with her eyes open. Suddenly the veil was drawn aside: she saw a knife, and behind the knife, holding it, his paunch bulging beneath a white apron, wearing for the occasion a bowler hat – the butcher.

"I'm dreaming," she said to herself.

With which statement the butcher agreed, closing the curtain. Then old Mother Mélie rushed into the wings, and off to the butcher's she trotted. On her way she passed the church.

"Mother Mélie," said the priest, "you're tripping along like a young girl."

"Yes, yes, *Monsieur le curé,* if you say so – like a young girl. But have you seen my old man?"

"I saw your old man and your calf, one joyful, the other pathetic."

"Oh, the poor dear! Oh, the ruffian! Pray for him, *Monsieur le curé.*"

And the old lady continued on her way. She arrived at the butcher's. The butcher, who had not had time to remove his hat, was surprised to see her again so soon.

"Good day, butcher. Where is my calf?"

"Good day, ma'am. I don't know your calf."

"Oh, don't you now!"

She paused in the doorway just long enough to blink her eyes. The morning was behind her, radiant, making the room in front of her dark. However, she was soon able to distinguish the carcasses hanging there.

"There are many calves here," said the butcher, showing her the carcasses. "Only they all look alike since we undressed them."

"I see one that seems to have kept its coat on."

"Where's that, Mistress Mélie?"

"Here."

And pointing her finger, she touched a very shame-faced Jean-Baptiste.

"That's your old man, Mistress Mélie."

"Cut me off a leg all the same."

"He's very skinny."

"Cut it off, I tell you!"

The butcher refused. The old lady took away his knife.

"Then I'll help myself to that leg."

Whereupon, Jean-Baptiste Caron intervened. "Don't act so foolish, Mélie. Your calf's here."

He handed her a rope; the poor dear animal was on the end of it, his eyes startled, his muzzle round and wet.

"Littl'un!"

"We weren't going to hurt him," said Jean-Baptiste Caron, "only cut him."

"A calf develops better that way," volunteered the butcher.

"Quiet, you liars! My calf shall remain entire, as the Lord made him."

Having made sure that he still had all his vital parts, including his little phallus, the old lady set off with him.

The priest, who had not yet finished his breviary, was still in front of the church.

"Well, Mother Mélie, I see you've found your calf."

"Yes, *Monsieur le curé*, but I got there just in time: they were about to cut him, the poor dear animal. I stopped their cruelty. You see, *Monsieur le curé*, he still has all his vital parts, including his little pointed phallus."

"So I see, Mother Mélie, so I see."

The old lady continued on her way, pulling her calf behind her. Soon afterwards the old man, Jean-Baptiste, appeared on the scene, looking very dejected indeed.

"It appears," said the priest, "that you're jealous of a calf. Your old lady showed me what you were planning to deprive him of."

"She showed you! Forgive her – she's not herself any more."

"Forgive her for what? I don't take offense at that. Surely you wouldn't expect her to put drawers on her calf?"

The bell for mass began to ring. The priest was obliged to leave the old man.

One month later the latter called at the presbytery. He was looking even more dejected; he walked bent double. When he saw down the priest noticed his face: he thought he seemed worried.

"Worried, no. Let's just say I'm weak."

"Well now! You're getting older."

"That may be, but it's not just age; for the last month I've eaten nothing but mash and grass."

"No!"

"Yes, mash and grass."

"The same as a calf?"

"You said it, *Monsieur le curé*; the same as a calf. I like meat, beans and lean pork. This food doesn't suit me at all and Mélie won't listen to me. She says we're all one nation."

"What language do you speak at home?"

"We still speak like people, but only because we don't know how to moo."

The priest began to laugh. "It's just the same with French Canadians; they still speak like people, but only because they don't know English."

Jean-Baptiste Caron nodded his head. "It's quite possible that calf is English," said he; "he's taking my place."

"Your place! You mean you live in the stable?"

"No, *Monsieur le curé*, we don't live in the stable. But the calf is living in the house."

"You don't say," said the priest. "He must be an English calf."

"He must be: he's not at all religious."

The priest rose to his feet. "We must drive him out."

This was also the opinion of Jean-Baptiste Caron.

"But how?"

Jean-Baptiste Caron also wondered how. The priest put a finger to his forehead, and this had the desired effect.

"Return to your house," he said to the old man. "But first pull yourself together and look cheerful. Once home, eat your mash as though you enjoyed it and be loving to the poor dear little animal."

"I won't be able to."

"You will. After a week or two, Mélie will think you share her feelings. At the same time, bring other animals into your house."

"You must be joking, *Monsieur le curé*!"

"Cats, dogs, mice, rabbits, even hens. I don't say you should bring in cows or pigs. Just domestic animals. Mélie will grow attached to them and so become less attached to the calf. Then it will be possible to use a stratagem."

Jean-Baptiste Caron: "A stratagem?"

The priest: "You will tell Mélie that you're worried about the calf's future."

"I'll tell her the truth: in six months he'll be a bull. It seems to me that's something to worry about."

"Exactly, this is what we must prevent. After all he's an English calf: mating isn't for him."

"All the same, we're not going to send him to school!"

"No, not to school: to a seminary."

The priest added: "A professional in the family is no disgrace."

"You're right, *Monsieur le curé*; a professional in the family is no disgrace."

At times advice is worth heeding, especially when it comes from one's priest. Jean-Baptiste Caron decided to make use of that offered him. Under the circumstances there was little else for him to do. He therefore declared himself to be in favour of calves, which won him the confidence of the old lady. Then he brought up the subject of education.

"Well now, it's no joke; a professional in the family is a worthwhile and honourable thing."

Mélie Caron knew it was no joke. But completely wrapped up in her calf, she was not particularly concerned about honour or the family; she wondered which of the two, the bull or the professional, would suit her best. Her heart inclined to the one, her reason to the other, and the animal looked at her puzzled. She too was puzzled.

"What are we going to do with you, poor little fellow?" she asked him.

"Moo, moo," replied the calf.

This reply did nothing to solve her dilemma. Then she reflected, not unreasonably, that once educated the animal would express himself more clearly. So she opted for the professional, telling herself that if by chance he did not like this condition he could always go back to being a bull. Without further delay she went to the priest and told him of her decision.

"A good idea, Mother Mélie! And since you want him to be educated, send him to the Quebec Seminary: that's where I studied."

The old lady looked at the priest. "You don't say!"

The priest was forced to climb down a little. "We mustn't exaggerate," he said. "But all the same, I do think, with his intelligence, this little fellow could become a lawyer or even a doctor."

The old lady seemed disappointed.

"A doctor, that's no joke!"

The old lady knew it was no joke. She simply said, "Pooh!"

"A lawyer then?"

She preferred the lawyer.

"Then the matter's settled, Mother Mélie; next week they'll come for your little one: a lawyer he shall be."

As had been arranged, one week later to the very day the Father Superior of the Quebec Seminary sent his representative, a great giant of a man, part beadle, part deputy, who arrived with much to-do in a carriage drawn by three horses. The carriage drew up in the courtyard of the presbytery. Immediately the postulant was brought forth.

"Ali baba perfectus babam," cried the representative.

Which is to say that at first sight, without further inspection, he had judged the calf fit to become a lawyer. On hearing these words the animal moved his ears. The priest noticed this.

"Well, well, he understands Latin!"

Mélie Caron did not understand it. She said "Amen," however, with a heavy heart.

This amen had an effect she had not foreseen: the representative rose to his feet and, standing up in the carriage, pointed his finger at her:

"Thou, *Melia, repetatus.*"

"Amen," repeated the old lady.

Then the giant of a man leapt from the carriage, seized hold of the calf, and carried him off into the church barn.

"He's not as good as the Father Superior of the Quebec Seminary," said the priest, "only being his representative, but you'll see, Mother Mélie, he still knows all about giving an education."

Indeed, no sooner had he entered the barn with the calf than he reappeared, alone, holding in his hands a long object, which he gave to the old lady.

"Thou, *Melia, repetatus.*"

"Amen," she said.

And the terrible pedagogue went back into the barn.

"But it's my Littl'un's tail!" cried Mélie Caron.

"Yes," replied the priest, "it is your Littl'un's tail. Keep it. He no longer has any use for it."

At that same moment the door of the barn opened, and who should appear but the calf, stiff, in a long black frock-coat, walking like a little man.

"Littl'un!"

He stopped and slowly turned his head toward the old lady. This head did not fit, it was shaky and too high, its features motionless. And he stared at her with vacant eyes.

"Littl'un!" the old lady called again.

He did not even twitch his ears. The old lady did not know what to think. What had they done to her little one in the church barn that he should come out looking so distant? They had cut off his tail, to be sure; they had put clothes on him, true; he was walking on his hind legs like a prime minister, so much the better! In short, they had educated him, but did that mean they had to make him blind and deaf? This being the case, education did make the farewell easier.

The seminarian calf, drawing a white handkerchief from his frock-coat, waved it, but distantly, oh so distantly: the fingers holding the handkerchief were already human. Mélie Caron made no attempt to hold him back. He climbed into the carriage beside the representative of the Father Superior of the Quebec Seminary, and there sat upright on his little behind, he who had never used it before. The carriage moved off and soon disappeared from sight.

"Well?" asked the priest.

Well, what? The old lady did not know, so she made no reply.

"Well, yes," the priest began again, "he is gifted, that little fellow! He's not even at the Seminary yet, and all there is left of the calf is its head. Education is for him. A lawyer he shall be, and what a lawyer!"

"What lawyer?" asked the old lady.

"Why, Lawyer Bull! A famous lawyer. Come, come, be proud: he'll be a credit to you."

Mother Mélie was holding the calf's tail in her hands, and it hung there pitifully. Proud? With her head down and her tail, so to speak, between her legs, she did not feel in the least like being proud. "I'm very happy," she said; and very sadly she went off. To see her leave like that worried the priest. The next day after mass, without stopping to have lunch, he went to call on her, and found her in the garden, feeding the hens.

"I was afraid I might find you in bed, Mother Mélie."

"I very nearly did stay in bed, *Monsieur le curé*. When I woke up I had no desire to do anything, only to die. Surely at my age I'm entitled to a rest. Then I heard the clucking of the hens, the barking of the dog, the animals making their morning noise, and I thought of my poor rabbits twitching their noses without a sound. Who else would have looked after all these animals but me? So I got up."

The priest took off his hat while he recovered his breath. His plan had worked, the calf was out of the way, the old lady cured; what more could he ask, under the circumstances? He was satisfied; he remembered then that he was hungry. Mélie Caron gave him a meal and he ate till he could eat no more. When he rose from the table she was still not satisfied: "Just one more little mouthful, *Monsieur le curé*?"

"So you're not cross with me, Mother Mélie?"

She was cross that he had eaten so little. Apart from that she had nothing against him, considering him to be a good Christian.

"But what about your calf, Mother Mélie?"

She saw no reason why she should be cross about that. Hadn't she parted with her calf so that he could become a lawyer? It had been for his own good; of what importance was the sacrifice she, poor woman, had made?

"Besides," said Mélie Caron, "I am used to these separations."

She was thinking of her thirteen children, well-fed all of them, full of ardour the boys, ripe and tender the girls, who had left her one by one. And where had they gone? One to Mani-waki, another to the States, a third out West.[1] As for the rest, she did not know. Besides, Maniwaki, Maniwaki... she had never been outside of Sainte-Clothilde de Bellechasse: what could Maniwaki mean to her? Or the States? Or Abitibi? Or the Farwest?[1] "I lost my children, *Monsieur le curé*; I can part with a calf. Besides, I still have my hens, some rabbits, a dog, a cat and some mice, enough to keep me going for some time yet. My supply still hasn't run out."

"You'll die one day, all the same."

"The worms will console me."

"Come, come, Mother Mélie. And what about the good Lord?"

"After, once the worms have eaten their fill."

The priest thought of his position; there was nothing in the Scriptures to prevent Mélie Caron having her bones cleaned off by worms before going up to join the Almighty. "Very well," he said, taking his hat and preparing to leave. Whereupon Mélie

---

[1] Ferron writes, mischievously: *Maniouaki*, *Stétes*, and *Farouest*.

Caron, still not satisfied, asked him if he thought that at the Seminary the little fellow would keep his head.

"His calf's head? Or course not."

"Then how shall I recognize him?"

The priest thought of his position and either because he had forgotten his theology or because the question had not been dealt with, he could think of nothing very Catholic to say in reply. He hesitated, feeling somewhat ill at ease in his cassock.

"Mother Mélie," he said at last, "there exists something which, as a young bull, your little fellow would have worn in all innocence, but which as a lawyer he will have to conceal; it's by that incorruptible root – for education cannot touch it – that you will recognize him."

And doubtless judging he had gone too far, without explaining himself at greater length, he went off, leaving the old lady with her curiosity, naturally, unsatisfied. So when Jean-Baptiste Caron came home she eagerly asked him for an explanation. Jean-Baptiste Caron, who was not inhibited by theology, answered without hesitation: "It's the phallus, pointed in the case of a calf that's become a young bull."

"And in the case of Littl'un?"

"Likewise, since education can't touch it. He'll keep his root even though he's a lawyer, and this way he'll be easy to recognize."

And so, reassured, Mélie went back to her daily routine, and the months passed, the winter months, then spring, and the cherry tree bloomed; then came the summer months, June, July, and the ripe hay was harvested. In August the newspapers announced the famous fair to be held at Quebec in the early fall, and which Jean-Baptiste Caron had been wanting to see for a long time.

"Old girl," said he, "we really should see the Provincial Exhibition before we die."

The old lady burst out laughing. "Have you gone crazy, old man?"

In order that she might judge for herself he handed her a page of the newspaper. On it she found this professional announcement: "Maître Bull, lawyer."

"Anyway," she said, "I've nothing against your crazy idea."

So to Quebec they went, their hearts anxious, their eyes wide. The city, the fair, amusement and pleasure soon lifted the anxiety. Fatigue came more slowly; however, after two or three days, they could hardly keep their eyes open, and were beginning to miss the peace and quiet of Sainte-Clothilde.

"But," said the old lady, "before we go back, there's someone I have to see."

Jean-Baptiste Caron was not in the least surprised.

"Someone you have to see?" he asked.

"Yes, old man! Just because we've never had any fallings out, which is no reason why we shouldn't see a lawyer before we die."

Old Mélie was right: they should see a lawyer. It was unfortunate, however, that the lawyer had to be Maître Bull. Jean-Baptiste Caron could see no good coming of the encounter. It is one thing to recognize a young bull under a gown, but quite another to get the lawyer to agree to the test. At any rate, Mélie should go alone.

"I'm thirsty," said Jean-Baptiste Caron. "I'll wait for you at the Hotel de la Traverse."

So Mélie went alone. To Maître Bull's office she came. "Come in," cried he in a beautiful deep voice. She went in and found, in a dusty little office, a young man dressed in black, handsome as an archangel, sad as an orphan, who, after the normal formalities, asked for her name, first name and place of residence: Mélie Caron of Sainte-Clothilde. And the purpose of her visit: whom did she wish to bring action against?

"No one," the old lady answered.

Surprised, he looked at her; and said, with relief: "Thank you."

It was the old lady's turn to express surprise. He relied to her that the lawyer's profession served as an alibi.

"Who are you then?"

"A poet," he replied.

"Oh," she said.

"I keep it a secret; if men knew they would look upon me as some kind of animal."

Mélie Caron lowered her eyes at this modesty.

"Your name again?" the lawyer asked her.

"Mélie Caron."

"I don't know why," he said, "but that name brings to my mind the image of a field and the sound of a river."

At these words, no longer doubting that this was her Littl'un, the poor dear animal, old Mélie pulled from her bag the pitiful object, which she had kept, and let it hang beside her. Meanwhile the archangel, the orphan, the young man in black, went on in his beautiful deep voice, saying that it was not the sound of a river, but that of the wind in the grass, the wind whose waters bleach it white in the sun.

"Earth's back is dark and stains the hand but when the wind passes she forgets her sorrow and, moved, turns over, showing her white belly, where the grass is soft as down, where each blade is a nipple gorged with milk."

"Poor dear," thought the old lady, "he badly needs to graze!"

"Do you sometimes hear a voice?" she asked him. "A voice calling you: Littl'un, Littl'un!"

"Yes, I hear it."

"It's mine," said Mélie Caron.

"I didn't know," said the lawyer. "Besides, I cannot answer. I am imprisoned in a cage of bone. The bird in his cage of bone is death building his nest.[1] There was a time when I hoped to free myself by writing, but the poems I wrote then did not render my cry."

"Poor dear," thought the old lady, "he badly needs to moo."

"Are you married, Littl'un?"

The young man gave a horrified start; his archangel's wings trembled; he was deeply offended at being thought capable of anything so low.

"Quite so, quite so," said the old lady. "I didn't mean to offend you. I only wanted to find out if you were free."

"I am free," he said, "subject only to the will of the ineffable."

She handed him the hairy member.

"Then take back your tail, Littl'un, and follow me."

She led him to the Hotel de la Traverse where Jean-Baptiste Caron was waiting for them.

"Old man, it's Littl'un!"

Of this she seemed so sure that the old man lowered his eyes, embarrassed. Together they returned to Sainte-Clothilde. "Well, well!" called the priest. "It's back to the land, I see!" And back to the land it was! Though they had surpassed the prophesied return. Indeed, once he had grazed, it was not long before Maître Bull had recovered his élan. Meanwhile his gown was falling to shreds. Soon there was nothing left of the fine education he had received at the Quebec Seminary. One day, at last, he was able to utter his poet's cry, a bellow such as to drive all the cows in the county mad. Faithful to his root, he had found his destiny. From that day on, before the wondering eyes of old Mélie, he led an existence befitting his nature, and left behind him in Bellechasse, where they called him The Scholar, the memory of a famous bull.

---

[1] *L'oiseau dans sa cage d'os*
 C'est la mort qui fait son nid.
These lines are taken from *Cage d'oiseau (Bird Cage)*, by the Quebec poet Saint-Denys Garneau (1912-1943).

SEÁN VIRGO

THE CASTAWAY

When a young priest in an old town fell into the sin of despair, his penance was to go back into the world and seek out his faith.

He stood in his room for the last time, with his suitcase half packed, and wondered what he should do. "You are only a castaway now," he told himself. He thought he might go back to the farm where his brother still lived, but the priest in the mirror called that cowardice. "That isn't the world," he said. "The world is a city now."

So the castaway rode the bus for a night and a day, and took a room in a cheap hotel near the station.

For a week he trudged the sidewalks, and rode the streetcars, and sat in cafés, watching and listening. He felt invisible, and was grateful for that. The people bewildered him.

He lay in bed with the sounds of other lives in the building around him.

"I am lonely for God," he whispered, and when the priest in him answered, "Perhaps God is lonely for you," he hated the glibness, the smugness of that.

He wandered through galleries and museums, but found himself most at home in the botanical gardens, with their misted glass walls and exotic vines. He bought crime novels from a second-hand stall and lost himself in their society.

Each evening he went to a shabby bar down the street and sat for an hour in the backroom sipping his beer. One night a little stumpy man came in and sat down on the other side of the room. Every time he looked up the man was watching him, smiling and nodding as if they shared in an unspoken joke.

When he got up in irritation and left, the priest in him chided, "He is only a simpleton—isn't this where charity should begin?"

The next night he found the man sitting in the corner he thought of as his own, smiling up at him when he came in. He sat at another table and opened his book, but the words were a blur on the page.

"There are great things to be found in books, they say." The little man's voice was like a bird's. He let out a warbling laugh, and jigged his stumpy legs under the table.

The castaway could not tell why the words galled him so. He would not look up. "This is childish," the priest in him said, but "No," he muttered, and got to his feet, "there is something too knowing about that smile."

As he walked up the street he heard someone following, but each time he turned round to look there was no one there.

He chose the hotel bar instead the next night, and sat undisturbed for an hour with his beer and his book. But when he went to the door, past the crowd of men at the bar, a head turned towards him and there was the moon face of the little stumpy man winking and smiling up at him as he passed.

"Perhaps you are right," the priest in him said. "There is something dangerous about that creature."

At daybreak he called the farm and asked if he could come home. "There's plenty of work for you," said his brother. "Something to show for what was spent on your education." It was not said unkindly.

Two nights later the castaway sat at the farmhouse table, eating the meal that his brother's wife had prepared. Soon after dark, he climbed the narrow stairs to the room where he'd slept as a child. He lay looking up at the window and found himself whispering the words of his innocence: *One to watch and one to pray / And two to bear my soul away.* The priest in him knew this was simple nostalgia, but for all that not worthless.

Through the wall he could hear them making love. He covered his ears, but she was a handsome woman with a generous mouth, several months pregnant, and the vision played out in his mind.

He could not meet her eye in the morning, and she understood. "We want you to stay," she told him. "Your brother works too hard on his own." She pointed across the field to the cottage where his grandmother had lived out her days. "That can be your home," she said, "but I hope you will eat with us." She touched his shoulder and he felt a rush of love for her kindness. "Don't worry," she smiled. "You'll be earning your keep, believe me."

The weeks that followed were like time turning back on itself. Each day it seemed he could manage heavier loads, and though his brother's old work clothes hung loose on his frame, he felt he was shedding a tired, dusty skin.

They were careful with him, not demanding too much, and as he grew stronger, he thought less and less – too weary each evening to do more than cross the field and fall deep into sleep. The old cattle dog took to following him; it slept by the cottage door.

They left for a weekend, and he was in charge. He looked out at the land, and imagined that it was his own. Next week they would start the first haying; at month's end the lambs would be sheared and shipped off to the sales. The seasons turned in his mind. When Spring came again, their child would be taking its first steps.

He finished the chores and went off with the old dog, along the concession road. He passed other farms, each a world of its own, and a loneliness overtook him. The old questions returned.

"You could stay here forever," the priest in him said, "but if you mean to serve God through the work of your hands, you should choose the monastic life." He walked on towards the river. "That's a very big *if*," he said. "I'm just feeling my way. Let it be."

He stood on the high bank, looking down at the water. An angler was fishing beside some willow trees, casting over and over downstream. His line formed loops and arabesques in the sunlight, floated for a moment on the surface, and then flashed back again. The castaway stood mesmerized by his skill and the flowing stream. He watched where the line kept falling and there, where the sunlight went down through the water, he saw a big trout, suspended above the gravel. The line flew across, and he saw the trout rise to the fly and held his breath, but the line was whipped away at that moment, and the man resumed casting. This happened not once but twice, and then again, and the mad fancy struck him that if the angler stepped out from the trees and looked up, it would be the little stumpy man.

He called the dog softly and went back the way he had come.

In a dream that night he stepped out from a barroom door and found three men beating someone who lay whimpering on the ground. The castaway rushed to his aid, but the men laughed in his face and went off down the alleyway singing. He dropped to his knees and saw the face of the little stumpy man, the round, child's eyes filled with tears and bewilderment.

He awoke, and lay shaken with grief. The cottage was still in thrall to the nightmare. The priest in him whispered *by Thy great mercy defend us from the perils and dangers of the night*, but the dread remained. He opened the door and stood dressing himself, looking out at the first pale light in the east. The dew was thick and cold on the grass as he walked to the farmhouse.

He climbed the stairs and lay down in his brother's room. He thought of their lovemaking, and the child who would be born in the Fall, perhaps in this bed, and he fell back to sleep. When he woke, the sun was high and he was far behind with the chores.

He ran out to feed the lambs and open their pen, and then worked till the late afternoon. By the time he went out with the dog to bring back the lambs, there were thick clouds in the west and the air was still, with a queer violet light everywhere. It grew dark too early, and when the wind came it swooped onto the farm, scouring the puddles in the yard and rattling the tin on the barn roof. He went down to the stable just as the downpour began. The trees were loud in the darkness, and the rain lashed his face.

But the stable felt all the more sheltered for the tumult outside. The milk cow had come in on her own and was waiting for him. He sat on the stanchion's edge and began to milk, breathing in the moist animal warmth, resting his cheek on her flank. The milk hissed into the pail, while all around the barn was the noise of a storm at sea.

The lights dimmed and flickered, grew bright for a moment and then left him in the darkness. Flashes of lightning picked out the yard and the house and lingered in his eyes. The cow shifted and grumbled, but he soothed her and kept the milk flowing. Through the open door he saw a light coming through the rain; a figure with a lantern appeared and stepped inside. The little stumpy man hung the lantern on a nail and his shadow climbed the wall, and then shrank back down as he knelt in the straw. His smile appeared under the cow's belly, as he set to work on the two far teats.

There was no denying the harmony of it, the steady pulse of the milk through their hands. The castaway thought of the times when his sister and he had milked together, racing through the chore to get free, to go out and play.

The milk foamed up in the pail. "I don't know who this is," the priest in him said, "but I think it may be the Devil." The castaway leaned into the cow's side and answered himself: "What use would the Devil have," he said out loud, "for a man who does not believe?"

The little man's laugh was a mad bird's filling the stable. His hands were so deft, though. In no time at all he was done with his share, and was stripping the teats of their last thin drops.

"Who are you?" the castaway asked. "Where do you come from?"

"Hereabouts, thereabouts," the little man said. "It's all the same, you know." He reached under and gripped the castaway's hands, so that two hands were milking each teat together. It was the strangest feeling.

Their eyes met over the milk pail. "Don't worry your head," chirped the stranger, and when the milking was done he took down the lantern and went out into the storm without looking back.

The castaway stumbled through rain and darkness, up to the house. At some point in the night he woke to a stillness all around. He opened the window to the sound of trees dripping, and smelled the earth washed clean.

There was a dance in the village hall the next Saturday night. "You have to come with us," she told him. "You must let people get to know you." She looked at him gravely. "We're allowed to have fun, you know." He dreaded the prospect, but he knew he should not refuse.

There were fiddles and guitars, and an out-of-tune, battered piano. People of all ages came and mingled; they all seemed to know each other, they made shyness feel like a sin. The castaway stood watching near the door, perplexed and ashamed, till his brother's wife beckoned him over. "Come on, sobersides," she said. "Just throw yourself into it." He saw how gracefully she moved, despite the child in her womb, and when a woman took his hand and turned him around, he felt something let go. The lilt of the fiddles crept into his heels, until he was laughing and moving without any thought of himself.

For a moment he thought he saw angels in all of those faces, caught up in the dance, and he closed his eyes in delight. When he opened them he was passing the band on the stage, and there was the little stumpy man, playing the fiddle, smiling his child smile, his eyebrows and heels keeping time with the tune. The castaway laughed out loud, and the fiddler got to his feet and played wildfire jenny.

The castaway danced through the night. He danced with women, he danced with children, he danced with his shadow outside on the lawn.

He looked up at the stars, and the priest in him held his peace.

MARIE-CLAIRE BLAIS

THE NEW SCHOOLMISTRESS

Translated by Vida Bruce

"Where does he live, this here school inspector?" Judith Prunelle asked Abbé Philippe Rougemont, who was shaking out his cassock with one hand and pulling his bicycle out of the ditch with the other. "Jesus Christ, I'm lost!"

"Lower your voice," said the Abbé, "I'm not deaf."

And that was how the new mistress of the School of Repentance entered this godforsaken village. (The absence of a teacher for the last three years had forced the Abbé to teach the children their catechism at home, an undertaking he had found both disappointing and ineffectual since not a single family welcomed him, with the except of Grand'mère Antoinette. And even she, probably hoping to conceal the depths of her poverty, received the Abbé on the doorstep trying to stop up the gaps in her household by placing her long stern silhouette on the stoop in front of him as if to forbid his entrance, imaging that the wall of shadow it created would hide the dearth within.) "Oh dear God! What kind of teacher is this you're sending us?" thought the Abbé, staring at the young girl who stood there in the middle of the road, a battered suitcase in her hand, saying in her rough slang, "Jesus, Mary and Joseph, where've I landed?" Descended from heaven no doubt, in a cloud of dust that still cloaked her from head to foot, dragging down with her all the saints – both male and female – she could name (Saint Chrysostom, Saint Luke, Saint Paul), running all the words together in an outrageous mouthful of profanity that included the sacred vessels of the church as well ("*Tabernacle*, I'd sure like to get out of here!"). Language perceived only through a prism of blasphemy whose rich colours, all gold and incense, seemed to inspire her revolt and enliven her vivid truck driver's imagination.

"My child," said the Abbé, lifting his shoulders, "please watch your language."

But what did she care about him, a man in whom she saw only a little boy, a playmate she could bully by poking a bony fist in his face? (Since childhood she had only known her eight wicked and quarrelsome brothers, had been happier among lumberjacks than girls her own age, was proud and disdainful because within her, hidden beneath the bony exterior, burned an insatiable energy – the girl in her living apart or sometimes not at all, appearing only fleetingly on the features of the tough adolescent who swore and spat all the time. But it was this young girl, nevertheless, who had obtained in some obscure school the yellowed diploma she now pulled from her pocket with a satisfied smirk: "Schoolmistress. There, I told you so, didn't I?") "Jesus Christ, I'll talk how I like," she said, threatening the priest with her fist.

A flood of invective then poured over the pale face of Abbé Philippe: "I don't like priests, they bore me."

The Abbé finally resigned himself to listening in silence, eyes closed. Having rattled off with gusto her entire vocabulary of oaths, Judith was silent. After a moment she asked for the time and for information about the inspector of schools.

"I'm sorry," said the Abbé, "I don't know where he lives. I'm new here. I'm not even sure we have an inspector general."

Judith couldn't imagine a school without an inspector, and besides, in her village they had advised her to knock on his door to find lodging. (She showed the Abbé a letter signed by the mayor of Sainte-Félice-du-bord, an illegible letter in which the Abbé pretended to take an interest.)

"You can come to my house," said the Abbé blushing. "There is a little room and a kitchen, no fire in the room in the spring but it still isn't too cold."

Letting herself suddenly collapse on top of her suitcase, legs stretched out in front of her, arms crossed, Judith Prunelle explained, her voice breaking like a young boy's, that she didn't need anyone, that she could very well find her own lodging. Snatching off her beret with a rough gesture, she started scratching her head.

"Well, what are you hanging around staring at me like that for?"

"I was resting," said the Abbé awkwardly. "I just came from catechism. But I'm on my way now. It's confession today..."

Before climbing on to his bicycle he seemed to hesitate a moment, then, all in a rush, he said to Judith – who was still watching him with a surly air – "Perhaps we can work an exchange. You find me some pupils for catechism and I'll give you a roof over your head and some grammar lessons."

"Don't need grammar," said Judith Prunelle. "Don't need you either."

"Mathematics, perhaps?"

"I know my sums," said Judith Prunelle. "Don't need you!"

"Oh! Well, fine," said the Abbé, "if that's how you feel."

The Abbé set off toward the woods. Judith heard his anxious voice in the distance: "It will be dark soon. Better go back."

"Ain't afraid. Ain't afraid of the dark," she replied to no one in particular to fill the silence. But when she found herself alone on the road and could see only the black fields in front of her and the darkening sky above, when she heard the whispering of the leaves in the wind, she began to tremble, and sighed hopefully: "Now then, this here inspector, Jesus Christ, I've gotta find him."

And she set out again.

The school was closed. Judith Prunelle opened it. There was no sign of the inspector general. Judith decided to make a bed for herself on the bare floor of the schoolroom. "Jesus Christ, it's freezing," she groaned all night long, covering her head with her coat, her neck twisted against the suitcase she was using as a pillow. "Tomorrow as soon as it's daylight I'll have to light that goddam stove! Then I'll go find me some pupils. No pupils, no school. What use is a diploma anyway, I wonder. My father was right, the north's so empty, hell, who needs diplomas? I'll stuff a little history and geometry into their heads. I know all them dates by heart, you bet I do. I'm no moron like that goddam little priest thought. I'm smart; he'll see. Charles II the Bald, Charles the Fat, Charles III, Charles the Handsome, I've got them all at my fingertips, yessir, mister priest. And then there's Charles the Great too! You wouldn't believe it could get so cold, and me with no mitts. I've got a suitcase full of carrots. Holy Virgin, useful maybe, but not much help keeping me warm. And then there's Charles IX and Charles X. I'll give them stupid goddam kids a beating and then we'll all eat carrots together. Holy smoke! I remember how all the boys in the village bawled like babies when they saw me leaving. And then they took off their caps. Jesus, that's respect for you! Maybe I should've gone back to the woods to cut trees, the sun's so warm there. Yeah, I used to drink a lot of beer there but I always stayed thin as a rake and the more I drank the thinner I got. And then there's Charles the Bold, they really oughta know that one. I'll hit them with the pointer if they don't get it. Well Jesus Christ, if it isn't the sun coming up; that's a surprise, eh? I'm sure glad to see it. I'll just shake myself up a little and eat a carrot and then bring in some wood. This is the life. Free as a bird, eh, and paid into the bargain. If only that goddam inspector general would get here."

Seated on her dusty desk, hair concealed under a large woollen beret, Judith ate a carrot. She was, to be precise, sitting on a part of the past of the School of Repentance, one of the school desks where Jean-Le-Maigre and Septième, in days gone by, had roughly carved their names with a knife and signed their amorous confessions with a black pencil *(Jean-Le-Maigre loves Martha the Hunchback – in life as in death... Septième begs Mademoiselle Lorgnette to wait for him after school... Dear Madame Casimir, would you be good enough to give me a match, you with your blouse bursting with treasure).* That fatal match was to be used to ignite a revolt and set fire to the school but this Judith Prunelle did not yet know. The new teacher swung her legs gently and happily welcomed the weak rays of sunlight that fell on her frozen knees. "Well by God, how about that for sunshine! Thank *you*, Saint Joseph. I was about ready to die of the cold in this place and wouldn't that've been cruel, by Jesus? Gotta put them through some of the Charlottes: Charlotte Elizabeth, Charlotte of Nassau, all that high society stuff. And I better get a rug for my school. They wipe their feet before they learn any history. I gotta teach the dirty little bastards some manners. Then I better clean up the goddam toilets. It's a real shame me arriving here like this without a word of welcome from the inspector general. I bet I know what's happened. They weren't expecting me because between times they've forgotten all about me coming. By Jonah, I'll teach them to remember with a few good clouts of the pointer. I'll show them."

It was six in the morning when Judith returned from the fields with her arms full of dry wood and children. From where they were sleeping in a damp, rat-infested barn, she had dragged a whole gang of kids seeking refuge for the night from a drunken grandfather, who was threatening to kill them. And from a wild-eyed mother, who was probably still wandering about as usual begging alms from the silent trees and a divine protection that the peaceful cloudless heavens could never grant her: "Alms for the love of God. My father's a drunk, my husband is sick, my children have no shoes."

"Mother was milking the cows one day," explained Josephine Poitiers, hanging on with one hand to the teacher's coat, "when suddenly, just like that, she went off her head and she's been like that ever since. It runs in the family, Grandpapa says," Josephine continued, walking along beside the teacher and her burden of children.

"Do you want me to fall, eh kid? Are you trying to knock me into the mud with all your goddam little brothers, eh?" But Josephine went right on pulling on Judith Prunelle's sleeve and trying with slow deliberation to explain:

"These things happen, Mademoiselle. It's a very great favour from God to have you in the school. We are certainly going to appreciate you. I had a vision yesterday in the barn. Our Lady told me you were coming."

"I don't understand a thing you're talking about," said Judith Prunelle in a sharp voice, and she abruptly deposited the children on the ground. "I'm not here to rescue orphans, for Christ's sake; I gotta look after my school."

"But she'll get better," said Josephine nodding wisely. Even thought she had always been poor and had been frequently beaten by her grandfather ("Grandfather loves us," she went on, taking hold of her little brothers' hands. "It's not his fault, it's just that when he's drunk he always wants to beat us up.") Josephine had none of the marks of a victim on her face: those profound scars that distinguish so easily the temporarily unfortunate of this world from those eternally doomed to wretchedness. She was, however, filthy from head to foot (the teacher could see the shadowy line of lice that separated the little girl's pigtails) but she wore her lack of cleanliness as if it were a handsome outfit, and her delicate manner and large china eyes, which she opened wide to utter her solemn phrases, came as something of a surprise. The phrases seemed not just to come from some other world but from some other person.

"You act as if you thought you were some kind of fine lady, for Christ's sake! I'm not sure we're going to hit it off," said the teacher with rough impatience. "And anyway, I'm not sure I've got enough carrots for the whole family. What's his name, that one over there?" she asked, singling out the smallest of the little boys who was blowing his nose with his fingers. "He doesn't look too bright."

"His name is Chester," said Josephine very politely, "and he's off his head too but he was born that way, Grandpapa says. There are lots of idiots in the village, Mademoiselle; you just have to get used to it. But with us it runs in the family. Chester, don't blow your nose in front of Mademoiselle. She doesn't like it."

"He can blow all he likes," said Judith Prunelle. "I'm no princess. You can see that easy enough."

Then flinging open the door of the school with a flourish, she cried out: "Well here it is, for Christ's sake! *My* school. And I'm gonna start teaching right away while it's still warm."

And Josephine, Chester, Marie-Ange Poitiers (and Hector Poitiers too) all seated themselves in a circle around Judith Prunelle and listened to her talk about one of her favourite subjects, the Creation of the World.

While Judith was creating the world, brandishing her thin fists at the blackboard, Chester Poitiers dreamed of his mother, wandering through the fields, the stones on the road tearing at her bare, bleeding feet that moved all alone on the white roadway. Josephine smiled and said every now and again into the ear of Chester or Hector, "Don't make so much noise with your nose. Mademoiselle doesn't like that."

Judith Prunelle interrupted her lesson to say shortly, "Jesus Christ, a nose doesn't bother me. Make whatever noise you want, Chester. I don't even hear it."

Josephine rose from her seat to explain. Mademoiselle asked her to sit down and the lesson continued. Chester closed his eyes.

"Just imagine, there wasn't a monkey, a mushroom, a drop of rain! I bet you can't imagine that, eh? Well, there was nothing, everywhere. Not an ant, not even a caterpillar."

"And God created the world in seven days," said Josephine, "and on the seventh day he rested. Monsieur le Curé Lacloche told me. Our Lady told me too. She talked to me yesterday. She was standing on the manure pile. She was very beautiful. She had golden hair. And she said, 'Josephine, would you like to boil some milk for my baby who is thirsty?' I ran to the house. There wasn't any milk left. When I came back, Our Lady wasn't there any more."

"Will you *sit down*?" said Judith Prunelle, knocking Josephine off her seat. "This isn't a classroom, it's a pigsty!"

"I saw her four times in the barn," said Josephine. "She promised to come back. She said to me: 'Josephine, you're going to be very unhappy. If I were you, I would hide my bread under the mattress every night. Because there's going to be a famine in the village. In the meantime, say your prayers.'"

"And there was no smoke and no fire in those days," continued Judith Prunelle passionately. "There was nothing. Then suddenly, it all began, all by itself, like someone starting to laugh in the night. The brooks, the seas, the rivers, everything began to bubble, like anger inside you, like soup boiling over the pot. My children, it was a beautiful sight to see."

"The lion lay down with the lamb," interrupted Josephine, "and the wolf in the arms of the deer. Our Lady shed many tears. I should tell you, Mademoiselle, that my little brothers don't wash very often. But there are lots of people don't wash, my grandfather says. Then I asked Our Lady what her name was. She said: 'Josephine, I am called Notre-Dame-Des-Petits-Sous.'"

Marie-Ange and Hector were asleep in their seats. Chester, whose square head stood out above the others, seemed to be meditating under the protective umbrella of his long eyelashes. While the teacher's conversation abounded in rippling images and seas overflowing their banks, saliva flowed from Chester's mouth copiously, soaking the collar of his shirt.

"It's nothing, Mademoiselle. He slobbers. It runs in the family."

"It runs in the family," Chester seemed to be saying, shaking his head.

But since Josephine talked so tirelessly and with such measured wisdom, her brothers, already encouraged by mental laziness, never opened their mouths unless to say with profound amazement – "Oh, Josephine!" – and even that rarely. Eventually they said nothing at all. As for poor Chester, he slobbered more and more, justifying Our Lady's prophecy to Josephine: "Josephine, your brother Chester has a pretty big head for his age. He'll end badly. He will be the village idiot. I hope you don't mind too much." So then Josephine said to Our Lady: "You're lucky, you are, that your baby doesn't have a big head like Chester's."

"And the fish danced," said the teacher, "and then the birds with their paper-thin wings flew all around in the springtime and there were giraffes walking very quietly on the new grass making no noise, no noise at all."

"Was there a sky up above?" Josephine stood up to ask the question. "Was God up there seated on a throne of clouds?"

"Yes," she replied, answering her own question, all-knowing. "He was there and he said, 'My beloved mountains, my beloved hills.'"

"Go to the toilet," shouted Judith Prunelle, pushing Chester toward the door. "If that isn't shameful, first day in my class and during the Creation of the World too, right in the middle of the storms and lightning!"

"These things happen, Mademoiselle," said Josephine, wiping up an incriminating puddle under the seat. "I should tell you it happens to him often, Mademoiselle, but I've always got a pocketful of handkerchiefs."

Josephine was still chattering like a mountain stream when Abbé Philippe appeared on the doorstep of the classroom, a woollen blanket under his arm, gazing at Judith with eyes dulled by lack of sleep.

"My child," he said, in a tone almost sinister, "I have just administered the last rites to poor Horace. He breathed his last in my arms."

Not knowing what to reply, Judith made a face indicating her disgust, then said coldly:

"Well now, M'sieur le Curé: me, I don't know this Horace of yours and anyway everybody's dying these days for Christ's sake! We've all got to go, me and you too, eh? It's not my fault if he's dead, this fellow."

"A moment of silence," begged Abbé Philippe, pressing his hands to his head. "Just a brief moment, please…"

"And anyway, is that all you've got to say to me about my school? Me expecting all kinds of congratulations. Well, lemme tell you I'm disappointed. I really am."

"I *do* congratulate you," said the Abbé. "It's admirable. Especially at seven o'clock in the morning. I apologize for bothering you in class, but I thought you might be cold and – "

Judith snatched the woollen blanket from the Abbé, murmuring a quick thank you and adding immediately, "You could have thought to bring us a little bread. These dirty little kids have to eat, y'know. Sit *down* everybody," she roared at the children who had stood up to greet the priest. "I don't want no ceremonies for a priest!"

Josephine alone remained standing.

"I am Josephine Poitiers," she said with authority. "It's a very great favour from God to have you in our parish, Monsieur l'Abbé. We are certainly going to appreciate you. The village has been very sad since Monsieur le Curé Lacloche left. Everybody is crying. But everybody's happy too, Grandpapa says. These are Chester, Marie-Ange and Hector Poitiers. They weren't with me in the barn when I saw Our Lady all dressed in red, holding her baby in her arms."

"Our Lady?" the Abbé asked in surprise.

"Of course," said Josephine. "Our Lady of the Blueberries. She sat down right beside me on the straw. We ate blueberries."

"We'll talk about all that again some time," said the Abbé calmly. "Do you know your prayers? Did your little brothers learn their catechism with Monsieur le Curé Lacloche?"

"I taught them their lessons," said Josephine. "I taught Monsieur le Curé Lacloche too when he came to our house to drink with Grandpapa Poilu. But Grandpapa told me not to talk to you because you don't drink."

"All right then," said the Abbé, "let's stop talking."

But Josephine went on chirping like a bird on a branch.

"I would like very much to confess," she said. "I know all the others' sins (Chester, wipe your nose; Monsieur l'Abbé doesn't like that). I met our Lady of the Green Peas in the field the other day (Chester, your nose!). She had lost her bowl. She said to me: 'Josephine, you ought to found a convent, right here among the peas and the radishes and gather around you all the village idiots to teach them God's law.' And then I saw fire in the sky. Our Lady said to me: 'Don't be afraid, Josephine, it's the dragon of faith coming down on your house. If I were you I'd go to the kitchen and see if your grandfather's breath is on fire.'

I ran into the house. Grandpapa had drunk a whole bottle of whisky. To put him to sleep, I told him the story of Saint Gondrian. 'Ah, Saint Gondrian,' said Grandpapa. 'Of course! I know that one. How is he? By the way, Josephine, where is your mother? She's getting so big,' Grandpapa said, 'what's to become of us all? If I wasn't so drunk I'd go look for her.' I took Grandpapa's hand and said, 'Let's go look for Mother. Our Lady will tell me where she is. Our Lady tells me everything.' Grandpapa cried and said, 'These day the saints don't give you anything. In the old days your Saint Gondrian used to put a bottle of whisky under my pillow every morning.' I said to him, 'Walk straight, Grandpapa. What will Mama think if she sees you like that?'

"'I've got a gun,' said Grandpapa. 'I can blow all your heads off and then – silence. I can drink in peace. There are too many children in this world. I'd like to sleep forever. Snore with happiness.' (Grandpapa was crying a lot, he was so sorry for having killed his dear little Josephine.) 'Hey, there she is, there's your mother,' said Grandpapa, wiping away his tears to see her better. 'Come to me, Rose. I open my arms, my house, my heart to you. What's the matter, Rose? You look so strange. Where did you cut your feet like that?'

"'My dear little Josephine,' Mother said, sitting in the middle of the road. 'Have you looked after the cow? Have you boiled the milk for the baby?' I should tell you, Monsieur le Curé, that when we got to the house we wiped up the blood that dripped from Mother's feet and put her to bed. But suddenly Grandpapa got all black with anger and took the gun down off the wall.

"'And Chester, where's Chester? I'm going to kill that kid,' he said.

"Chester, Chester," Josephine moaned, crying suddenly in the middle of her story, to the dismay of Abbé Philippe and

Judith Prunelle who were watching her. "Poor Chester. Grand-papa filled his body full of holes."

Seeing himself dead, Chester began to cry and all the Poitiers children imitated him noisily, so that Judith had to give two loud raps with the pointer on the blackboard to command silence.

"Jesus Christ," she cried. "What have I got myself into? You, mister priest, can you tell me what we're ever gonna do, you and me, with this here school?"

Abbé Philippe shrugged his shoulders and did not reply.

HUGH HOOD

BROTHER ANDRÉ, PÈRE LAMARCHE AND MY GRANDMOTHER EUGÉNIE BLAGDON

On the north slope of the mountain, a view of the city neglected by tourists, Saint Joseph's Oratory dominates the city inescapably. He who remains below, on the south side, the river side, of the mountain, may explore the dockside and the principal bridges, the galleries and most of the best restaurants, all those things you can find in cities across the river to the south. But unless the visitor has driven in from the west, or flown in, he likely never gets around the mountain at all, in summer, and in winter only if he means to ski in the Laurentians.

Coming in from the north or west though, the Oratory is the first thing you see, lying up on the western spur of the mountain, a classical Basilica on the grandest scale, with an absolutely enormous floodlit dome.

The airline buses come in that way, and their passengers spot the dome early, and the university tower next to it. And if you've been up the Autoroute for a drive in the country, on the way back you'll see the dome lying at the end of the road while you're still twenty miles from town. When the road curves the dome appears to move; sometimes it's to the west, on your right hand, sometimes dead ahead. Never on your left. It's as though the entire island were a moving bearing, swinging as you swing, as your car follows the road.

You can't ignore it, or get around it, if you come in that way. It's huge, huge, huge. God, but that's a big building. It's very appropriately located on *Reine Marie*, that is, Queen Mary Road. To the English, the street name suggests the wife of the late King George V. To the French, one judges, it means the queen of angels and of saints, and the wife of Saint Joseph, to whom the Oratory is dedicated, the good husband and father or, as the critically enlightened hasten to point out, the Vulcan-figure of Christianity, the cuckold of the Holy Spirit. One prefers to think of Saint Joseph as the good husband and father, though of a child not his own. The Oratory is across the street from the largest wax museum in North America, which has some devotional figures in it, and some topical saints and martyrs and statesmen and newsy murderers. A chain of tourist buses comes up this way, in summer with open roofs, so that the pedestrian is treated to a free spiel. After you've heard it a few times it palls, but the carnival atmosphere envelopes wax museum and Oratory... "biggest, biggest, biggest, ladies and gentlemen, more statues, more miracles, the most accurate, holiest," they run together in the imagination.

In front of the Oratory there is a steep flight of a couple of hundred stairs which the petitioner is supposed to ascend kneeling, reciting the Rosary betimes. I have never seen anybody on his knees on that staircase; perhaps like many other pious devotion of a less sophisticated age, the penitential intention is dying. Who needs it?

One would look a fool going up the stairs on his knees. Who confesses his sins publicly these days? Nobody! On your knees, for God's sake?

Like other famous shrines, Lourdes, Saint Anne de Beaupré, the Oratory has a number of credits for miraculous cures, which makes one think of all those jokes:

"And then what happened?"

"I threw away me crutches?"

"And then what happened?"

"Fell flat on me arse and broke the other leg."

There have been cures and investigations and inexplicable oddities, and the cures have been given a scientific name: "inexplicable oddity."

Also in the antechambers of the Oratory, once you've negotiated the two hundred and fifty steps, whether on your knees or afoot, on crutches or on somebody else's back, are to be found souvenir stands where the sale of religious articles flourishes. Last time my mother was over there, she bought a glass globe with a snowstorm and a miniature Oratory in it, as a present for somebody, I believe one of our kids. You shake the globe and the snowstorm gives you quite an effect of the Oratory in winter. You can get all kinds of rosaries there, and medals... they have a very good selection of Saint Joseph statues.

There is also the crypt, the resting place of Brother André, the porter (doorkeeper) who lived on the site in a tiny shack or cabin of his own construction during the three decades and more that the Oratory was abuilding, 1845-1937. Brother André's birth and death dates exactly circumscribe a simpler age than our own, when kinds of belief and devotion were possible that are no longer possible: we see only with an effort of the historical imagination how it is that the humble anonymous unlettered porter should have conceived the notion of this great building, should have persuaded his superiors in religion to undertake its construction, should have raised the money for it himself, at first in pennies and nickels and only later in greater amounts. 1845-1937. You couldn't get away with it now. See how perfectly the dates fit the achievement! Brother André's calling was that of a saint, and anybody born much after 1845 won't very likely have such a calling. He died at the right time too. If he'd lived fifteen years longer, somebody would certainly have sued him for something. Saints are the natural targets of lawsuits, as I see it.

Brother André's "cause," as they call it technically, is on file in the Holy City, and is being investigated with deliberate speed. Eventually he'll very likely be canonized, particularly if a few more "inexplicable oddities" turn up for the record. Meantime he lies in the crypt, venerated but not idolized by visitors to the shrine, dead twenty-five years now, and very much alive.

I saw him once, when I was a boy of eight or nine, probably in the last summer of his life, at the summer camp I began to go to in 1934 at the age of six. I might have been nine years old when I saw him, which would put it in the summer of 1937, the year he died. I can remember the occasion fairly well although his personal appearance tends to blur with that of old Brother Rogatian, F.S.C., the principal of my school in Toronto during my first years there. School and camp were conducted by the Christian Brothers (not Brother André's order, by the way), who also ran a high school in Montreal. Many of the teaching brothers were regularly shuttled back and forth between Toronto and Montreal, depending on the needs of the given academic year, and they were therefore closely in touch with the devotional life of both cities.

Brother André looked like our principal, as I say, a very old, lined, grey-haired man. Frail. He was past ninety and was already greatly venerated by all who knew him and his story. I wish I could separate him from Brother Rogatian in my mind's eye. It seems to me that he presented me with some religious article, as he may have done all the kids. I do remember distinctly that his visit made a great impression on all the children, even the half-grown adolescents who dwelt in the Seniors' Cabin.

Brother André was surrounded by a stable of advance men, agents and handlers, who did his public-relations work. They

weren't described or thought of as such in naïve 1937, but that's
what they were all right, his bodyguard and retinue. As this was
my first and probably last chance to meet an authentic saint, I
want to get the impression down accurately, for the record.

Two or three weeks before he arrived at the camp to meet us
and our parents, his name was mentioned prominently in the
Sunday sermon, and in the succeeding weeks we were briefed
on who he was, and the great work he was accomplishing in
Montreal. They showed us photos of the half-completed Basilica, with the tiny wooden shack in its shadow. We were admonished to write to our parents about the forthcoming visit. The
weekend before he came, as a matter of fact, numbers of parents
turned up at the Guest Lodge, as well as one extremely rich and
prominent Catholic layman who was, I think, a widower, the
late Senator Fitzgerald, a fan of Brother André's. A lot of these
people stayed at the camp right through the week, so as to be
on the ground when the holy man arrived.

There were priests of his own order, nominally his superiors,
hanging around the camp for days, and a number of enthusias-
tic mothers of families who had attached themselves to his
cause, and a trio of Catholic journalists who had been assigned
to the Brother André story on a more or less permanent basis,
and two tub-thumpers for the Oratory fund. When he arrived
on a midsummer Saturday afternoon, it was kind of a shame to
see this feeble old man hung round with such a graceless mob.
He was led on a tour of the campsite and then seated in the
middle of a field on a kitchen chair, to give his blessing to the
long line of souls that instantly formed in front of him. On a
table at his left was a cheap cardboard carton full of cloth scapu-
lars and medals, which he distributed to young and old. I think
I got a scapular but I'm not certain.

He had faced and blessed long lines of the faithful for three
decades, or four, my mother tells me. Once when she was stay-

ing in Lachine with her mother, at the summer home of their
very rich friends the Cormiers, she happened to express the wish
to visit Brother André, or at least to see him at a distance.

Madame Cormier was a rich bold meddlesome bourgeoisie
who had given very large sums to the Oratory fund, and who
imagined that this gave her a privileged entrée to Brother
André's company. "Why, I'll introduce you," she declared, and
she whisked my mother and grandmother in from Lachine,
halfway across Montreal, up to the site of the building where
Brother André was, as it happens, seated at the head of just such
another line of petitioners.

Up to the head of the line trotted tall Madame, with my
mother and grandmother in tow. "I'll introduce you. Here we
are." But everyone who exalts himself shall be humbled; the
Brother simply moved a hand, indicating the end of the line
without a word, and Madame Cormier had to take the lowest
place, and at that she went on giving him money.

Even at nine years of age, I suspected that he was something
special, whether because the counselors had drilled this into us,
or because of some obscure natural intimation of reverence I
can't be sure. The memory is not as clear as some others from
that time in my life, but it's pretty prominent, and fits directly
into our family history, making it seem very accessible.

My mother, who was born in 1896, is French Canadian by
birth but early in life, at the age of six in fact, she changed her
name from Marguerite to Margaret. She grew up on the sidewalks of old midtown Toronto where the English-speaking kids
would tease her:

"*Marguerite, across the street,*
We can smell your dirty feet."

The teasing was partly, even mainly, because of her French
extraction. At six she decided to assimilate herself to the domi-
nant group and at sixty-eight she enforces the decision. Yet for

years after she made her choice she was lodged fast in the Toronto French minority community, the world of old Sacré Coeur – Père Lamarche's parish – and didn't really escape until she went to the university. While my mother, little Marguerite, was worrying about her dirty feet, Brother André was the biggest name in Paroisse Sacré Coeur, in 1906, in 1916, all the time my mother was growing up on Amelia Street as Marguerite and then as Margaret Blagdon.

Her father had an English surname because he was born in Lévis, Quebec, of mixed French and English parentage, and *his* mother had the lovely, the superbly musical name of Aubeline Lemieux. "Aubeline," little child of the dawn. He had tried to get away from the French community too. After taking his baccalaureate preparatory to studies at Laval, he'd fled across the continent and had taught school for a while in Montana. Something drew him back though, and he ended up stuck, as my mother didn't want to be stuck, in Père Lamarche's little kingdom. There he married Eugénie Sauriol, a great strong solid heavy-jawed obstinate girl when she was in her twenties, in the 1890s, handsome as the day is long. When she died last fall at ninety-two she still had some brown hair, the big strong stubborn jaw, and the terrible French-Canadian pertinacity.

She used to beat the hell out of my father at auction bridge, by executing a series of stunning misplays. He, who played by the book, and very able, would find her impossible to predict or understand, and naturally they didn't get along. He therefore hated French Canadians, by reflex association, not by conviction. He certainly didn't understand the folkways of Sacré Coeur; he used to wax hilarious over his visits with my mother to *la famille Prideaux*, old friends of her family who lived down Sackville Street.

"I was sitting in the parlour," he'd tell the story for the hundredth time, "and I turned around and saw this thing grinning at me from the kitchen. I jumped a mile. 'What's that?' I said. 'That? Why that's Coq l'oeil!' Then they tapped their foreheads. 'He's a bit simple, *notre pauvre 'tit frère!*'"

This *Coq l'oeil* was unlined, rosy and looked thirty, when he was past seventy and his brothers and sisters were gnarled and aged. He's sat behind the stove in the kitchen all his life, affectionately tended by his mother and sisters. Nowadays the Mental Health lobby would rehabilitate him and have him out driving a cab so that at seventy he'd look as harried as the rest of us. *Coq l'oeil*, cockeyed. Who's the cockeyed one?

When my mother visited us in Montreal last fall, we took her for some drives up the Autoroute, always with the Oratory on the horizon in the background. Once about noon we were approaching a small town in the Laurentian foothills, and as we passed a signpost that said *Saint-Lin*, my mother hollered at me to stop for a second. There was some sort of placard at the side of the road just behind us. I backed the car up to it. *Birthplace of Sir Wilfrid Laurier*, it said, giving the location of the historic site.

"Ha," said my mother decisively, "I knew it, Saint-Lin. This is where Père Lamarche was born."

Of course I knew who she meant, because Père Lamarche was one of the tribal elders of my infancy, the pastor of the French church, old Sacré Coeur, just east of Sackville on King Street, around the corner from the House of Providence, and that's real authentic *old* Toronto... going back to around 1850.

In the 1930s the parish moved a little way uptown to the new church at the corner of Sherbourne and Carlton, and even that isn't far uptown. But when my mother was a little *pied noir*, when my great-aunt Liz McKinnon was the organist, Sacré Coeur was located in the heart of the French enclave. The original building is now a Ukrainian-rite church, still in use, and what was formerly a small French minority is beginning to throw a little weight – one of the CBC radio stations is switching over to full-time French-language broadcasting, in the teeth of considerable opposition.

Anyway, we had lunch in a clean pretty little restaurant on the main street of Saint-Lin and afterwards went over to see the Laurier house, which was worth seeing in a number of ways. It's a very fine example, partly unobtrusively restored, partly in the original condition, of a French rural dwelling house of about 1835, with some wonderful furniture and woodwork, and a remarkable and very ingenious little staircase. Nobody seems to know the house is there, but there's a full-time attendant maintained by I don't know whom. He wore a uniform, and was shaving the beautifully tended lawn as we arrived. He let us in and gave us some leaflets and the prepared talk. But when my mother asked him about Père Lamarche he abandoned the script and treated us like members of the family.

"*Mais on parlait toujours des deux, Pères Lamarche.*"

"*Vous avez parfaitement raison,*" said my mother, "*frères également de Saint-Lin. Et j'ai connu l'aîné, notre cureé pendant des années et des années.*"

The attendant was grinning widely, handing us doilies and bits of woodwork off the furniture; he really opened up. It was magical. When we left I asked him to take two dollars as a favour to me. I don't know that I've ever seen anybody try harder to be agreeable. In fact, we all did; we did ourselves credit, *une bonne entente, paisable et douce.* Père Lamarche was pretty widely known in Quebec and Ontario because he had the important Toronto appointment, in a parish where a minority in a hostile city flocked for protection in mutual solidarity, just as they did to the secular arm, as represented by Mr. L.V. Dusseau, of the Gendron Carriage Works.

That isn't by any means an exaggeration. In my own childhood I harboured mixed and puzzled feelings about my French

relatives and their friends and the apparently interminable chain
of family ties amongst them: Archambaults, Prideaux, Sauriols,
Levesques, Lemieux. My father was not militantly anti-French;
he would permit them in the house and he maintained my
grandmother Blagdon for several years after she was widowed.
And though he wouldn't have admitted it, he was particularly
fond of my great-aunt, Mrs. McKinnon, who despite her married name was born a Sauriol and very French. She was the
organist at Sacré Coeur for over thirty years, the mother of an
only child, Charlie McKinnon, a boy with a beautiful tenor
voice who used to sing in the drawing-room, evenings, while his
mother played. He became a priest afterwards, and my father
nursed a violent and unreasoning distaste for him. He used to
cite the occasion of cousin Charlie's ordination, when old Mr.
Blagdon, my grandfather, had presented him with two twenty-
five-dollar gold pieces in a little purse. Cousin Charlie (according to Dad) at once extracted the pieces and inspected them.

"That'll come in handy," he said curtly, putting them into
his fob without taking any notice of their festive or souvenir
character, and with no word of thanks. My father believed, as I
do for the most part, that the clergy, with certain important
exceptions, considered themselves exempt from the received
rules of politeness; he always instanced this occurrence. He did
not like cousin Charlie, but went to his funeral and was very
impressed that the Cardinal presided.

Mrs. McKinnon, widowed from her twenties, came to our
house after Sunday Mass at Sacré Coeur about twice a month all
through my childhood, until her health failed. She was white-
haired as long as I can remember, and resembled a small pussy-
cat. She had an incipient moustache of fine white hairs, only a
few but long, which intensified the impression of the feline. She
always accepted a drink of straight Scotch whisky, about two
ounces in a highball glass. I regarded this as definitely odd, a

romantic wickedness, out of character. When she had finished he drink, Dad would press her to have another.

"Just a touch," he would say, proffering the decanter, "a smell."

Aunt Liz would nod deprecatingly. "Now, Alex, a nip, no more." In the end she would take another finger, and then we would all go in and have Sunday dinner and rancorous theological disputation.

She played Arcadelt motets, and florid nineteenth-century French Masses. On Palm Sunday for a recessional, she invariably gave us Fauré's *Les Rameaux*. I have a record of John McCormack singing this in English as *The Palms*, and each time I play it, I'm transported to the shadowy old church on King Street, purple shrouding the statues in the gloom, and Aunt Liz manipulating the stops overhead. She was not a bad musician either, not as good-looking a woman as her sister, my grandmother, Mrs. B. Always known as Mrs. B.

Mr. B. and Mrs. B. When my mother was a girl, she and my grandparents dwelt on Amelia Street to the north and east of what used to be called Cabbagetown, in Toronto. I don't know that many people recollect that picturesque name. Irish and English it was, labouring class and small tradesmen, south of Gerrard and east off Parliament. But Amelia Street was separated from Cabbagetown by maybe six blocks and a pretty considerable status barrier. It ran east off Parliament, parallel with Winchester Street but a few blocks north, as far as the cemetery or necropolis that lay on the western slope of the Don Valley. In those days, the first three decades of the century, the east end of the city lay mostly to the south of Bloor Street; the Prince Edward Viaduct hadn't been built. You could pick your way down through the necropolis to the river valley, walk north a quarter of a mile and be in the open country described by Morley Callaghan in the opening pages of *Strange Fugitive*.

Nowadays the city stretches thirty miles further north, but then
it huddled down by the lakeshore. My grandparents' world lay
along Amelia Street and Winchester Street, east and west, and
along Sackville and Sumach Streets north and south, and Sacré
Coeur was more or less the South Pole at Sackville and King.
Almost everyone they knew lived in the district, which was
solidly middle class and perhaps upper middle class. On the corner of Winchester and Sackville were three or four mansions,
the Eastwood house, the Freyseng house (Freyseng of Freyseng
Cork) and in fact this was no slum. I walked to look at Amelia
Street last spring; it persists, not greatly changed, inhabited now
by speakers of the Central European languages, and a bit more
cosmopolitan than it used to be, a solidly respectable neighbourhood still, whose sons and daughters might aspire to the
university, as my mother did. But pretty old-world and ingrown
in those days; everybody in the French community knew everybody else and minded their affairs, and when someone began to
behave peculiarly that was community property, a family concern.

Like the time that Brother André visited Père Marche, long
long before I was born, back around 1910 when the saint was
in his heyday. That visit was *toto coelo* distinct from the later
appearance at my summer camp. Whenever he visited the
Toronto French it was a gala, an occasion for a demonstration
of community loyalties. Greater efforts were made at collecting
for the Oratory than at any other time. Presents were
exchanged, and the good Brother was much occupied with the
life of the flock of his friend the pastor, with paying visits,
renewing family connections, visiting the sick and the infirm.

Now as it happens there was much concern along Amelia
and Sackville Streets just at this time at the behaviour of Mrs.
Moore, my grandparents' next-door neighbour. Like Mrs.
Blagdon and Mrs. McKinnon, she had married an English

surname, or rather an Irish, and like them was *vraie Canadienne*. But she hadn't been frequenting the Sacraments or even the church, hadn't even been leaving her house for the last several months, perhaps as much as a year.

"It's my belief she intends to set up for a witch," remarked my grandfather one fine Saturday morning during Brother André's visit; he was half teasing, half in earnest.

My grandmother, a woman of extraordinary firmness of character, took the suggestion at face value, and fastened an even closer watch on her neighbour's windows. It wasn't as if they were strangers, as if she were prying. Mrs. Moore was a Chambly girl, Réjeanne Lajeunesse, and a connection of hers, Emma Lajeunesse, was an international famous star of concert and opera, under the name of Madame Albani. My grandmother knew everybody in Chambly, and all about Mrs. Moore's antecedents and family history. She therefore knew perfectly well that there was a serious question of property and testament bothering her neighbour. In effect she had been jobbed out of her share of an inheritance, and was taking out her resentment on God. She kept her shutters half-drawn so that Mrs. B. could only see inside with great difficulty.

"Witchcraft," said my grandfather peaceably. He was an extraordinary man, able to do any delicate task with his hands, a self-taught painter and sculptor, very quiet, the reverse of his spouse.

"Very dangerous and idle!" said Mrs. B. brusquely; she went out and began to put questions all along the street about what should be done with a woman who hadn't been to Mass in a year, who lurked malevolently in the dark behind her shutters, who stuck out her tongue at those who might help her.

"Someone must visit her," said a grocer a little way down Sackville Street, M. Labadie, when my grandmother consulted him, "forcing an entry if necessary."

Mrs. B. hefted a sack of flour with nonchalance. "One would be justified in your opinion?"

"She has not been in the store for weeks. How does she eat?"

"Wretched woman," said my grandmother, and she marched out of the store and around the corner. When she came abreast of her neighbour's veranda, she strode up the steps, where she halted, crying out in a loud voice, "Réjeanne, Réjeanne, come out! I have to speak to you." There was no answer from the shadowed house, so she mounted the steps and shook the screen door with energy. "I know you're in there, you wicked girl. Come out!" The lock pulled free of the doorframe and she went into the house, into the parlour which was a maze of bric-a-brac, china elephants, ferns, narrow looking-glasses. Mrs. Moore was crouched fearfully on a sofa in a defensive posture when my grandmother stormed in.

"Oh, I've been bad, Eugénie," she said appealingly, beginning to weep. "I'm afraid of Père Lamarche. I haven't been to Communion in a year. I didn't make my Easter Duty. What can I do?" She had been terrified of dying alone in there without Extreme Unction, but had been afraid, on the other hand, to confess herself.

"What made you do it, Réjeanne? How could you lock yourself in here?"

"I cursed God. I blasphemed. I'm afraid." she began to shake, obviously on the point of hysterics. "It's those nephews of mine in Chambly; they've done me out of everything."

"*Les Thériault?*"

"Who else? They've insinuated themselves into the store, and my cow of a sister won't stand up to them. I haven't had a cent from the store in two years, and I have no husband. I vowed not to go to church until it all came right, but God denies me the favour. Very well," she folded her arms determinedly, "God may damn me if He likes; it'll be His own fault."

Horrified, my grandmother eyed her with severity. "Mortal sin, Réjeanne," she said loudly, making the other woman tremble visibly, "that's what you're in, and you'll burn for it." She began to expound the torments of Hell, as then understood.

"Oh, Eugénie, stop!"

"Eternal torment. Lakes of fire!"

"No, please, *je t'en supplie!*"

"Your only recourse is a general confession."

"Oh, I couldn't, I couldn't. Père Lamarche? I couldn't."

"Why not?"

"Ah, he's a friend of the family. I've had him here to dine. I can't say all that to him, and besides, I'm afraid."

"What will you do?"

"I'll just stay in here until the end."

"Are you eating?"

"Not much, and my poor canary died." It was true, the poor creature was lying in a cage, toes turned up.

"Foolishness, foolishness," said my grandmother who was fond of pets. "I'll tell you what, Réjeanne, I'm going to get Brother André to visit you." This was a stroke of genius, and the abandoned Mrs. Moore fell back on the sofa in amazed alarm. "Brother André?"

"Why, yes, he's in the city, staying at the rectory. When you get back to the Sacraments, you can make a big big contribution to the Oratory; it'll smooth your path. I'll fetch him this afternoon."

"Brother André in this house?" She might as well have named Sir Wilfrid Laurier.

"Here in this house," declared my grandmother. "He'll exorcise your silly fears. I'll see him this afternoon." She turned and left the house, leaving poor Réjeanne Moore staring fearfully into the twilit hall.

Down she went on the old Winchester Street car line, clank-
ing and rumbling with many jogs and starts and stops, as far as
Queen and Church, where she transferred to a Queen car which
took her to within a couple of blocks of the rectory, of which
she was an habitué. She was a great manufacturer of altar linens
and a confidante of Père Lamarche's housekeeper Mme. Des-
patie from Saint-Lin, whom she found in the kitchen.

"Where is Brother André?"

"Paying a call on L.V."

"Ahhh," said my grandmother, impressed. That would be
L.V. Dusseau, the most successful member of the local French
community, the director of the Toronto branch of the Gendron
Carriage Works, of Toledo, Ohio, and a kind of paternal and
benevolent despot who had employed almost all the French
males in the city at one time or another. Even if they could do
no more than push a broom, he would put them on at the
Gendron, and then they would bring their relatives from
Montreal. "Ahhh," said Mrs. B. "I must see Brother André
about Réjeanne Moore."

"Is she misbehaving again?"

"She hasn't been to church in a year, and must be compelled
to go, for her own good." The two women were in complete
agreement over the plan of campaign. When the saint came
back to the rectory, they fell at his feet, almost tripping him,
beseeching him to rescue their sister from her plight.

Brother André was then a vigorous sixty-five, not the frail
ancient that I remember. He accepted the challenge instantly it
was explained to him, and rode back uptown on the Winchester
car with my grandmother. As they approached Sackville, he was
recognized and a small crowd began to collect. They got off
the streetcar at Sackville and Winchester and walked north
together, my grandmother in the lead and the thaumaturge
behind, smiling and nodding at the children who plucked at his

cassock and their elders who bowed or knelt as he passed. Nowadays they would all ask for his autograph, prompted by a remote crew from Channel Nine, but then they simply crossed themselves and smiled. It became a little procession, coming up Sackville Street toward Amelia. They paused for a moment at M. Labadie's while Brother André went inside to say hello and tuck a couple of dollars in his worn purse. The grocer came to the door with him.

"I'll send more when business picks up," he said, and off they went. In front of Mrs. Moore's everybody stopped and there was a hush. The saint went up the walk, perfectly in command of the situation; *c'était son métier*. He put a firm hand on the doorknob and disappeared. My grandmother faced the crowd and led them in the *Veni Creator Spiritus* in her powerful unmusical voice. The good Brother was in the house perhaps twenty minutes; suddenly the door flew open with a bang and he appeared on the porch with a radiant and joyful woman at his side. She laughed and wept all at once, knelt and clung to his hand, was surrounded at once by amiable old friends, while Brother André detached himself and left as unobtrusively as possible, a kind smiling upright, ordinary-looking sixty-five-year-old man.

"Oh, he is a saint, a saint," sobbed Mrs. Moore joyfully, "and he comforted me in my worst need. I must go to Confession this afternoon and receive at Mass tomorrow."

"I'll go with you," said my grandmother.

"Would you, Eugénie? *Comme tu es gentile*! But where is Brother André?"

He had quietly withdrawn. Mrs. Moore was a daily communicant for the rest of her life, until she grew too feeble to go out, but she never saw Brother André again.

I have retained this image very clearly from my mother's tales in my infancy. I have a vision of him walking erect and

smiling along Amelia Street with something in and around him
larger than he seemed visibly to be, some numinous envelope
greater than life.

The question after all is of the size of a man, whether he is
what he seems, or less than he seems, or more. When I saw
Brother André in the last year of his life, inarticulate, worn-out,
with that knotted ropy neck, those palsied hands, on exhibition
like any other curiosity and at the mercy of his retinue, he
seemed to me a lot smaller than life and certainly incapable of
transforming it from within.

But as he strode triumphantly and humbly down the humble street in 1910, when belief and hope came easier, he must
have seemed visibly greater than life, and its master. He must
have walked like a giant in the eyes of the simple faithful. The
French are not like that nowadays, whether in Toronto or
Montreal, and we may think them – us, because I'm half one of
them – well rid of ignorance and superstition, well birthed into
the twentieth century; but the question isn't so easily closed.
Ignorance and superstition are rightly banished, and priestcraft;
but what Brother André was, was none of these.

His Oratory is still there, ugly, monumental, dominating,
and it will remain so, in danger from neither left nor right.
Ignorance and superstition are one thing, and holiness another,
which we touch sometimes, rarely, and half-miss. At nine years
of age, how could I find the saint in the dying old man? Yet he
brought poor Mrs. Moore friendship and hope and peace.
Saints. What are saints?

MORLEY CALLAGHAN

SISTER BERNADETTE

When Sister Bernadette, who had charge of the maternity ward in the hospital, wasn't rebuking a nurse in training for some petty fault, she was having a sharp disagreement with a doctor. She was a tall woman with a pale face; she looked very handsome in her starched white headpiece. To her, the notion that her nun's habit might be protecting her from sharp retorts from the nurses was intolerable. But she simply couldn't hold a grudge against anybody, and if she had a tiff with a nurse she would wait till she saw the girl passing in the corridor and say innocently, "I hear you're offended with me," as she offered the warmest, jolliest smile. When young nurses in training, who were having a bit of idle gossip, saw the sister's tall, gaunt form, so formidable in the black robes, coming toward them they often felt like a lot of half-guilty schoolgirls as they smiled good-naturedly. Of course Sister Bernadette had sympathy for all the women who were suffering and bearing children and she was like a mother to them, but it was the small things in the ward that were most important to her. If she saw a man in the corridor carrying a parcel carefully, she would watch him go into a patient's room, wait till he had departed, then rush into the room and look around to try and guess at once what might have been in the parcel. It was not hard for her to guess correctly, for she seemed to know every object in each private room. All the mothers liked her but were a bit afraid of her. Sometimes forgetting that women were paying expensive doctors to look after them, she would give her own instructions and insist they be carried out completely, as if she knew more about the patients than the doctors did. There was a Doctor Mallory, a short dark fellow with a broad face, a shifting, far-away expression in his eyes, and a kind of warm, earthy tenderness in his manner, who often quarrelled bitterly with Sister Bernadette because she ordered a patient of his to take a medicine he had not recommended. He did not know that Sister Bernadette loved him for quarrelling openly with her instead of being just cuttingly polite because she was a nun.

One day Doctor Mallory, looking very worried, waited in the corridor, watching Sister Bernadette's tall form with the dark robes coming toward him. When he looked into her face he couldn't help smiling, there was so much fresh, girlish contentment in her expression. But this time he spoke with a certain diffidence as he said, "Sister, I'd like to talk with you a minute."

"Please do, Doctor," she said. "You're not offended again, surely?"

"Oh no, not this time," he said, smiling warmly. "I wanted to tell you about a patient of mine I'd like to bring to the hospital to have her baby."

"Now, don't tell me you're so afraid of me you have to ask my permission to bring a patient here?" she said, laughing.

"Not at all. Only this girl doesn't want to come. She's ashamed. She's of a good family. I know all about her. But she's not married and won't come here under her own name. I said I'd speak to you and you'd fix it up, Sister. Won't you?"

Sister Bernadette frowned. The doctor was smiling at her, as if he couldn't be fooled by a harsh refusal. It gave her pleasure to think that he was so sure of her sympathetic nature. But she said sharply, "It's against the rules to register anybody under a false name, you know that, Doctor."

"I know it, that's why I wanted to speak to you, Sister."

With ridiculous sternness Sister Bernadette said, "What do I care? Do what you want to do. Register the woman as Mrs. Macsorley, or anything else, it's all the same to me," and she turned and walked away as though greatly offended. The doctor, chuckling, watched her hurrying along the corridor without looking back.

Sister Bernadette could hardly wait to see Doctor Mallory's new patient. Five minutes after the woman was brought to the hospital, Sister Bernadette was in the room looking at her with eager curiosity and speaking in a soft reassuring voice. The patient was only a girl with big scared blue eyes and fluffy blond hair whose confidence had been completely destroyed by her predicament. Sister Bernadette was desperately afraid that the young girl, who had been such a sinner and who was now suffering and disgraced, would be afraid of a woman like herself, a nun, who had given her life entirely to God. For some reason she wanted this scared girl to love her. That night, while the baby was being born, Sister Bernadette was in the corridor many times.

During the two weeks the girl remained at the hospital she was treated with a special attention by the nurses who thought she was an old friend of Sister Bernadette. No one suspected that Mrs. Macsorley wasn't married. Sister Bernadette got a good deal of pleasure realizing that she and the doctor were the only ones who shared the secret. Every morning she paid a visit to Mrs. Macsorley's room talking about everything on earth, praised the baby, and tried to make the girl feel at home by strutting about like a blunt, good-natured farm woman. The fair-haired, blue-eyed girl, who was really a self-possessed, competent person, was so im-pressed by the sister's frank, good-natured simplicity, she sent word out to the baby's father that there was no reason why he shouldn't come to see her.

When Sister Bernadette was introduced to the father, a well-dressed soft-spoken, tall man, she shook hands warmly, called him Mr. Macsorley and showed the baby to him. His embarrassment disappeared at once. He felt so much at ease with Sister Bernadette during that first visit that he decided to come every day at noontime. At first Sister Bernadette was delighted by the whole affair; it seemed so much like the kind of thing that was always going on in her ward, making her world seem so rich with experience that she didn't care whether she ever went outside the hospital. But when she heard that the girl's lover was a married man, it bothered her to see that he was still so attentive. Though she honestly liked the man and liked the girl too, she said to Doctor Mallory with awkward sincerity, "I don't like to see that man coming to see the girl so much. Evidently they're still in love."

"Does he come often?"

"Every day. And they are both so sure of themselves."

"It isn't very nice. It isn't fair to you," the doctor said.

"No, no, I don't mean that," Sister Bernadette said. "But you know that man is married and has two children. I just mean that the girl at least ought to respect his wife and children and not let him be so devoted to her." Then Sister Bernadette began to feel self-conscious as though the doctor was misunderstanding her. "Don't misinterpret me," she said at once. "The girl can run around with single men as much as she likes and come here as often as she likes as far as I'm concerned..."

"I'll tell them about it," the doctor said.

"No. Please don't. You'd better not say anything," she said.

Then it was time for Mrs. Macsorley to leave the hospital. Doctor Mallory came to Sister Bernadette and explained that he, himself, was going to find someone to adopt the baby. Coaxing and pleading, he asked if it wouldn't be all right to leave the baby in the hospital nursery for two days at the most.

Such a request didn't actually worry Sister Bernadette, but she snapped at the doctor, "It's absolutely against the rules of the hospital to leave a baby who's in good health in that nursery after the mother has gone." In the brief argument that followed she was short- and hot-tempered, and in the end she said, "All right, have your way, but only for one day, mind."

She didn't think it necessary to worry till the baby had been left in the nursery for a week. Doctor Mallory was trying very hard to get someone to adopt the baby girl. Sister Bernadette began to think that the child would remain in her nursery till she, herself, did something about it. Every time she looked at the brown-eyed baby she was reminded that she had done wrong in letting the mother register at the hospital under another name. After all, it was just vanity, her eagerness to have the doctor believe her a good-natured person, that was not causing trouble. Perhaps she ought to reveal the whole matter to the Mother Superior, she thought. In her prayers in the morning and in her evening prayers she asked that someone be found who would take the baby at once.

In the evenings, after ten o'clock feeding-time, she would go into the nursery when the lights were turned down looking at one small crib after another with an expert eye that made the nurse in charge wary. But she stood by Baby Macsorley's crib, frowning, puzzled by her own uneasiness. She lifted the baby up as though to see it for the first time. The baby was wearing a little pink sweater coat one of the nurses had knitted. Sister Bernadette knew that Baby Mac-sorley had become the pet of the nursery. Only last night one of the nurses had performed a mock marriage between the baby and another fine baby boy who was being taken home that day. When she put the baby back into the crib she found herself kissing her on the forehead and patting her back, as she hoped, quickly, that no one had seen her.

As soon as she saw Doctor Mallory next day she blurted out, "If you don't get that baby out of here by tomorrow, I'll throw it in the snowbank."

Doctor Mallory was a bit afraid of her now, for he knew that she was a determined woman, so he said, pleading, "Wait till tomorrow. I'm trying to get one particular lady to adopt it. Wait till tomorrow. I'm working with her."

"You'll have to work faster, that's all," Sister Bernadette said, without even smiling.

Instead of one day, she waited two days longer, but now she was so angry that whenever she went into the nursery and saw the baby, she felt herself resenting the young mother with the candid blue eyes and the baby blond curls and the bold straight-forward lover who came so openly to the hospital and felt no shame. Once Sister Bernadette picked the baby up and then put it down hastily for she felt with disgust that the sordidness in the life of the mother and father might be touching her through the baby and disturbing her too much. "I can't go on thinking of those people," she muttered, "the baby is out of here tomorrow."

But Doctor Mallory was avoiding her and she didn't have a chance to speak to him for three days. She saw him turn a corner and duck into an elevator. "Doctor," she called, "listen to me. I'm going to put that baby in the rear seat of your car and let you drive off with it. We're through with it."

"Why, what's the trouble now, Sister?" he said.

"It's demoralizing my nursery. I'll not have it," she said. "It's the pet of the whole place. Every nurse that goes in there at night picks it up. The baby's been here too long, I tell you."

"But just thinking about it surely doesn't bother you?"

"It certainly does. It's staring me in the face every moment."

"Here's some cheerful news then. Maybe you'll be rid of the baby tomorrow. I'm getting an answer from the lady I wanted to adopt it tonight."

"Honestly, Doctor, you don't know how glad I am to hear that," she said, taking a deep breath.

There was such light-hearted relief within Sister Bernadette when she entered the nursery that night that she had a full, separate smile for each baby as she moved, a tall, black-robed figure, amount the cribs. When she stood beside Baby Macsorley's crib, she began to chuckle, feeling it might now be safe to let the baby have some of the warm attention she had sometimes wanted to give. She seemed to know this baby so much better than all the other babies. Humming to herself, she picked up the baby, patted her on the back and whispered, "Are you really going away tomorrow, darling?"

Carrying the baby over to the window she stood there looking down at the city which was spread out in lighted streets with glaring electric signs and moving cabs, the life of a great city at night moving under her eyes. Somewhere, down there, she thought, the bold young girl with the confident eyes and her lover were going their own way. As she held their baby in her arms, she muttered, frowning, "But perhaps they really are in love. Maybe they're out dancing." The girl and her lover belonged to the life down there in the city. "But that man ought to be home with his wife," she thought uneasily.

Sister Bernadette began to think of herself as a young girl again. For the first time in years she was disturbed by dim, half-forgotten thoughts: "Oh, why do I want so much to keep this one baby? Why this one?" Her soul, so chaste and aloof from the unbridled swarm in the city streets, was now overwhelmed by a struggle between something of life that was lost and something bright and timeless within her that was gained. But she started to tremble all over with more unhappiness than she had ever known. With a new, mysterious warmth, she began to hug the child that was almost hidden in her heavy black robes as she pressed it to her breast.

HUGH GARNER

THE CONVERSION
OF WILLIE HEAPS

I could see Willie coming along the road from his place, walking fast like he always did. His long legs were jerking back and forth above his broken shoes and his tangled hair hung in a bang just above his wide-staring eyes, where it had been cut by his mother, Mrs. Heaps. His mouth was hanging loose like it usually was, and even from a distance you could see his long brown teeth that were always wet like a panting dog's.

Although he was thirty years old he didn't seem much older than me. My father said it was silly for a full-grown man to play with a twelve-year-old boy, even if Willie *was* a little simple, but he was the only real friend I had, and we had lots of good times together. In the winter I went with him on trips to town, and during the summer we would go fishing down to Allison's dam, or woodchuck hunting in the fields around our place.

He was an expert at gelding colts, and once or twice a month during the summer he would take me with him to other farms around the district. I used to watch him with my tongue between my teeth as he operated on the young horses, his hands as gentle as a mother's, hating to cause them any more pain than was necessary.

The first time I saw him working on a colt it made me sick and I vomited in a corner of the yard. Willie told me I couldn't go out with him again if I acted like that, so I was careful from then on and it never bothered me again.

When Willie got up to our place he stood in the road and shouted to me to come with him.

Where to?"

"Down to Angus Gordon's place."

"I'll have to ask my mother," I said.

"Hurry up then. I want to get going before it's dark," he shouted impatiently.

My mother heard our voices and came to the screen door, wiping a plate with a dishtowel.

"Can I go with Willie?" I asked.

"Oh – I guess so," she answered, not wanting me to go, but not wanting to stop me either. She shouted, "Hello, Willie!" as she spied my friend standing in the road.

He didn't answer. It seemed that he could never get used to talking to grown-ups.

"Don't you be late home, young man," my mother warned me as we set off up the road.

I waved to her and hurried along, trying to match my stride with Willie's.

He was excited about something, and he kept turning his head in my direction, trying to make up his mind to tell me what it was. Sometimes he acted like that, worrying about a secret thing until he almost burst with the burden of it.

"We've got a new preacher at the Pentecostal," he said finally, grinning with relief now that it was out.

We climbed the torn wire fence that separated our land from the old unused railway spur.

"The preacher's name is Reverend Blounsbury," he said as we slid down the grassy bank to the tracks.

"What happened to the other one?" I asked.

"Who, Mr. Oldsworth? He's gone to the city. Reverend Blounsbury is a better preacher anyways."

"Is he a real minister, with minister's clothes?"

"He don't need 'em," answered Willie.

"Why don't he? My minister wears them."

"He's God's servant. He don't need 'em."

On Sundays Willie went with his mother and father to the Lost Souls Pentecostal Mission in Brantford. They never missed a service there, and Willie had told me several times about people being saved by the blood of Jesus Christ, which would cleanse you of all impurities and make you ready to meet your Maker on the judgment day.

Willie was thinking hard about something, and now and then he'd swallow and his neck would twitch with excitement. After a long silence he said, "I got saved last Sunday."

"How do you get saved?"

"You go and kneel down at the front of the Mission," he answered.

"Is that all?"

"Everybody sings, and sometimes the women cry."

I cut off the tops of some wild mustard with a long willow whip I'd picked up. "How many times you been saved, Willie?" I asked.

"Oncet. Oncet is all you can be saved," he said, looking at me as if I should have known.

"Were you scared much?"

"Nope. Ain't nothing to be scared for."

"Do you believe in that, Willie?"

"Sure I believe in it — hell!" he answered, with mild disgust at my ignorance.

"That makes you sure you're going to heaven, don't it?" I asked.

"Yep," he answered. He walked very fast and I had a hard time keeping up with him on the old cinder roadbed.

"Does the new minister save anybody at all?"

"Yep. He's a better preacher than the other one."

"Is that all they do at the Pentecostal, Willie?" I asked. We went to the Presbyterian Church in Simcoe, and I had always wondered why his church was so different from ours.

"No, they sing and the minister says a sermon. On Sunday he talked about sinning. He says it's a sin to go out with a woman 'cause Jesus didn't do it, and it's sinful when men do it."

I couldn't imagine our minister talking about that stuff in church. I thought about this as we hurried along the track, the cinder dust billowing up from our feet and the old musty-paper smell of the burdocks filling the narrow right-of-way.

"I wish we didn't have to go down to Angus's place," I said. "Some of the fellows are down catching bullfrogs at the dam. Perry got one last night as big as a saucer."

"They don't know nuthin' about catching frogs," said Willie. "You wait and see what *we* catch tomorrow night."

He told me how he would do it. He would sneak up behind them and throw rocks into the swamp ahead of the frogs. Then when they jumped in his direction he would catch them in a long strip of weighted lace curtain. Willie sure knew lots of tricks like that. I was glad he was my friend and let me go places with him. There'd be no fun at all without Willie.

When we reached the bridge across the tracks he pulled me up to the road. He was thin but he had a lot of strength. He lifted me clean off the ground with one hand.

"How old is the colt at the Gordons', Willie?" I asked as we turned up the road to the farm.

"I dunno. There's two of 'em, Angus said."

"It must hurt them, eh, Willie?"

"For a while, I guess. They get over it."

"What does it do, Willie?"

"Makes 'em big and quiet. They can't work good unless they're cut."

The dirt road was warm through the rubber soles of my sneakers. It was the kind of summer evening that usually comes before an electrical storm. The sun was lying low behind a grove of hardwood, and high in the sky the clouds we called "washboards" were pink in the evening light. Over the low spots in the fields high-climbing swarms of gnats boiled and tumbled in the warm air. The crickets whistled at us from every fencepost as we hurried along the road.

"I feel sorry for the colts," I said. "It don't make me sick no more, though."

"Don't you get sick again or else I won't bring you."

"I ain't gonna be sick no more," I answered. I didn't want to get Willie mad at me.

There didn't seem to be anyone home at the Gordons' when we got there. We could hear the cattle and horses stamping in the stable beneath the barn.

Willie knocked on the kitchen door, but there was no answer.

"I hope they're at home," he said. "I don't want to hafta come over here again next week."

"Maybe they'll be back soon."

"We ain't got much time to wait, 'cause it'll soon be dark."

"They'll come in a minute," I said hopefully.

Willie was getting mad, and I could see the big blue veins in his neck beating like the devil. When he was mad there was nothing to do but keep out of his way. One time it took three men to hold him when he was mad.

"I won't come over again next week," he muttered, kicking at the bottom step beneath the door.

"Maybe they'll come home soon, Willie."

"Why didn't they wait! Why'd they go away when they knew I was coming over!"

He was getting madder every minute. It would be dark soon and I didn't want to be alone with him if he got real mad.

"Can't you do it anyways, Willie?" I asked, trying to quiet him down.

"Oh, why didn't they wait!" he cried. He kicked at the step again, harder this time.

"Let's do it, Willie," I pleaded. "My mother told me not to be late getting home."

He was no longer listening to me. "They could have stayed in!" he cried. "Angus Gordon is a sinner anyways!"

I could see his shoulders working under his denim jacket and I was afraid to have to go home with him unless he calmed down. He wouldn't hurt me when he was all right, but his mother told me once to stay away from him when he took a spell.

"I'm going to fix them colts anyways," he said, striding towards the barn.

"That's right, Willie. We might as well," I answered as I tried to keep up with his grown-up strides across the yard.

Willie opened the stable door, and the colts whinnied from the darkness. I groped around on the shelf near the doorpost, trying to find a stable lamp.

"I can't find a lamp, Willie!" I shouted at him, my voice showing me how scared I was. I tried to follow him with my eyes so I'd be ready to run if he turned on me.

"I've got one," he said, and I could see him in the light of a struck match as he struggled with the chimney of a lantern.

When the lamp was lit I looked around the stable. The colts were tied at the end of a short row of stalls. There was also a team of horses and a big Holstein bull.

"Help me out with them," he shouted, and in the light from the lamp he looked crazier than he ever had before. I hesitated near the door.

"Come on, come on, we can't stand here!" he cried. "There is too much sin around here! Angus is a poor sinner an' we gotta help him before he's punished by God!"

"Let's wait until another time, Willie," I pleaded.

"We may be too late. Now is the time!"

"I don't want to," I said, afraid to leave the open doorway.

"You gotta. There's too much sin. Oh, Lord, help the poor sinner!" he cried.

The horses were scared, lifting their feet from the floor, their heads high and their eyes bright in the lantern light.

He brought one of the colts into the yard and we got him down and hitched his feet. Willie was singing a hymn as he walked around in quick little jerks, doing all the work himself. He worked fast. The colt snorted and stretched his neck when it was done.

"You'll never sin!" Willie cried. "You'll never sin, little horse!"

The sight of Willie moving around the yard with the short knife in his hand, singing his crazy hymns all out of tune, scared me half to death. This was a different Willie than I had known before.

He turned the colt loose and I opened the gate, letting him through. The next colt was harder to manage, but with my help Willie got the rope around his legs.

"Glory!" Willie cried when his singing stopped. "No more sin! There'll be no more sin!" He fitted the words into another crazy tune.

He did the other colt, but it took him much longer this time. While I held the lantern I shivered at the sight of his crazy hands and at the sound of his tuneless mumblings. It was quite dark now outside the pale circle made by the lantern and heavy clouds were blotting out the sky.

When he finished his job I led the colt out through the gate and came back to Willie. "Now we can go, Willie," I said eagerly.

"Hallelujah! I'll not let them sin!" he shouted. "I can stop all the sin in the world!"

"Sure you can, Willie," I agreed. "But let's go home now."

"Not yet. I've got work to do. Glory!"

"Come on, Willie, please!"

"No, not yet."

I stared around me at the darkened buildings, praying that the Gordons would come home soon. Across the fields I could see a light in the kitchen of the Turner house a quarter of a mile away. Though it was far it made me feel a little better to know that I wasn't completely alone.

Willie ran into the stable again, shouting about sin. I followed him as far as the door, and when I looked inside I nearly fainted at the sight. The lantern was standing on a ledge and Willie held the knife in front of him. His body was stooped and he was walking slowly towards the big black and white bull.

"No, Willie!" I cried in terror. "No!"

"The world is full of sin! Oh, Lord, help me to stop the sin of the world! Glory!"

"Please, Willie! I think I hear Mr. Gordon coming!" I lied.

"Angus Gordon is a goddam sinner! We're all sinners! I have the power to stop all sin! Oh, hallelujah!"

He caught the bull by the tail, and it bellowed and swung its haunches against the wall. A cloud of dust rose from the floor and the stable was filled with the noise of the big beast banging against the timbers. The horses were stamping in their stalls. I saw Willie trying to get into position to use his knife and I began to scream.

Then I turned my head so I couldn't see him any longer, but I could hear the bull bellowing and banging around and the snorts of the frightened horses.

Suddenly he came running towards the door, the lantern swinging in his hand. "The Lord be praised!" he cried. "No more sin!"

I ran across the yard as fast as I could and climbed over a fence into a pasture. Hiding behind a post I watched Willie standing there with the lantern lighting his legs.

He began circling the yard. His hymns and the bellows of the bull were so loud that I thought every living thing in the neighbourhood must be listening. I watched him heading towards the pigsty and I shouted to him, but he made no sign that he heard me. There was the click of the latch on the pigsty door, even above the other noises, and the lantern disappeared inside lighting up the cracks between the boards.

There were some grunts at first, then startled squeals. The bellows of the bull grew weaker, but the night was filled with the squeals of the hogs and the noise of them butting against the walls of their pens. Now and again there was the sound of Willie's singing, but his songs no longer had any understandable words.

I looked around me in the darkness, hoping I'd see some-body coming across the fields. Willie stayed in the shed a long time, the pigs squealing and grunting, and his crazy tunes rising and falling across the yard.

I wondered what Mr. Gordon would do to us. We'd be arrested! I'd tell them that I didn't have anything to do with it. Anyways, I was only a boy. I wouldn't do a thing like that.

The place was a bedlam. Every animal seemed to sense what was happening and they were all trying to break out of their pens and stalls together.

Willie came out of the pigsty, swinging the lantern around his legs. I wondered what he was going to do next. Then I heard another door opening, and there was the sound of hens cluck-ing and the swish of wings against wood.

The hen-house door swung open and he came out again, the lantern held high so that I saw his face. He was completely crazy now, his eyes bugged out from his head and his mouth slobbering as he sang his tuneless songs. He peered around him in the darkness, and the light from the lantern shone on a frantic white hen that was running back and forth against the wall of a building. He ran towards it and his lamp blinded the hen so that it stopped running long enough for him to grab it. He dropped the lantern to the ground and picked the bird up by the neck. Then he stared into the sky and screamed at the top of his voice, at the same time pulling the head from the hen. He threw the wriggling body from him, where it flopped along the ground, and, stooping, picked up his lantern once more.

He held the light high and began calling my name. At times he got mixed up and called the names of other people who lived in the neighbourhood, crying out that they were all sinners. He began to search for me in the darkness, and I pressed myself down in the grass to hide. When he came closer to me I stood up and backed away from the fence. He saw me then and his face broke out in a horrible grin. "Come on, poor little sinner," he coaxed as he stumbled in my direction.

"No! Go away!" I screamed, hating him now so that I forgot I had ever liked him. He was a complete stranger to me, a crazy loathsome stranger I'd never seen before.

His look changed from crafty friendliness to horrible rage and he roared a string of filthy curses. His mumbling lips were covered with spit, and he threw himself against the fence, crying and cursing together.

I turned and ran as fast as I could across the uneven ground, trying not to scream and give away my position in the darkness. I don't remember all of my flight, but I was so scared that I took a large patch of skin off my back going through a rail fence, and I didn't realize it until later. In my imagination Willie was right behind me with his knife.

I don't know how long it took me to get to the Turner place. I was sobbing and panting with fear as I made for the house, slapping at the Turner's dog which was barking at me and trying to grab my legs. Bert Turner let me in the door, and I collapsed on a chair in the kitchen.

"What's the matter, boy?" he asked, staring at me.

"It's Willie – Willie Heaps! He's gone crazy! He – he's cutting all the animals at the Gordons'. He's killed the pigs and chickens too!"

"What did he say?" asked Mrs. Turner, entering the kitchen.

"It's Willie Heaps," Bert answered. "I'd better telephone his father."

After they bolted the door I sat on the chair crying and shivering with fright. Mrs. Turner gave me a cup of coffee but I was too weak and shaky to lift it to my mouth. Bert called my family on the phone, and my father and Edgar the hired man came for me in the car.

A search party was out all night looking for Willie and warning the neighbourhood to be on guard against him. Early next morning Mr. Summerville, the police chief in Cumberford, got a message that Willie had been found in a ditch by a farmer, self-mutilated and nearly dead from loss of blood. An ambulance was sent from Brantford and they took Willie to the hospital there. He died the following night.

My mother made me go to the funeral, but I refused to look at Willie in his coffin. Mr. and Mrs. Heaps were crying and carrying on, and shouting to God to call Willie to His side.

A tall skinny man in a black shiny suit introduced himself to my mother and father as the Reverend Blounsbury, Willie's minister. He had a turned-on smile and a long thin nose that seemed to be running but wasn't.

"And this is Willie's little friend, is it?" he said, putting his hand on my shoulder.

My mother nodded.

"Poor child, to be bereft of a friend so soon in life," he said. "But don't grieve, lad, Willie now sits at the right hand of his Maker. He had been saved, you know."

My mother nodded again.

"And how about you? Have you been converted yet, young man?"

"No!" I cried, shaking his hand from me and edging to the door.

"My, what's come over that boy!" exclaimed my mother.

I ran out of the house and down the road towards home. I hated them all: Willie, Mr. and Mrs. Heaps, my mother and father, and especially the Reverend Blounsbury. Why couldn't they have left Willie alone, I asked myself. Why couldn't everybody in the whole wide world leave everybody else alone?

BARRY CALLAGHAN

THIRD PEW TO THE LEFT

A man of about seventy came into a downtown bar every late
afternoon, a small man who wore slacks and a sports shirt in the
summer and a cardigan sweater over his shirt in the winter. His
hair was white. There was a feeling of wry beneficence in his
smile. He seemed to wish people well and to wish himself well.
This had something to do with his being an old priest who
drank, and sometimes he drank a lot if people at the bar bought
him drinks.

The woman who was the bartender always called out cheer-
fully when he came in, "Hello, Father Joe." He smiled, pleased
to be welcomed, but perhaps not wanting everyone to know
that he was a priest. He took a chair by a small table in a corner, a table almost no one ever sat at unless the bar was
crowded and usually it was crowded late at night, long after he
had gone home to St. Basil's, a residence close to the bar and
close to the university, a home for young seminarians and old
retired priests.

I had gone to the university, and I had been married in St.
Basil's Church so I called out, too, "Hello, Father Joe." He
smiled but it was the smile of a man who expected to be left
alone. Sitting by myself at the bar I always sent him a drink, a
scotch and soda over ice.

"Cheers," he said quietly.

One day I was feeling so alone at the bar that I couldn't help
myself. I sat down beside him. He was surprised, but at ease.

"You're a fine-looking amiable old priest," I said. I had been drinking since noon.

"You're a fine-looking ruin of a man yourself," he said.

"Perfidy's upon us," I said.

"Not likely," he said. "Relax."

I did. I told him that I'd been a student. He said that he'd been a teacher. I'd studied languages and literature, I said. He said he'd taught philosophy. I asked him how, after all these years, he liked being a priest. He said he liked it fine. I asked how he liked the new right-wing bishop, Father Ambrosionic.

"I dunno," he said.

"The mad Pole's given us a stern Serb," I said. "Now, now," he said. "Let's be looking on the bright side, at least you know now exactly where you stand. You can thank the Pope for that."

"Thank you, Pope," I said.

"Have you been drinking?"

"A little," I said.

"I drink a lot," he said. Then he touched my hand. "Don't worry," he said. "It has nothing to do with any spiritual crisis. I don't go in for that class of thing."

"Where you from?" I asked.

"Pittsburgh," he said. "Many long years ago, when it was a tough town. My father was a tough man, a steel worker. How about you?"

"Here," I said.

"You're from here?"

"Here."

"I haven't met anybody from here for years," he said.

"Well, you have now," I said.

"Good. It's good to be in touch with roots," he said.

"I'll tell you the truth, Father, as far as I'm concerned, that's a shoe store."

"Well, at least you've got your feet on the ground," he said, trying to stifle a laugh. I wagged my finger at him and he winked at me and I waved at the bartender, telling her to bring us two more drinks.

"I've a weakness for cheap jokes," he said.

"I've a weakness for cheap whiskey," I said.

"You might say that makes it even between us," he said. "Myself, I lean to the good whiskey, when I can get it."

"Well, they don't serve you slouch whiskey in here," I said.

"No, they do not," he said.

We smiled at each other.

"Well, now that we've got that settled," he said, sipping his fresh scotch and soda, "what's your claim to fame?"

"Advertising. Consulting," I said.

"Which is it?"

"Both," I said. "When I'm not consulting I advertise I do."

"You do?"

"Yes."

"And this is where literature gets you?"

"Like a patient etherised upon a table," I said.

He laughed.

"I used to know some poems by heart," he said.

"What happened?"

"My heart gave out," and he laughed again, saying, "forgive me, I can't help it."

"Neither can I," I said.

"Do you know what forgiveness is?" he asked.

"No," I said.

"When you know you have nothing left to lose and you pass it on."

"Boy, I should've studied with you," I said.

"Maybe not," he said.

"What'd you teach?"

"Philosophy, for openers. Plato, Aristotle, Thomas Aquinas... it was wonderful, talking about how God's mind worked, and then I used to leap right up to the twentieth century, to our own time, to Maritain..."

"What happened to what's in between?" I asked.

"Nothing," he said.

"Yeah but where'd it go? Where'd Descartes go?"

"Nowhere. I left him right where he was."

"You can't do that," I said.

"I did," he said.

"Didn't anybody say anything?"

"They did not. Anyway, I used to tell them, 'We all know the trouble with Descartes, he put de cart before de horse!'"

"Oh, God, you didn't!"

"I did," he said. "And why not? It's a corny joke, but it's got me out of some tricky situations. Anyway, when you think about it, this business about 'I think therefore I am' is rather profoundly dumb. After all, God thought and therefore we are and since we are, we think. What else could we do but think – go bowling? And if we think too much we probably end up like your man Woody Allen, talking ourselves to death. It's what the wise boys call ennui..."

"The wisdom of hell," I said, laughing with him.

"I don't know a lot about hell," he said. "That's why I drink. Any time I get anywhere close to hell I take a drink. "

"But you're in here every day," I said.

"Yes," he said.

"Jesus."

"Yes," he said, lifting his glass, "and isn't He a help, a wonderful fellow. Forgave us, and died for our sins."

"You're kidding," I said.

"I don't kid about Jesus," he said.

"I don't mean that, I mean the way you said it."

"How'd I say it?"

"Like He was the guy next door."

"You drink too much," he said.

"Says who?" I said, drawing a circle with my finger in the dampness on the table.

"Never mind, I don't want to ruin our nice talk. I don't want to know why you think you drink."

"No?" I asked, disappointed.

"I might be interested to know why you think you love," he said. "But that would take a couple more drinks and they're not going to give me any more. Orders from on high, eye in the sky."

"You really think I drink too much?" I asked.

"How do I know? I hardly know you."

"Maybe it's true," I said.

"Maybe."

"Maybe a lot of things are true."

"Could be, you never know. Not until you know."

"Not until the fat lady sings," I said.

"The only fat lady I ever knew," he said, "was my mother, and she lived to a ripe old age. Ninety-two. She had a fine philosophical bent," he said.

"I used to like talking philosophy," I said.

He smiled, his mouth taking a little turn, wishing me well.

"You did, did you?" he said.

"Yep," I said.

"If a tree falls in a forest when there's no one there, does the tree make a sound?... That kind of thing?" he said.

"Yeah, that kind of stuff," I said. "And poetry, the half-deserted streets, the muttering retreats of cheap one nights in sawdust hotels... Something like that."

"I never went in much for poetry. Limericks were my speed," he said.

"There was a priest who taught me, Dore or Dorey, something like that," and Father Joe nodded as if he knew who I was talking about, "and he had that whole poem off by heart. He'd stand up in front of us and roar that thing out, I never liked to admit it back then but I envied him, he had this light in his eyes like he was lifted right out of himself. And then, he said something I've never forgotten. I mean he said about the end, where you feel like you're a pair of ragged claws scuttling across the ocean floor – and I don't know about you, Father, but that's exactly how I feel when I've drunk too much – he said, Hell probably isn't fire or anything like that, it's probably being those claws inside your own head and hearing them..."

"Don't be so hard on yourself," he said.

"Hard?" I asked.

"Yeah," he said.

"My father always said I was too easy on myself."

"Well, it's a matter of perspective. The truth is tricky."

"Do I dare to eat a peach?" I blurted out.

"There's a time for everything," he said.

"I guess there is."

"Time for me to go," he said, standing up, "I think."

"...am not Hamlet, nor was meant to be," I cried. "Am an attendant player—"

"Thanks for the drinks," he said, straightening his shirt collar.

"Right. Any time," I said.

"And the chat," he said.

"Any time."

I was wounded. I was sure that he had grown tired of me. Then he said gravely, "It's a long time since you've been to confession. I can tell, a long time."

"I suppose it is," I said, startled.

"After a long long time it's harder," he said, leaning to me.

"I don't know."

"Listen, the time'll come when you'll want to go to confession..."

"I doubt it," I said.

"Sure. It'll come, but don't worry about it. When the time comes, I'm your man."

"You think so?"

"I know so."

I stared at the circle I'd drawn on the table. Then I said, "Yeah well, do you want me to go to confession or do you want me to tell you the truth?"

"Confession," he said, laughing. "I told you, the truth is tricky."

Over the next three or four months, we saw each other almost every day. We got used to knowing that at the end of the afternoon, for about forty-five minutes, we were together in the same room. We said a word or two but we never had a long talk again. I never went to confession. I bought him drinks. He drank them. I consulted. I drank and told myself one or two small truths and turned down a free ticket to see the new Woody Allen film. "It's got to do with Descartes," I told my friends. "He and Woody... put de cart before de horse." Nobody laughed. "Get off the bottle," one of them said.

Then, Father Joe was not there. I asked the bartender if she knew where he was. She said, "Father Joe's been sick, he died, the funeral's tomorrow." I went to the funeral at St. Basil's Church. The bishop, Father Ambrosionic, didn't go. I didn't mind. I knew where I stood. Third pew to the left.

DIANE KEATING

THE SALEM LETTERS

April 6, 1692
After the waggon
left for Jail

To my Mistress Elizabeth Proctor,

I be out on the stoop scraping plattes into the slop pail when I heerd the wheels clanging over the froz'n mudd & dung of the barneyard. Shading my eyes from the sun I stood in the door-waie to watch you & Mr. Proctor drive off. While I be staring at the back of your hooded cloak & his huge shoalders my week'r eye began drifting upward so at the same time I be glim-sing tops of trees & blue skie.

Thats when the'Angels appeer'd at the edge of my sight. Thous-ands of them. Dancing acrosse th'Heavens. Dancing like a path of sunlight across water.

I fell to my nees. Cover'd my face with my armes. But 'twas as tho I be seeing with my Soule. Befor me rised up a bull bigg'r than Gallows Hill with hornes the shape of new moons. Chained to his shoalder a mightie bird of prey be ripping at his flesh.

Then it all disappeer'd in a whirlwind of fethers & blood & I fellt words like handes of the Lord being laied upon my hed – Feer not, Mary, they saied, thou hast found favour with the Lord. Thru thee the unseen shall be seen. Thru thee the bound shall be freed.

Next I remember I be lieing on my back in a puddel from the overturn'd slop buckett & staring up at the skie thru chinks in the roof.

Rite awaie I know'd 'twas a Revclashun cuz of the dazzeling dark befor my eyes. Also I know'd, Mrs. Proctor, that the bull chained to the bird of prey be Mr. Proctor chained to you. Husband to wife. Erthe to Hell.

With my heart pounding hard as hoofs I pickt up my sopping skirt & ran outside. I want'd to warn Mr. Proctor to wait for the Constabul. Not to take you by himself to Jail. Altho I ran all the waie to the gate the waggon be too farr downe the road for him to hear me calling.

After much thot & pray'r I hav decided, Mrs. Proctor, to tell you of my vishun. 'Tis a warning to you as much a promise to me. Take heed. Tho I am only eighteen and your servant I am speshull. The Lord hast chosen me to reveel your witchcraft.

When my left eyeball comes unbound I hav seconde sight. I can see th'invisibel world bulging in from th'edges of thinges. You be scared of what I will find out. Thats why you beet me 'bout the hed saieing eyes must work together same as ox'n in a yoke. That why you tell everyone my eye be a signe of weeknesse in the hed and not to take serieusly what I be seeing.

But now I am not alonne. Them other girls hav cried out at you. Now they will beleev that when you be lifting your arme to beat me I truely didd see a brown growth like a nippel in your arm pitt. Abbie saies while you be in Jail it will be prick't with a needel & if there be no sensashun that proves 'tis a witches teat for suckeling imps & demons.

For a long time peepul have suspecked that magpie of yourn, Mrs. Proctor, be a demon helper. 'Tis unnatural for a wild bird to swoop out of nowhere & perch on a personnes shoalder.

My Soule shivers to think of it. The waie it glares with them round black eyes – lifeless as beeds sewn to the sides of its hed – while chatt'ring in your ear a language without words. A language only you understand.

In a few daies there will be a Heering to decide if the evidence against you warrants a trial at the Court of Oyer & Terminer. Altho I am one of those you torment Mr. Proctor will not allow me to go. He saies us girls be acting madd as March hares to get attenshun & if tied to our spinning wheels we will be cured fast enuff.

Since you both refused to attend the Heering for them oth'r three witches you did not see how we swoon'd & writh'd & howl'd when the accused be brot in. The magistrates called us bloodhounds of the Lord.

Soon everyone between Salem & Boston shall know who I am. Then the Governor himself shall listen to me. Even Mr. Proctor. Tho since you be accused of witchcraft he does not speek but lookes unutterabel thinges at me. Eech time I feel kikt in the'head.

In truth & trust
I remain your servant
Mary Warren

April 9, 1692
After Morning Prayers

To my mistress Elizabeth Proctor,

Now that Mr. Proctor be taking a pacquet of vitalls every daie to the Jailhouse 'tis eesy to slip in your letters. He warn'd me not to tell anyone – not even the littel ones – so he must hav brib'd the guard.

I hav much to saie & you best not laff like you alwaies donne when I spoke the truth to you. Speshully I hated how – if Mister be 'round – you would roll your eyes & chuckel so it seem'd you be indulging me. And that soft hollow chuckelling, Mrs. Proctor, be like an echo of your magpie. 'Tis not human sound.

Abbie agrees with me. She been here yesterdaie for tea & the haires on her armes stood up when she herd the magpies evil laffing in the branches of the bigge elm. That bird deserves to be hanged she cried out. Without a dowt, Mrs. Proctor, you will soon be hanged & donn't want you crying out at me when meeting the Lord, face to face, for your Final Reckoning.

Since the Revelashun I no longer feer you. With the help of the'Almightie I shall stopp you from destroying Mr. Proctor. I know how much you feer him. His animal strength. His animal lawes. Being almost seven feet high he alwaies gettes his own waie. Peepul shake their head & saie he be more like Sam-son than Solomon.

I beleev them. I beleev he be the strong'st man next to God. Not alwaies good but then why should he be? God be not good. God be God.

And you Mrs. Proctor? You be like Delilah. You want to find the secrett of his power. Thats why you be pacting with the Devil tho Mr. Proctor donnt beleev it. He beleevs only what he sees.

I remember the first time I seen your specter self. 'Twas last summer after you rode off to a Quilting Bee on the Meetinghouse Green. An xcuse, Mr. Proctor saied, for gathering heersaie from the other goodwives. Tho I had not left the farme for som months you told me to staie with the babee who be weak'nd by the Bloody Flux.

While heeting water in the bigg iron cauldron to wash its clouts & coverlettes my wand'ring left eye cawt somethinge moving. I thot your cloake hung by the open door be blowing in the wind. But no, Mrs. Proctor, 'twas your specter. Same as you but loos'r looking as tho your bones be made of jelly.

As you slid toward me I seen your eyes be emptie holes. Your face twist'd & white like it be burnt by acid. My holl'ring brot Mr. Proctor running from the house. As I throw'd myselfe into his armes I fellt you strangeling me. Your handes on my neck greesy & cold as intestines pull'd from a fresh kill'd goat.

Mr. Proctor must hav been standing on the hem of my skirt cuz when he tried to push me awaie he rippt it. I lost my balance & fell to the floor with him on top of me. Thats when your specter self crosst my legges with so much force they poppt out of joint & Mr. Proctor for all his strength could not uncrosse them. Not without breaking them he saied.

Even then he wouldn't beleev me. Even when I point'd to your specter standing beside him he saied 'twas his shaddowe. Threten'd to ram a hott pok'r down my throate if I diddn't stopp screeming your name.

Thats why now I be too scared to tell him 'bout the Revelashun. For sure he would wopp me. Perhaps send me awaie.

Later
After Cockshut

I am sitting near the winddoe listening for Mr. Proctors hors.
The only sounds be the bull kiking at the slattes of his small stall
& the calling of a whip-poor-will down by the creek. Makes me
bone lonely to hear it.

Mr. Proctor saies its whisiling be an omen the frost has gon
from the ground. Time to start plowing but he & the two old'st
nev'r be here. They ride farr as Ipswich trying to gett persons to
signe a petishun saieing you be a dilligent attend'r upon Gods
Holy Ordinances.

Wonnt do no good, Mrs. Proctor. Again this afternoon
the'Almightie reveel'd He be on my side by helping me find that
strawe doll of yourn.

I be in the smoakhouse unhooking a legge of bacon for dinner when I seen it wedg'd in a crack between the chimney &
wall. 'Twas wearing clowthes made from Mr. Proctors shirt &
the pinnes thru its body be winded with his graye haires.

I wager you leern'd the Black Artes from your Grandma who
be accus'd of witchcraft twentie yeares ago. Tho the charge be
dropp't many people in Salem remember & saie where theres
smoak theres fire.

Perhaps thats why Mr. Proctor wonnt lett me com to the
Heering & see you xamined by them Magistrates. He hates
their high-fallutin waies. Powder'd pigges in wigges he calls
them.

He must be scared I will cry out in publick just like that
starkel'd nitwitt daughter of Reverent Parris cried out on their
slave & then fell into a fitt. Abbie tell'd me she laie on the floor
gasping & writhing like a long white fish thrown up on the
shore.

Since you be taken to jail, Mrs. Proctor, the wave of afflict'd
girles growes bigg'r. They saie it be cuz erly April comes midwaie
between winter & summer solstis when the influence of the
moon be the great'st.

Mrs. Proctor save yourself. Admitt to the blastings. The worst being Goodwife Putnams babee who died in the womb. The midwife told Goodwife Jacobs who told her servant Sarah, my friend, that while she be pulling the babee out by the legges they broke off – shrivell'd as the forkt root of mandrake – but the wee blind face be perfect as a pansy. And that blue.

Everyone agrees 'twas you who blasted it. Or else why at the Burial did that magpie of yourn keep chatt'ring & chorteling from high on a neerbye tree. No one could stopp themselves from listening. Like in a waking dream they forgot what they be doing & follow'd it from tree to tree. Reverent Parris & Goodwife Putnam be left alonne to low'r the coffin.

Confess, Mrs. Proctor, that Satan took you for his bride. The Lord shall forgive you. So shall I. So shall all of Salem – town & village.

Confess & they shant hang you. They knowe we be born damn'd. All of us lost from the Lord. Lost as leeves that loosn'd from a tree be blowing forever in the wind.

> With trust & hope
> Mary Warren
> Bloodhound of the Lord

April 10, 1692
Forenoon, Sitting on the stoop

To My Mistress,

The first warm breezes be coming from the West. Day &
Night I heer them slith'ring thru the willows & now the budds
be the sise of a mouses ear.

Your littel ones be on the creek bank cutting branches to
feed the bull. I can heer 'em laff abov the peep of froglings and
the faroff ringing of an axe. Must be Mr. Sheldon cleering land
on the other side of Gallows Hill.

Erly this morn while hanging out the wash I pegg'd my petticoat to Mr. Proctors breeches. As I be watching them cling &
sway in the wind – dancing togeth'r as we nev'r can – I glim'st
out of the corner of my week eye flashes of hellgreen flames by
the back steppes. Turn'd out 'twas crocus leeves poking up from
dirty crusts of snowe.

As I pickt the wee purple blooms I thot of them sleeping
curl'd in their bulbs all winter. Then I thot of my heart sleeping
curl'd in my body. Waiting like these flow'rs donne for the
warmth of the sun. Waiting for Mr. Proctor.

Since you be in jail eech time I put my hand on my con-
shence it comes out black as pitch. I must confess I love Mr.
Proctor. Thats the truth. Last week I tell'd him when he looks at
me I go week as a rained-on bee. He laff'd & laff'd & ask'd me
if I tell'd you.

I donnt care, Mrs. Proctor, I knowe he loves me even tho he
donnt showe it. He cannt help him selfe. The Lord ordain'd it.
Diddnt He give me the gift of seeing the visibel & th'invisibel
meeting at th'edges of my sight? That be so I could reveel your
witchcraft.

Take heed Mrs. Proctor. 'Tis no sinne to cheet the Devil. Old Hornie, Mr. Proctor calls him.

Yours truthfully
Mary Warren
Bloodhound for the Lord

April 11, 1692
Spring Feest Daie

Dear Mrs. Proctor,

All night I toss't & turn'd like butter in a churn. Theres no relying on a starrie evening to giv one plesant dreems.

Donn't recall much xcept the wind singing save him save him as I soared abov the treetops. 'Twas night but the moon had stopp't shining. The starres be round white stones & I pluck't one out of the skie as I flied bye.

In front of me Gallows Hill rised into a dark platform. Perching on top of the Hanging Tree I seen your littel ones tied to a low'r branch. Their naked white bodies dangeling like geese with broken neckes.

On the ground beneath them you be squatting, Mrs. Proctor, gnawing on a dogge bone. Just as I reech't out to droppe the ded starre on your hed the tree start'd to shake & I woke to Mr. Proctors footsteppes on the stairs. Even in his stockings he qwakes the howse. That heavy menacing walk of his'n alwaies seems 'bout to gather into a rush.

This be the third morn Mr. Proctor has rode awaie befor the cock crow'd. So farr twentie-seven persons sign'd the petishun on your behalf. But nobodie from Salem village. They saie Mr. Proctor ownes 4 howses & 700 acres of the best lands & still he donn't paie his ministrie tax.

Two daies ago Reverent Parris stopp't him on the Village Green & saied to xpect a heavy fine. They argued & Mr. Proctor lost his temp'r. Poking the Reverent in the chest with his forefinger he saied no man whose eyebrows meet could be trust'd. Not even an ordain'd Minister.

After the Reverent yell'd that he be a devilish churlish uncivil dogge Mr. Proctor accus'd him of being mor interest'd in his salarie than in saving Soules.

Then the Reverent clasp't his handes togeth'r & throw'd back his hed crying O Lord protect us from blasfeemers. At that moment he be shat on from above by a big pidgin. Nobodie could stopp themselves from laffing.

Abbie who been there saied the Reverent grow'd green-looking as an erly apple & seem'd 'bout to vomitt. Todaie she tell'd me he plannes to file for sland'r. Being the Reverents neece she knowes all 'bout the goings-on at the Parsonage. And being best friends we tell eech oth'r everythinge.

Did you remember, Mrs. Proctor, this be the annual Spring Feest Daie to celebrate the end of our long winter & the incoming of shippes with salt & sugar & foreign news? They saie Governor Phipps return'd afer five yeares perswading King James to giv our colony a new charter.

I am longing to go to the Meeting-Howse but Mr. Proctor saies the maddness of one be making many madd. He forbiddes me to take the littel ones.

Since you be gon they keep crying off & on. They paie me no heed. Mor like littel caged animales they eet what they will & sleep where they fall. They cann't be missing you, Mrs. Proctor, cuz you never be 'round. You staied all daie in front of the house overseeing the Taverne Room. Gossiping with the men.

I nev'r told you this but Abbie overherd Mrs. Parris saie your licents as a taverne keep'r might be revoked even tho the front roome be only Ordinarie to wet one's whistle between town & village.

Did you knowe Mr. Ruckes report'd you to the town council? He tell'd them when he couldnn't paie for his fifth pint of cider you demanded his gold tooth. Made him yank it out. Abbie saies Mrs. Parris claims you be lowe as a Sodomite woman who did nothinge but eet & drink & sell & plant & build.

Mrs. Proctor why donnt you paie attenshun to what peepul saie 'bout you? Speshully to what I saie. You never com to the Meeting-Howse with Mr. Proctor & me & the littel ones. On Lecture Daies you be too busy in the Ordinarie. To Labour be to pray you alwaies saied.

On the Sabbath you be too tired xcept it be a Feest Daie. Then you would gett gussied up in that wool'n cloak you order'd from Boston & them leather gloves with the pearl buttons.

Do you knowe what Abbie tell'd me the goodwives saied when they seen you gathering up the front of your skirt & flouncing up the steppes to the Meeting-Howse? They saied ill-gott'n, ill-spent.

There still be time to sav your Soule. Confess, Mrs. Proctor. Confess that the Devil holds you in the hollow of his hande. Confess befor his hande closes into a fist & you be broken to bits like a clod of erthe.

> In truth & loyalty
> Mary Warren
> Bloodhound of the Lord

April 12, 1692
After boiling up deer fat for candels

Dear Mrs. Proctor,

For over two winters I hav been living in your shadowe
under the roof of a man who be neither my father nor my husband. Alwaies I be in the back of the house doing a wifes chores.
Waiting for Mr. Proctor. Waiting since the daie I arriv'd & he
lift'd me out of the waggon. Staring at me with them eyes –
black & wild as any hunting animal – while my heart flippt-
floppt like a scared bird in a cage.

Do you remember the first winter, Mrs. Proctor? In the
evenings after th'Ordinarie closed & the littel ones been in bed-
dle I would quilt on the bigg frame in the corner of the middel-
room while Mr. Proctor & you sat in the warmth of th'in-
glenook. He in his deep chair whitteling them flee trappes we
wear'd 'round our neckes. You in your rocker clucking over the
book where the tavern ernings be recorded.

You wouldn't knowe how I used to stare at Mr. Proctor.
Outlined in the crimson glowe of the fire he be so strong & soli-
tarie & solem looking. Like the Angel who pour'd the Lords
Seeds into Marys ear.

Do you remember Mrs. Proctor? How you would be clap-
perclawing about something that happen'd in the Taverne when
he would reach over & tapp your nee. Elizabeth, he would saie,
you could talk the Devil out of a witches howse. Then you
would look at eech other & smile.

You didnn't knowe Mrs. Proctor how that look – that smile
– splitt my heart in two. Just like one of them aspens behind the
howse splitting in the cold. Its dry crack echoing from tree to
tree.

Even after all this time when I heer his stamping outside the
backe door – three times with eech boot to knock off the mudd

or snowe – I cann no more stoppe my heart from pounding than a dogge upon his masters return cann stoppe his wagging tail.

Specially in winter when he has been hunting cuz then I gett to rubb polecatt oil into his feete to cure the rheumatisme. Who would guess with his face weather riven'd as a hilltop that his feete be so pink & smooth & warm. Like fresh skinn'd rabbits in my handes.

I wager you haven't seen the scarr – shaped like a wee clov'n hoof – on the outside of his left foot. Nobodie but me knowes he be born with six toes. His Mama birth'd alonne while hiding in a root cellar during an Indian raid. Feering they would saie she been diddel'd by a demon she bit off the xtra toe.

Mrs. Proctor, do you remember the Feest Daie last New Years? We be going to the Corys pigge roast but the sleigh been too full. I saied that I would ride ov'r with Mr. Proctor when he got backe from deer hunting.

Upon heering his hounds I closed the shutters & lit the candels. Then I took off my bonnet & lett out my haire. I knowe you warn'd me to keep my head cover'd cuz my haire be redd. You alwaies be saieing Judas had haire redd'r than fire.

But I donn't care. Mr. Proctor cann nev'r keep his eyes off me when my haire be sett free. This be specially true last News Year Feest. When he came in I be standing with my back to the fire. My haire falling 'round me soft & heavie & long like a shawl. All the time he be taking off his cloak & hat he stared at me. Ask't me what happen'd that my eyes had grow'd mor green than a catte stalking a mouse. I giv'd no reply. Just smil'd.

Soon as he sat in his chair by the hearth I nellt to pull of his bootes & stockings. Then hidd'n my haire I slowly caresst his feet while I rubb'd in the warm oil. He paied no heed. The only sound been the crackel of the fire & the wethercock screeking as it turn'd on the roof.

Thinking how Mary show'd her love by kissing the feet of
Jesus I began gently to run my tongue along his soles. And then
to mouthe his toes as I snugell'd his feet like a newborn babee
to my breasts.

I thot the moaning been the wind coming thru the keyhole
of the doore but 'twas Mr. Proctor. Suddenly he giv'd a slite
shudder & grabbing my haire yank'd back my hed. I remember
how he kept mutt'ring so sweet an evil ov'r & ov'r as he be spitting in my face & then covering it with kisses. It fellt as tho a
burning arrowe peerc'd my heart – melting it like hott wax into
my bowelles. Darling, I wisper'd, pressing clos'r to him. He
jumpt up. Kickt me awaie. I be scared cuz his face had gon
white as leprosy. When I start'd crieing he pickt up the spinning
wheel & smash'd it against the wall.

You be the Gatewaie to Hell, he yell'd, charging out of the
howse.

When I heerd his hors galloping awaie I be sertain he had
gon to sign a warrant for my arrest as a harlott. I tried to pray
for my sinne but when I closed my eyes it be red as fire inside
my hed. And the mor hot it grow'd the mor I want'd Mr. Proctor.

At sundowne he return'd with you & the littel ones. Tho he
pretended nothinge had gon on I could feel his coal black eyes
burning into me with all the pent up force of Lucifers last look
at the Lord.

You nev'r notis'd but ever since that daie, Mrs. Proctor, I
havnt been abel to look you in th'eyes for feer you would see
how I yearn'd for him. But now that I hav been bless'd with the
Vishun I need not feer breaking the Ten Commandments. In
my armes – with my lippes – I shall comfort Mr. Proctor. Yea,
tho he be made to walk thru vallies of dry bones & dust I shall

be with him. For the heart, Mrs. Proctor, the heart cannot be divided from the flesh.

Yours truthfully
Mary Warren
Bloodhound of the Lord

ALDEN NOWLAN

MIRACLE AT INDIAN RIVER

This is the story of how mates were chosen for all the marriage-able young men and women in the congregation of the Fire-Baptized Tabernacle of the Living God in Indian River, New Brunswick. It is a true story, more or less, and whether it is ridiculous or pathetic or even oddly beautiful depends a good deal on the mood you're in when you read it.

Indian River is one of those little places that don't really exist, except in the minds of their inhabitants. Passing through it as a stranger you might not even notice that it is there. Or if you did notice it, you'd think it was no different from thousands of other little backwoods communities in Canada and the United States. But you'd be wrong. Indian River, like every community large and small, has a character all its own.

The inhabitants of Indian River are pure Dutch, although they don't know it. Their ancestors settled in New Amsterdam more than three hundred years ago and migrated to New Brunswick after the American Revolution. But they've always been isolated, always intermarried, so that racially they're prob-ably more purely Dutch than most of the Dutch in Holland, even though they've long ago forgotten the language and few of them could locate the Netherlands on a map.

The village contains a railway station which hasn't been used since 1965 when the CNR discontinued passenger service in that part of northwestern New Brunswick, a one-room school that was closed five years ago when the government began using buses to carry local children to the regional school in Cumberland Centre, a general store and two churches: St. Edward's Anglican, which used to be attended by the station agent, the teacher and the storekeeper, and the Fire-Baptized Tabernacle of the Living God, attended by practically everyone else in Indian River.

The tabernacle, formerly a barracks, was bought from the Department of National Defence and brought in on a flatcar. "Jesus Saves" is painted in big red letters over the door. A billboard beside the road warns drivers to prepare to meet their God. There is an evergreen forest to the north, a brook full of speckled trout to the west and, in the east, a pasture in which a dozen Holstein cattle and a team of Clydesdale horses graze together. The pastor, Rev. Horace Zwicker, his wife, Myrtle, and their five children live in a flat behind the pulpit.

Pastor Zwicker was born in Indian River and, before he was called of God to the ministry, was a door-to-door salesman of magazine subscriptions and patent medicines, chauffeur for a chiropractor, and accordionist in a hillbilly band that toured the Maritime provinces and Maine.

Services are held in the tabernacle Wednesday night, Sunday morning and Sunday night. During the summer evangelists arrive, usually from Alabama, Georgia, or Tennessee, and then there are services every night of the week. Almost every one of the evangelists has some sort of speciality, like painting a pastel portrait of Christ as he delivers his sermon or playing "The Old Rugged Cross" on an instrument made from empty whiskey bottles. Once there was a man with a long black beard and shoulder-length hair who claimed to have gone to school with Hitler; another time a professed ex-convict named Bent-Knee Benjamin preached in striped pajamas, a ball and chain fastened to his leg.

Fire-Baptized people worry a good deal about sin – mostly innocent little rural sins like smoking, drinking, watching television, and going to the movies. Fire-Baptized women, of whom there are several thousands in northwestern New Brunswick, are easy to identify on the streets of towns like Woodstock and Fredericton because they don't use cosmetics and wear their hair in a sort of Oregon Trail bun at the backs of their necks. Fire-Baptized girls are made to dress somewhat the way Elizabeth dressed before she met Philip. There is a legend, invented presumably by Anglicans and Catholics, that Fire-Baptized girls are extraordinarily agreeable and inordinately passionate.

A few years ago there happened to be an unusually large number of unmarried young men and women in Indian River.

Pastor Zwicker frequently discussed this matter with his Lord.

"Lord," he said, "You know as well as I do that it isn't good to have a pack of hot young bucks and fancy-free young females running around loose. Like Paul says, those who don't marry are apt to burn, and when they've burned long enough they'll do just about anything to put the fire out. Now, tell me straight, Lord, what do You figure I should do about it?"

The Lord offered various suggestions and Pastor Zwicker tried them all.

He had long and prayerful conversations with each young man and woman. He told Harris Brandt, for example, that Rebecca Vaneyck was not only a sweet Christian girl, pure and obedient, she made the best blueberry pie of any cook her age in Connaught Country. "Never cared much for blueberries myself, Pastor," Harris said. He told Rebecca that Harris was a stout Christian youth who wouldn't get drunk, except perhaps if he were sorely tempted of the devil on election day, and wouldn't beat her unless she really deserved it. And she replied: "But, Pastor, he has such bad teeth!"

His conversations with the others were equally fruitless. The Lord advised stronger methods.

"Look here, Brother," the pastor admonished young Francis Witt's father, "it's time that young fellow of yours settled down and got himself a wife. I was talking it over with the Lord just the other night. Now, as you're well aware, Brother, the Scriptures tell us that a son should be obedient to his father. So if I was you—"

"Need the boy," replied the father. "Couldn't run this place without him. Talked to the Lord about it myself. Wife did too. Lord said maybe Francis wouldn't ever get married. Might be an old bachelor like his Uncle Ike. Nothing wrong in that, Lord said."

Other parents made other excuses. If even one couple had responded favourably to his efforts, Pastor Zwicker might have decided that he was worrying himself and the Lord needlessly. But to be met everywhere by disinterest! It was unnatural. Was the devil turning his flock into a herd of Papist celibates?

He had talked once with an escapee from a nunnery in Ireland. A tunnel to the rectory. Lecherous old men, naked under their black nightgowns. Babies' bones in the walls.

His body trembled and his soul – although he did not know this and would have been horrified had he known – made the sign of the cross. What was there left for a man of God to do?

God moves in a mysterious way His wonders to perform. The following Sunday night the power of the Holy Ghost shook the tabernacle to its very foundations. The Day of Pentecost described in the Acts of the Apostles was re-enacted with more fervour than ever before in Indian River.

Pastor Zwicker had summoned a guitarist from Houlton, Maine, and a fiddler from Fredericton. He himself played the accordion and his wife the Jew's harp. Old Sister Rossa was at the piano and little Billy Wagner was sent home to fetch his harmonica and mandolin.

There was music — music even as the pastor laid aside his accordion and preached, music and singing and, as the service progressed, a Jericho dance up and down the aisle.

Later, old men said it was the best sermon they had ever heard. "Brother Zwicker just opened his mouth and let the Lord fill it," they said.

His theme was the sins of the flesh. As near as Woodstock, as near as Fredericton, as near as Presque Isle, half-naked women with painted faces and scented bodies prowled the streets seeking whom they might devour. He had looked upon their naked thighs, observed the voluptuous movements of their rumps, had noted that their nipples were visible through their blouses. In King Square in Saint John he had stepped aside to allow a young lady to precede him onto a bus and had discovered to his horrified amazement that she was not wearing drawers. Saint John was another Babylon where before long men and women would be dancing together naked in the streets.

There was much more of the same kind of thing, interspersed, of course, with many quotations from the Bible, particularly from Genesis, Leviticus and Revelation. The Bible was almost the only book that Pastor Zwicker had ever read and he knew great stretches of it by heart.

"Praise the Lord!" the people shouted. "Hallelujah! Thank you, Jesus!"

Old Ike Witt stood on his chair and danced.

"Oh, diddly-doe-dum, diddly-dee-doe-dee," he sang. "Oh, too-row-lou-row-tiddly-lou-do-dee! Glory to Jesus! Diddly-day-dum! Glory to Jesus! Tiddly-lee-tum-tee!"

Matilda Rega threw herself on the floor, laughing and crying, yelling: "Oh, Jesus! Christ Almighty! Oh, sweet Jesus! God Almighty! Oh, Jesus!" She began crawling down the aisle toward the altar.

The Jericho dancers leapt back and forth across her wriggling body.

We are marching to Zion!
Beautiful, beautiful Zion!
We are marching to Zion,
The beautiful City of God!

Kneeling before the altar, Timothy Fairvort whimpered and slapped his own face, first one cheek, then the other.

"I have sinned," he moaned.

SLAP!

"I have lusted in my heart."

SLAP!

"I will burn in hell if I am not saved."

SLAP!

"Oh, help me, Jesus."

SLAP!

The Jericho dancers sang:

Joy, Joy, Joy. There is joy in my heart!
Joy in my heart! Joy in my heart!
Joy, Joy, Joy. There is joy in my heart!
Joy in my heart TODAY!

It was as if the midway of the Fredericton Exhibition, Hank Snow and the Rainbow Ranch Boys, Oral Roberts, Billy Graham, A Salvation Army band, Lester Flatt and Earl Scruggs, Garner Ted Armstrong and a Tory leadership convention were somehow all rolled into one and compressed into the lobby of the Admiral Beatty Hotel in Saint John.

Then it happened.

Sister Zwicker began speaking in an unknown tongue.

"Elohim!" she yelled. "Elohim, angaro metalani nega! Gonolariski motono etalo bene! Wanga! Wanga! Angaro talans fo do easta analandanoro!"

"Listen!" roared the pastor. "Listen!"

The Jericho dancers sang:
When the saints go marching in!
When the saints go marching in!
How I long to be in that company
When the saints go marching in!

"Elohim!" screamed Myrtle Zwicker. "Wanga! Ortoro ortoro clana estanatoro! Wanga!"

"Listen!" bellowed the pastor. "Listen!"

Others took up the cry. At last the Jericho dancers returned to their seats, exhausted, sweat pouring down their hot, red faces. The music faded away. Old Ike Witt climbed down from his chair. Matilda Rega lay still, quietly sobbing, at the foot of the altar. Timothy Fairvort put his jacket over his head, like a criminal in a newspaper photograph. There was silence except for the voices of the pastor and his wife.

"The Lord is talking to us!" shouted the pastor, who had by now taken off his jacket and tie and unbuttoned his shirt to the waist. "Harken to the voice of the Lord!"

"Elohim!" cried his wife. "Naro talaro eganoto wanga! Tao laro matanotalero. Wanga!"

"It is Egyptian," the pastor explained. "The Lord is address-ing us in the language of Pharaoh, the tongue that Joseph spoke when he was a prisoner in the land of Egypt."

"Egyptian," murmured the congregation. "Thank you, Jesus."

"Taro wanga sundaro—"

"The Lord is telling us that His heart is saddened."

"Metizo walla toro delandonaro—"

"His heart is saddened by the disobedience of His people."

"Crena wantano meta kleva sancta danco—"

"The disobedience and perversity of His young people is heavy upon His heart."

"Zalanto wanga—"

"For they have refused to marry and multiply and be fruit-
ful and replenish the earth, as He has commanded them."

"Toronalanta wanga—"

"In His mercy He has chosen to give them one more chance
to escape the just punishment for their disobedience."

"Praise His name! Thank you, Jesus!"

"Willo morto innitaro—"

"It is His will that His handmaiden, Rebecca Vaneyck,
should become the bride of—"

"Altaro mintanaro—"

"Yes, yes, the bride of Harris Brandt. This is the will of the
God of Abraham and of Isaac and of Jacob, for it was He who
brought you out of the land of Egypt."

"Yes, yes," chanted the congregation. "It is the Lord's will.
Let it be done. Hallelujah!"

Rebecca and Harris were led to the altar. They looked at one
another with dazed, wondering faces. After a moment he
reached and took her hand.

Within half an hour, three other couples stood with them.
The Lord had revealed His will. Puny mortals such as they had
no say in the matter.

The Jericho dancers leapt and cavorted in thanksgiving. So
did Ike Witt and Timothy Fairvort, whose face was still hidden
by his jacket. He stumbled blindly around the tabernacle,
knocking over chairs, singing behind his jacket:

When the roll is called up yonder!
When the roll is called up yonder!
When the roll is called up yonder!
When the roll is called up yonder,
I'll be there!

Pastor Zwicker fanned himself with a copy of the *Fire-
Baptized Quarterly*. Next week, there would be four marriages
in his tabernacle. The Lord's will had been accomplished.

"Thank you, Jesus," he murmured.

Then he remembered Ike Witt and Matilda Rega, the old bachelor and the old maid. Could it be the Lord's will that they, too, should be joined together? He would discuss it with Myrtle. Perhaps next Sunday the Lord would reveal His thoughts about the matter.

ALEXANDRE AMPRIMOZ

TOO MANY POPES

As if flooding the previous year were not enough, a summer drought came to the countryside. It was the year grandfather ate a bacon omelet on Good Friday. We heard the thunder as he took the first bite. He jumped up from the table and threw his plate out the window.

"You make such a fuss, just for an omelet!" he cried, shaking his fist at the clouds, full of anticlerical rage.

My mother made the sign of the cross and we heard a deep, almost inhuman scream: the Mayor, a pious man, was lying on the pavement. Though not seriously hurt, he promised revenge.

That evening we heard the devil walking across the attic floor. My mother called the priest who, after all, couldn't refuse a former nun. He came on Easter Monday to bless the house and rid it of all evil spirits.

My grandfather spent that afternoon in the barn singing obscene couplets to Margherita – his favourite cow. I remember a verse about the Pope keeping his glasses on while sodomizing a Cardinal in a Vatican trattoria.

The priest pretended not to hear, but emptied two bottles of wine and ate a pound of mortadella and three fresh mozzarellas. Then he demanded coffee and, after three cups of grandmother's finest espresso and a couple of panettone cakes, he finished his seventh glass of *Vecchia Romagna* brandy.

"Seven to disinfect the seven deadly sins," he ended with a burp. Then, to show off his English, he recited:

Candy
Is dandy
But liquor
Is quicker.

"Blessed Father," grandmother said, "you are a real scholar. I have never heard anyone speak Latin so well!"

We heard fragments of another romance from the barn, something about the Pope and Mussolini and acrobatic exercises on satin pillows. A few minutes later the priest left and we heard footsteps in the attic again.

"It didn't work," my mother said. "We'll have to call him again tomorrow."

"Priest lover," mumbled grandmother.

The exorcist came to our house every day for the next two weeks. Grandmother contracted mononucleosis. As for mother, she kept complaining of a sore back. But all the praying didn't work and everyone in the village suggested it might be better if we left a house haunted by the devil.

Finally, grandfather decided he would wait for the intruder upstairs.

"You think you're smarter than the priest?" asked my mother. There was resentment in her voice. "We'll have to go and stand in church to pray from now on."

The day my grandfather decided to face the devil three things happened: Margherita gave birth; my mother found out she was pregnant; and my grandmother bought a dwarf. She kept the little man in a cage under the kitchen sink during the day, but at night she took him up to her room (I have never heard of any other village where one could buy a dwarf and a solid cage at a reasonable price). On that day, I told everyone I was not afraid to go with my grandfather to catch the devil.

The old man took his gun, a bottle of grappa, and his grandson to the dark hiding place. We waited. Suddenly, a rat crossed

our path, visible in the moonlight. We heard someone or something coming toward us, majestic footsteps echoing against the
hard wooden floor. I clenched my fists while my grandfather
took aim in the darkness. I saw an incredible figure, some kind
of huge owl! I heard a shot and a scream.

My grandfather wounded the Mayor in the shoulder. The
village sided with the Mayor; they wanted to drive us out of
our home, out of the village, back to Rome, to Oran. The
Mayor was justified. Since grandfather's plate of bacon omelet
had hit him on the forehead, he had begun to grow a horn.
Looking ridiculous was only half the Mayor's problem. The
children of the village ran after him, screaming, "Cornuto!
Cornuto!" as they stroked their own little horns and pointed
at his wife.

The priest said the next Sunday that God was punishing
everyone for my grandfather's sin, that the drought was going to
last until the man who had eaten meat on Good Friday left the
village.

A month later, there was still no rain. The Mayor and his
friends came to beat us up – me and grandfather. My mother
and grandmother tried to defend us, but after a rolling-pin and
frying-pan battle, we were overpowered.

The village idiot who witnessed the scene commented,
"Holy Saint Eulalia of the Severed Breasts, I smell a stag party
coming on."

But for us, things were not amusing. The Mayor punched
the idiot, closing his left eye, and the villagers threw us into the
back of an army truck and drove up the winding hillside roads,
hoping we would never find our way back and would die of
thirst.

Those dunes were reddish sand, an ocean of sand in the
heart of Tuscany, a dry red sea, a silent storm of dust with the
sun polishing the bleached ribs of the land. No horses. No

camels, only a distant drum. Bells from steeples? It was only our hearts beating in our ears.

"This wind can wither a man in twenty-four hours," grandfather said. "Worse than a bitch, worse than the Church."

I was seeing silver balloons, shiny silver balloons, floating in the air. I had a disgusting taste like chalk in my mouth. My eyes were full of visions. I kept my mouth shut. The peasant on his donkey at the top of a dune didn't look real, but he said, "I just happened to be out here doing the devil's work," and he laughed in his own devil-may-care way. He took us home, back through the land of drought, the hawthorn bushes like piles of dust (reminding me of my heretic ancestors' scattered ashes), the umbrella pines brown as the parasols of abandoned cafés, and the patches of fur of dead rabbits, all smelling like the corpses of bats I had once seen in Roman catacombs.

We were looking for relief, for straws in the wind. A visit from the Pope of Slugs did not work to our advantage once we were home. He was a tall, grey-haired man, who carried a long stick that vaguely resembled a bishop's crosier. He could have been mistaken for an unkempt Franciscan monk. This Pope of Slugs had never liked grandfather, who had once told the village priest he was a fool for compromising with the forces of superstition.

The Pope, who was always half drunk, began to give the news from the neighbouring villages. Then, he passed the hat three times and began his prophecies. The Pope was a good politician and told the people what they wanted to hear.

"The devil's bacon-chewer nests among you. Sister Rain won't come until you drive this son of the devil away!"

He burped loudly and passed the hat a fourth time. Before leaving, he ordained three new Village Idiots. Now every religious denomination was against us.

Finally, grandfather had to leave the village. Despite the heat, the Mayor said severe frosts were expected and so the villagers lit smudge fires around our house every night, the dwarf began to howl all day, and Margherita's calf died of smoke inhalation. Mother miscarried and the priest, who let out a huge sigh of relief as he leaned over the little pine box, said, "Dust to dust and ashes to ashes," and then he hissed at grandfather, "Now, get out, or they'll never find your dust in the ashes of your house." So, we went to the train station (grandmother traded the dwarf and his cage to another old woman for a framed stereoscopic photograph of the village) and sat on a long bench by what was once the train station's flowerbed. A beggar slept in the bed in the sun with his mouth open. My grandfather and my uncle Fred were locked in endless conversation about a fabulous future waiting for them in Canada.

There was an empty wine bottle beside the beggar in his bed. It attracted flies that kept disturbing him. He woke up and swore loudly.

Our conversation stopped dead; we looked at his unshaven face, his greasy grey hair and blue eyes, so strange, so full of fire.

"You've never seen me before?" he asked.

No one answered.

"Then let me introduce myself..."

He stood up, turned around, and dropped his threadbare trousers.

"Now line up; it's only a hundred liras for a big kiss..."

No one moved.

"Come on! Are times so damned dry you can't kiss any more? Come on, the bacon-chewer's buggering off! Come on! It's going to rain!"

They arrested the beggar. He tried to resist.

"I have every right to preach. I am the Pope of Cockroaches. Why don't you arrest the other Popes, too?"

"The others," shouted the captain of the Carabinieri, "the others have permits of permission from the priest and the Mayor. Now give yourself up, and if you dirty our uniforms you'll pay for it!"

He went away like a lamb.

"That's the problem," mumbled grandfather. "Too many Popes, too many Popes..."

When our train pulled out of the station, rain began to fall on the village my grandfather was seeing for the last time.

GLORIA SAWAI

THE DAY I SAT WITH JESUS ON THE SUNDECK A WIND CAME UP AND BLEW MY KIMONO OPEN AND HE SAW MY BREASTS.

When an extraordinary event takes place in your life, you're apt to remember with unnatural clarity the details surrounding it. You remember shapes and sounds that weren't directly related to the occurrence but hovered there in the periphery of the experience. This can even happen when you read a great book for the first time, one that unsettles you and startles you into thought. You remember where you read it, what room, who was nearby.

I can remember, for instance, where I read *Of Human Bondage*. I was lying on a top bunk in our high school dormitory, wrapped in a blue bedspread. I lived in a dormitory then because of my father. He was a religious man and wanted me to get a spiritual kind of education: to hear the Word and know the Lord, as he put it. So he sent me to St. Paul's Lutheran Academy in Regina for two years. He was confident that there's where I'd hear the Word. Anyway, I can still hear Mrs. Sverdrup, our housemother, knocking on the door at midnight and whispering in her Norwegian accent, "Now, Gloria, it is past midnight, time to turn off the lights. Right now." Then scuffing down the corridor in her bedroom slippers. What's interesting here is that I don't remember anything about the book itself except that someone in it had a club foot. But it must have moved me deeply when I was sixteen, which is some time ago now.

You can imagine then how distinctly I remember the day Jesus of Nazareth, in person, climbed the hill in our backyard to our house, then up the outside stairs to the sundeck where I was sitting. And how he stayed with me for awhile. You can surely understand how clearly those details rest in my memory.

The event occurred on Monday morning, September 11, 1972, in Moose Jaw, Saskatchewan. These facts in themselves are more unusual than they may appear to be at first glance. September's my favourite month, Monday my favourite day, morning my favourite time. And although Moose Jaw may not be the most magnificent place in the world, even so, if you happen to be there on a Monday morning in September it has its beauty.

It's not hard to figure out why these are my favourites, by the way. I have five children and a husband. Things get hectic, especially on weekends and holidays. Kids hanging around the house, eating, arguing, asking me every hour what there is to do in Moose Jaw. And television. The programs are always the same. Only the names change: Roughriders, Stampeders, Blue Bombers, whatever. So when school starts in September I bask in freedom, especially on Monday. No quarrels. No TV. The morning, crisp and lovely. A new day, a fresh start.

On the morning of September 11, I got up at seven, the usual time, cooked Cream of Wheat for the kids, fried a bit of sausage for Fred, waved them all out of the house, drank a second cup of coffee in peace, and decided to get at last week's ironing. I wasn't dressed yet but still in the pink kimono I'd bought years ago on my trip to Japan, my one and only overseas trip, a five-hundred-dollar quick tour of Tokyo and other cities. I'd saved for this while working as a library technician in Regina, and I'm glad I did. Since then I've hardly been out of Saskatchewan. Once in awhile a trip to Winnipeg, and a few times down to Medicine Lake, Montana, to visit my sister.

I set up the ironing board and hauled out the basket of week-old sprinkled clothes. When I unrolled the first shirt it was completely dry and smelled stale. The second was covered with little grey blots of mould. So was the third. Fred teaches science in the junior high school here in Moose Jaw. He uses a lot of shirts. I decided I'd have to unwrap the whole basketful and air everything out. This I did, spreading the pungent garments about the living room. While they were airing I would go outside and sit on the deck for awhile since it was such a clear and sunny day.

If you know Moose Jaw at all, you'll know about the new subdivision in the southeast end called Hillhurst. That's where we live, right on the edge of the city. In fact our deck looks out on flat land as far as the eye can see, except for the backyard itself, which is a fairly steep hill leading down to a small stone quarry. But from the quarry the land straightens out into the Saskatchewan prairie. One clump of poplars stands beyond the quarry to the right, and high weeds have grown up among the rocks. Other than that, it's plain, just earth and sky. But when the sun rises new in the morning, weeds and rocks take on an orange and rusty glow that is pleasing. To me at least.

I unplugged the iron and returned to the kitchen. I'd take a cup of coffee out there, or maybe some orange juice. To reach the juice at the back of the fridge my hand passed right next to a bottle of dry white Calona. Now here was a better idea. A little wine on Monday morning, a little relaxation after a rowdy weekend. I held the familiar bottle comfortably in my hand and poured, anticipating a pleasant day.

I slid open the glass door leading onto the deck. I pulled an old canvas folding chair into the sun, and sat. Sat and sipped. Beauty and tranquility floated toward me on Monday morning, September 11, at around 9:30.

First he was a little bump on the far, far-off prairie. Then he was a mole way beyond the quarry. Then a larger animal, a dog perhaps, moving out there through the grass. Nearing the quarry, he became a person. No doubt about that. A woman perhaps, still in her bathrobe. But edging out from the rocks, through the weeds, toward the hill, he was clear to me. I knew then who he was. I knew it just as I knew the sun was shining.

The reason I knew is that he looked exactly the way I'd seen him five thousand times in pictures, in books and Sunday School pamphlets. If there was ever a person I'd seen and heard about over and over, this was the one. Even in grade school those terrible questions. Do you love the Lord? Are you saved by grace alone through faith? Are you awaiting eagerly the day of His Second Coming? And will you be ready on that Great Day? I'd sometimes hidden under the bed when I was a child, wondering if I really had been saved by grace alone, or, without realizing it, I'd been trying some other method, like the Catholics, who were saved by their good works and would land in hell. Except for a few who knew in their hearts it was really grace, but they didn't want to leave the church because of their relatives. And was this it? Would the trumpet sound tonight and the sky split in two? Would the great Lord and King, Alpha and Omega, holding aloft the seven candlesticks, accompanied by a heavenly host that no man could number, descend from heaven with a mighty shout? And was I ready?

And there he was. Coming. Climbing the hill in our backyard, his body bent against the climb, his robes ruffling in the wind. He was coming. And I was not ready. All those mouldy clothes scattered about the living room, and me in this faded old thing, made in Japan, and drinking in the middle of the morning.

He had reached the steps now. His hand touched the railing. His right hand was on my railing. Jesus' fingers were curled around my railing. He was coming up. He was ascending. He was coming up to me here on the sundeck.

He stood on the top step and looked at me. I looked at him. He looked exactly right, exactly the same as all the pictures: white robe, purple stole, bronze hair, creamy skin. How had all those queer artists, illustrators of Sunday School papers, how had they gotten him exactly right like that?

He stood at the top of the stairs. I sat there holding my glass. What do you say to Jesus when he comes? How do you address him? Do you call him Jesus? I supposed that was his first name. Or Christ? I remembered the woman at the well, living in adultery, who'd called him Sir. Perhaps I could try that. Or maybe I should pretend not to recognize him. Maybe, for some reason, he didn't mean for me to recognize him. Then he spoke.

"Good morning," he said. "My name is Jesus."

"How do you do," I said. "My name is Gloria Johnson."

My name is Gloria Johnson. That's what I said all right. As if he didn't know.

He smiled, standing there at the top of the stairs. I thought of what I should do next. Then I got up and unfolded another canvas chair.

"You have a nice view here," he said, leaning back against the canvas and pressing his sandalled feet on the iron bars of the railing.

"Thank you," I said. "We like it."

Nice view. Those were his very words. Everyone who comes to our house and stands on the deck says that. Everyone.

"I wasn't expecting company today." I straightened the folds of my pink kimono and tightened the cloth more securely over my knees. I picked up the glass from the floor where I'd laid it.

"I was passing through on my way to Winnipeg. I thought I'd drop by."

"I've heard a lot about you," I said. "You look quite a bit like your pictures." I raised the glass to my mouth and saw that his hands were empty. I should offer him something to drink. Tea? Milk? How should I ask him what he'd like to drink? What words should I use?

"It gets pretty dusty out there," I finally said. "Would you care for something to drink?" He looked at the glass in my hand. "I could make you some tea," I added.

"Thanks," he said. "What are you drinking?"

"Well, on Mondays I like to relax a bit after the busy weekend with the family all home. I have five children you know. So sometimes after breakfast I have a little wine."

"That would be fine," he said.

By luck I found a clean tumbler in the cupboard. I stood by the sink, pouring the wine. And then, like a bolt of lightning, I realized my situation. Oh, Johann Sebastian Bach. Glory. Honour. Wisdom. Power. George Fredrick Handel. King of Kings and Lord of Lords. He's on my sundeck. Today he's sitting on my sundeck. I can ask him any question under the sun, anything at all, and he'll know the answer. Hallelujah. Well now, wasn't this something for a Monday morning in Moose Jaw.

I opened the fridge door to replace the bottle. And I saw my father. It was New Year's morning. My father was sitting at the kitchen table. Mother sat across from him. She'd covered the oatmeal pot to let it simmer on the stove. I could hear the lid bumping against the rim, quietly. Sigrid and Frieda sat on one side of the table, Raymond and I on the other. We were holding hymn books, little black books turned to page 1. It was dark outside. On New Year's morning we got up before sunrise. Daddy was looking at us with his chin pointed out. It meant be still and sit straight. Raymond sat as straight and stiff as a soldier, waiting for Daddy to notice how nice and stiff he sat. We began singing. Page 1. Hymn for the New Year. Philipp Nicolai, 1599. We didn't really need the books. We'd sung the same song every New Year's since the time of our conception. Daddy always sang the loudest.

> *The Morning Star upon us gleams;*
> *How full of grace and truth his beams,*
> *How passing fair his splendour.*
> *Good Shepherd, David's proper heir,*
> *My King in heaven, Thou dost me bear*
> *Upon thy bosom tender.*
> *Nearest. Dearest. Highest. Brightest.*
> *Thou delightest still to love me,*
> *Thou so high enthroned above me.*

I didn't mind actually, singing hymns on New Year's, as long as I was sure no one would find out. I'd have been rather embarrassed if any of my friends ever found out how we spent New Year's. It's easy at a certain age to be embarrassed about your family. I remember Alice Olson, how embarrassed she was about her father, Elmer Olson. He was an alcoholic and couldn't control his urine. Her mother always had to clean up after him. Even so, the house smelled. I suppose she couldn't get it all. Anyway, I know Alice was embarrassed when we saw Elmer all tousled and sick-looking, with urine stains on his trousers. Sometimes I don't know what would be harder on a kid having a father who's a drunk, or one who's sober on New Year's and sings "The Morning Star."

I walked across the deck and handed Jesus the wine. I sat down, resting my glass on the flap of my kimono. Jesus was looking out over the prairie. He seemed to be noticing everything out there. He was obviously in no hurry to leave, but he didn't have much to say. I thought of what to say next.

"I suppose you're more used to the sea than to the prairie."

"Yes," he said. "I've lived most of my life near water. But I like the prairie too. There's something nice about the prairie." He turned his face to the wind, stronger now, coming toward us from the east.

That word again. If I'd ever used *nice* to describe the prairie, in an English composition at St. Paul's, for example, it would have had three red circles around it. At least three. I raised my glass to the wind. Good old St. Paul's. Good old Pastor Solberg, standing in front of the wooden altar, holding the gospel aloft in his hand.

> In the beginning wass the Word,
> And the Word wass with God,
> And the Word wass God.
> All things were made by him;
> And without him wass not anything made
> That wass made.

I was sitting on a bench by Paul Thorson. We were sharing a hymnal. Our thumbs touched at the centre of the book. It was winter. The chapel was cold an army barracks left over from World War II. We wore parkas and sat close together. Paul fooled around with his thumb, pushing my thumb to my own side of the book, then pulling it back to his side. The wind howled outside. We watched our breath as we sang the hymn.

> *In thine arms I rest me, Foes who would molest me*
> *Cannot reach me here. Tho' the earth be shaking,*
> *Evry heart be quaking, Jesus calms my fear.*
> *Fires may flash and thunder crash,*
> *Yea, and sin and hell assail me,*
> *Jesus will not fai-ai-ail me.*

And here he was. Alpha and Omega. The Word. Sitting on my canvas chair, telling me the prairie's nice. What could I say to that?

"I like it too," I said.

Jesus was watching a magpie circling above the poplars just beyond the quarry. He seemed very nice actually, but he wasn't like my father. My father was perfect, mind you, but you know about perfect people busy, busy. He wasn't as busy as Elsie though. Elsie was the busy one. You could never visit there without her having to do something else at the same time. Wash the leaves of her plants with milk or fold socks in the basement while you sat on a bench by the washing machine. I wouldn't mind sitting on a bench in the basement if that was all she had, but her living room was full of big soft chairs that no one ever sat in. Now Jesus here didn't seem to have any work to do at all.

The wind had risen now. His robes puffed about his legs. His hair swirled around his face. The wind was coming stronger now out of the east. My kimono flapped about my ankles. I bent down to secure the bottom, pressing the moving cloth close against my legs. A Saskatchewan wind comes up in a hurry, let me tell you. Then it happened. A gust of wind hit me straight on, seeping into the folds of my kimono, reaching down into the bodice, billowing the cloth out, until above the sash, the robe was fully open. I knew without looking. The wind was suddenly blowing on my breasts. I felt it cool on both my breasts. Then as quickly as it came, it left, and we sat in the same small breeze as before.

I looked at Jesus. He was looking at me, and at my breasts, looking right at them. Jesus was sitting there on the sundeck looking at my breasts.

What should I do? Say excuse me and push them back into the kimono? Make a little joke of it? Look what the wind blew

in? Or should I say nothing, just tuck them in as inconspicu-
ously as possible? What do you say when a wind comes up and
blows your kimono open and he sees your breasts?

Now there are ways and there are ways of exposing your
breasts. I know a few things. I read books. And I've learned a lot
from my cousin Millie. Millie's the black sheep in the family.
She left the Academy without graduating and became an artist's
model in Winnipeg. And she's told me a few things about bodily exposure. She says, for instance, that when an artist wants to
draw his model he has her either nude and stretching and bending in various positions so he can draw her from different
angles, or he drapes her with cloth, satin usually. He covers one
section of the body with the material and leaves the rest
exposed. But he does so in a graceful manner, draping the cloth
over her stomach or ankle. (Never over the breasts.) So I realized
that my appearance right then wasn't actually pleasing, either
aesthetically or erotically, from Millie's point of view. My breasts
were just sticking out from the top of my old kimono. And for
some reason that I can't explain, even to this day, I did nothing
about it. I just sat there.

Jesus must have recognized my confusion, because right
then he said, quite sincerely I thought, "You have nice breasts."

"Thanks," I said. I didn't know what else to say, so I asked
him if he'd like more wine.

"Yes, I would," he said, and I left to refill the glass. When I
returned he was watching a magpie swishing about in the tall
weeds by the quarry. I sat down and watched with him.

Then I got a very, very peculiar sensation. I know it was just
an illusion, but it was so strong it scared me. It's hard to explain
because nothing like it had ever happened to me before. The
magpie began to float toward Jesus. I saw it fluttering toward
him in the air as if some vacuum were sucking it in. When it
reached him, it flapped about on his chest, which was bare now

because the top of his robe had slipped down. It nibbled at his little brown nipples and squawked and disappeared. For all the world, it seemed to disappear right into his pores. Then the same thing happened with a rock. A rock floating up from the quarry and landing on the breast of Jesus, melting into his skin. It was very strange, let me tell you, Jesus and I sitting there together with that going on. It made me dizzy, so I closed my eyes.

And I saw the women in a public bath in Tokyo. Black-haired women and children. Some were squatting by faucets that lined a wall. They were running hot water into their basins, washing themselves with white cloths, rubbing each other's backs with the soapy washcloths, then emptying their basins and filling them again, pouring clean water over their bodies for the rinse. Water and suds swirled about on the tiled floor. Others were sitting in the hot pool on the far side, soaking themselves in the steamy water as they jabbered away to one another. Then I saw her. The woman without the breasts. She was squatting by a faucet near the door. The oldest woman I've ever seen. The thinnest woman I've ever witnessed. Skin and bones. Literally, just skin and bones. She bowed and smiled at everyone who entered. She had three teeth. When she hunched over her basin, I saw the little creases of skin where her breasts had been. When she stood up the wrinkles disappeared. In their place were two shallow caves. Even the nipples seemed to have disappeared into the small brown caves of her breasts.

I opened my eyes and looked at Jesus. Fortunately, everything had stopped floating.

"Have you ever been to Japan?" I asked.

"Yes," he said. "A few times."

I paid no attention to his answer but went on telling him about Japan as if he'd never been there. I couldn't seem to stop talking about that old woman and her breasts.

"You should have seen her," I said. "She wasn't flat-chested like some women even here in Moose Jaw. It wasn't like that at all. Her breasts weren't just flat. They were caved in, as if the flesh had sunk right there. Have you ever seen breasts like that before?"

Jesus's eyes were getting darker. He seemed to have sunk farther down into his chair.

"Japanese women have smaller breasts to begin with usually," he said.

But he'd misunderstood me. It wasn't just her breasts that held me. It was her jaws, teeth, neck, ankles, heels. Not just her breasts. I said nothing for awhile. Jesus, too, was not talking.

Finally I asked, "Well? What do you think of breasts like that?"

I knew immediately that I'd asked the wrong question. If you want personal and specific answers, you ask personal and specific questions. It's as simple as that. I should have asked him, for instance, what he thought of them from a sexual point of view. If he were a lover, let's say, would he like to hold such breasts in his hands and play on them with his teeth and fingers? Would he now? The woman, brown and shiny, was bending over her basin. Tiny bubbles of soap dribbled from the creases of her chest down to her navel. Hold them. Ha.

Or I could have asked for some kind of aesthetic opinion. If he were an artist, a sculptor let's say, would he travel to Italy and spend weeks excavating the best marble from the hills near Florence, and then would he stay up all night and day in his studio, without eating or bathing, and with matted hair and glazed eyes, chisel out those little creases from his great stone slab?

Or if he were a patron of the arts, would he attend the opening of this grand exhibition and stand in front of these white caves in his purple turtleneck, sipping champagne and nibbling on the little cracker with the shrimp in the middle, and would he turn to the one beside him, the one in the sleek black pants, and would he say to her, "Look, darling, did you see this marvellous piece? Do you see how the artist has captured the very essence of the female form?"

These are some of the things I could have said if I'd had my wits about me. But my wits certainly left me that day. All I did say, and I didn't mean to, it just came out, was, "It's not nice and I don't like it."

I lifted my face, threw my head back, and let the wind blow on my neck and breasts. It was blowing harder again. I felt small grains of sand scrape against my skin.

> *Jesus, lover of my soul,*
> *Let me to thy bosom fly.*
> *While the nearer waters roll,*
> *While the tempest still is nigh.*

When I looked at him again, his eyes were blacker still and his body had shrunk considerably. He looked almost like Jimmy that time in Prince Albert. Jimmy was a neighbour of ours from Regina. On his twenty-seventh birthday he joined a motorcycle gang, the Grim Reapers to be exact, and got into a lot of trouble. He ended up in maximum security in p.a. One summer on a camping trip up north, we went to see him, Fred and the kids and I. It wasn't a good visit, however. If you're going to visit inmates you should do it regularly. I realize this now. Anyway, that's when his eyes looked black like that. But maybe he'd been smoking pot or something. It's probably not the same thing. Jimmy LeBlanc. He never did think it was funny when I'd call him a Midnight Raider instead of a Grim Reaper. People are sensitive about their names.

Then Jesus finally answered. Everything seemed to take him a long time, even answering simple questions.

But I'm not sure what he said because something so strange happened that whatever he did say was swept away. Right then the wind blew against my face, pulling my hair back. My kimono swirled about every which way, and I was swinging my arms in the air, like swimming. And there right below my eyes was the roof of our house. I was looking down on the top of the roof. I saw the row of shingles ripped loose from the August hailstorm. And I remember thinking, Fred hasn't fixed those shingles yet. I'll have to remind him when he gets home from work. If it rains again the back bedroom will get soaked. Before I knew it I was circling over the sundeck, looking down on the top of Jesus' head. Only I wasn't. I was sitting in the canvas chair watching myself hover over his shoulders. Only it wasn't me hovering. It was the old woman in Tokyo. I saw her grey hair twisting in the wind and her shiny little bum raised in the air, like a baby's. Water was dripping from her chin and toes. And soap bubbles trailed from her elbows like tinsel. She was floating down toward his chest. Only it wasn't her. It was me. I could taste bits of suds sticking to the corners of my mouth and feel the wind on my wet back and in the hollow caves of my breasts. I was smiling and bowing, and the wind was blowing in narrow wisps against my toothless gums. Then quickly, so quickly, like a flock of waxwings diving through snow into the branches of the poplar, I was splitting up into millions of pieces and sinking into the tiny, tiny holes in his chest. It was like the magpie and the rock, like I had come apart into atoms or molecules, or whatever we really are.

After that I was dizzy, and I began to feel nauseated. Jesus looked sick too. Sad and sick and lonesome. Oh, Christ, I thought, why are we sitting here on such a fine day pouring our sorrows into each other?

I had to get up and walk around. I'd go into the kitchen and make some tea.

I put the kettle on to boil. What on earth had gotten into me? Why had I spent this perfectly good morning talking about breasts? My one chance in a lifetime and I'd let it slip through my fingers. Why didn't I have better control? Why was I always letting things get out of hand? Breasts. And why was my name Gloria? Such a pious name for one who can't think of anything else to talk about but breasts. Why wasn't it Lucille? Or Millie? You could talk about breasts all day if your name was Millie. But Gloria. Gloria. Glo-o-o-o-o-o-ri-a in ex-cel-sis. I knew then why so many Glorias hang around bars, talking too loud, laughing shrilly at stupid jokes, making sure everyone hears them laugh at the dirty jokes. They're just trying to live down their name, that's all. I brought out the cups and poured the tea.

Everything was back to normal when I returned except that Jesus still looked desolate sitting in my canvas chair. I handed him the tea and sat down beside him.

Oh, Daddy. And Philipp Nicolai. Oh, Bernard of Clairvaux. Oh, Sacred Head Now Wounded. Go away for a little while and let us sit together quietly, here in this small space under the sun.

I sipped the tea and watched his face. He looked so sorrowful I reached out my hand and put it on his wrist. I sat there a long time rubbing the little hairs on his wrist with my fingers; I couldn't help it. After that he put his arm on my shoulder and his hand on the back of my neck, stroking the muscles there. It felt good. Whenever anything exciting or unusual happens to me my neck is the first to feel it. It gets stiff and knotted up. Then I usually get a headache, and frequently I become nauseated. So it felt very good having my neck rubbed.

I've never been able to handle sensation very well. I remember when I was in grade three and my folks took us to the Saskatoon Exhibition. We went to see the grandstand show the battle of Wolfe and Montcalm on the Plains of Abraham. The stage was filled with Indians and pioneers and ladies in red, white, and blue dresses singing "In Days of Yore From Britain's Shore." It was very spectacular but too much for me. My stomach was upset and my neck ached. I had to keep my head on my mother's lap the whole time, just opening my eyes once in a while so I wouldn't miss everything.

So it really felt good having my neck stroked like that. I could almost feel the knots untying and my body warmer and more restful. Jesus too seemed to be feeling better. His body was back to normal. His eyes looked natural again.

Then, all of a sudden, he started to laugh. He held his hand on my neck and laughed out loud. I don't know to this day what he was laughing about. There was nothing funny there at all. But hearing him made me laugh too. He was laughing so hard he spilled tea on his purple stole. When I saw that, I laughed even more. I'd never thought of Jesus spilling his tea before. And when Jesus saw me laughing like that and when he looked at my breasts shaking, he laughed harder still, till he wiped tears from his eyes.

After that we just sat there. I don't know how long. I know we watched the magpie carve black waves in the air above the rocks. And the rocks stiff and lovely among the swaying weeds. We watched the poplars twist and bend and rise again beyond the quarry. And then he had to leave.

"Goodbye, Gloria Johnson," he said, rising from his chair. "Thanks for the hospitality."

He leaned over and kissed me on my mouth. Then he flicked my nipple with his finger, and off he went. Down the hill, through the quarry, and into the prairie. I stood on the sundeck and watched. I watched until I could see him no longer. Until he was only some dim and ancient star on the far horizon.

I went inside the house. Well, now, wasn't that a nice visit. Wasn't that something. I examined the clothes, dry and sour in the living room. I'd have to put them back in the wash, that's all. I couldn't stand the smell. I tucked my breasts back into my kimono and lugged the basket downstairs.

That's what happened to me in Moose Jaw in 1972. It was the main thing that happened to me that year.

ERIC MᶜCORMACK

KNOX ABROAD

The voyage is over. John Knox stands, sways a little, with Clootie, his cat, on the forest-ragged banks of the river (more like the shore of the ocean), on land at last. It is October, and this is an alien place. He looks around and smiles. Nothing has changed, even after a wilderness of sea. His shoes touch dead leaves, the discreet vomit of the trees. He observes the paralysis of the rocks. The winds still blast down from directly above, threatening to hammer him, like a stake, into the ground, drive him under, bury him alive. Every night of the voyage, he saw (he has seen the same thing for twenty years of nights) the planets and the stars desert, rush centrifugally away into the outer universe, as though fleeing a plague. In the mornings, as always, the sun searched him out, singed his ever so delicate grey skin. Again he smiles. Even amongst the trees there is no refuge. He bends over and lightly strokes Clootie's black coat. Together they turn and walk along the beaten path, fade into the forest gloom.

"An etymological footnote on the name Canada. John Knox, the founder of Scottish Presbyterianism, was apprehended in 1547 by the French and sentenced to service as a galley slave in the French navy. After eighteen months, he escaped. A Breton legend, however, suggests that before escaping he served some months on an exploration ship to New France. This is not impossible. A less reliable tradition supplies the information that, many years later, after his return to Scotland, one of his disciples asked him for his opinion of the New World, which had now become a refuge for the persecuted. Knox is said to have replied, 'I *canna dae wi'* it, I *canna dae wi'* it,' thus, albeit inadvertently, giving the country its name."

M. Gobert, *Memoîres des Ecossais*,

(Geneva, 1897)

In the galleys he was supposed to be the slave, but he was master, he knew it and they knew it. The same on the expedition ship. The mate lacked the nerve to make him holystone the decks alongside the others, for fear of his tongue. No ears could endure the monstrous words (predestination! election! reprobation!) he would hurl against them. Still, he was no burden: when the barber-surgeon drowned in a storm, two weeks out of St. Malo, Knox took his place – no one else had the stomach for the job. Though he loathed the unbearable closeness of other living bodies on the ship. Give him solitary confinement, a narrow dungeon, and he would have been more content.

The captain, knowing his prowess as a controversialist, tried often, on this tedious journey, to entice him to his cabin for dinner, to dispute on matters theological. Knox spat at him as an idolater like all the others, and refused the bait.

Knox jettisoned the statue of the Virgin. It was on a Sunday, and the crew assembled for the weekly statue-kissing, a good-luck ritual. Knox grabbed the statue from its perch by the main-mast and hurled it, head over tail, halo of stars over serpent's head, out into the ocean. Where it sank like a stone. The sacrilege horrified the French sailors, but they kept their hands off him. He joked to his cat: "The Queen of the Sea cannae swim, Clootie." But they kept their hands off him.

Physically, Knox was scrawny. He was an aggressive talker, except to his cat, Clootie, a black creature, sleek with wicked eyes. The cat was a growler, a hisser, and in the minds of the sailors, was Knox's familiar demon. Knox, too, was a growler, but never growled at Clootie.

"Well, Clootie, my wee man, did you ever see a country so naked of churches? It won't do. I can already imagine a forest of steeples along this riverbank. Churches could make this obscene river a lovely thing." (Knox could speak perfectly good English, ungnarled by "ach's" and "dinnae's" whenever he felt like it.)

The cat would purr its admiration of his voice, winding itself around his narrow shins. The man would squint about. If they were alone, he would allow the rubbing to continue, melting into it. If someone was watching, Knox would boot the cat out of his way, its tail swishing angrily.

Thank Christ I am off the ship at last. That fat pig-wife of the captain's spying on me everywhere with her pig eyes. The only favour I ever did for her was to tear the dead baby out of her by the feet. Now she wants me. The black sows farrowing on my father's farm sickened me less. And thank Christ to be out of that stinking fo'c'c'le. Filth and corruption everywhere. Men opening their breeches to show off the size of their organs. Ship's boys acting as their fancy-women.

But during the storms, the truth flared up in them. Fear bulged in their eyes, and I taunted them all, every single one of them, with the burning fires of hell. I was on deck during the great storm in mid-ocean, admiring the fury of the waters. They were trying to lower sail when a boom snapped, the sail ripped, and sheets flogged everywhere. A young sailor, the worst balls-strutter of the lot, caught his arm in the grip of a ratchet. The bone was half-broken, like a snappy branch, and all the flesh torn, the muscles severed. I took the surgeon's saw and sawed the arm away from his jerking body, then I carried him below

and dipped the stump in boiling tar. For days, I was the one to
bite off his rotten flesh and suck out the pus. I even swallowed
it if they were watching. They couldn't match me. As long as I
can remember, death and sickness, sickness and death have been
my allies.

Now the voyage is over. This was a good place to land. All
around me, beautiful sites for churches, plain churches, with
plain cemeteries, no flowers if I can help it. I have planted
already the men nobody else would touch, who died of cholera
on the voyage. I've manured the soil with corpses the way we
did with the dead cattle on the farm. I buried their sad priest,
sick when we left France. Only Clootie and I attended his
funeral. We commended his body to the devil. Back on the
ship, I cleaned the shit and the vomit of the sick from the decks.
It gives me an advantage over them all, they are so concerned
about staying alive.

The sailor presented the natives with pieces of coloured broken glass, brown wooden beads, pieces of rope, and scraps of
cloth. The natives seemed uninterested. One gift only, an iron
knife, they all admire. The captain insisted it go to the chief,
Quheesquheenay, to win his favour. They offered the natives
pieces of Breton cheese, quite rank after the voyage, which the
natives, in turn, gave to their dogs; fried chicken legs (chickens had been kept aboard), which the natives relished; boiled
chicken eggs, which they spat out. Wine they treated as con-
taminated water, and could not understand why the sailors
drank it when there was so much water around. They munched
cautiously on some lumps of black bread from the captain's
pantry. The natives gave little in return, no gold or silver,
which was really what the sailors hoped for. They did give them
amulets full of rats' giblets and bones. The sailors objected to

the smell and threw the amulets into the river while the natives looked on. They invited the crew to eat a sort of stewed beef that smelt very appetizing, but the sailors were afraid it was made of human meat. Some of them vomited spontaneously at the very sight of it. The natives watched all this impassively.

Finally the chief's council offered, as a special treat to the captain, a bowl full of fresh assorted testicles of forest creatures, from the huge rubbery testes of the moose and the bear to the tiny soft beads of rats and rabbits. The captain hid his nausea and diplomatically accepted the gift. He took it back to the ship, and, after dark, flung the testes overboard. They caught in an eddy, and floated around the ship for days, swelling grotesquely till they burst and sank.

The male natives were tall, for the most part, well muscled, dressed in neatly stitched animal skins. Sickness was unusual amongst them. There were no wens, no leprosy, no bloody flux, no stopping of the stomach, no gout, no strangury, no fistulas, no tissicks, no spotted fever, no head-mould, no shingles, no rickets, no scurvy, no griping in the guts. There were no congenital deformities. There were no pest houses.

The skin of the warriors was bronze and clear, except for battle scars. They had flashing dark eyes, and they all seemed to be superb athletes, capable of feats the puny Bretons could only envy. They could lope with ease along tangled forest paths, hurl their spears gracefully, paddle their bark canoes at amazing speeds. They wrestled with ferocity, not hesitating to break an opponent's limb if the opportunity offered.

The natives had heard about the French from neighbouring tribes who had been visited by earlier ships, but this was the first they themselves had seen the strangers. Clearly they were disappointed for they found it impossible to respect men whose physical prowess was so defective. But they did respect the power of the arquebuses 'and the ship's cannon, which the Frenchmen quickly demonstrated.

The French sailors learnt to be careful in their approaches to the native women. A warrior's wives were private property and it was death for a stranger to tamper with them. All the other women were available to all the tribe, and were quite free with their sexual favours, even widows and grandmothers. Which was as well for the Frenchmen, since the young women, golden-skinned and lithe, would have nothing to do with them. They had the bodies of dancers. Their clothing was provocative, their breasts dangling loose, their nipples erect when excited, which was often. Their skirts were split to the waist. When they ran, their hairless crotches were visible. Often, while they were relaxing, or just sitting down, they would finger their groins unconsciously, or sometimes consciously if they saw the Frenchmen squinting at them.

At night the warriors would flit around their bonfires, whooping fearsomely. Or they would stretch on beds of skins moodily sucking on their tobacco pipes with glassy eyes. If the visitors were present, there would be an air of tension. The chief of the tribe, Quheesquheenay, would sit there on his deerskin mat, making no effort to communicate, staring intently at the Frenchmen. The solemn beat of drums would resound, echoes by other drums great distances away across the river.

"Oomhowoomareoomthcioomaliensroom?"

"Oomtheyoomstinkoomouroomvillageoomoutoom."

"Oomkilloomthemoom."

"Oomweoomunlikeoomyouoomonlyoomkilloomworthyoomenemiesoom."

"Oomcutoomthemoomupoominoompiecesoom."

"Oomevenoomifoomcutoomthemoomupoominoompiecesoomandoomsewedoomalloomtheoombestoompartsoomtogetheroomweoomstilloomwouldoomnotoomhaveoomaoom-

realoomenemyoomforoomtheiroompenisesoomareoom-
likeoomwormsoom."

"Oomuseoomtheiroompenisesoomtooomcatchoom-
fishoom."

"Oomtheoomfishoominoomouroomriveroomareoom-
toooomsmartoomtheyoomknowoomwormsoomareoom-
notoomthatoomsmalloom."

I have the heathen under control. They despise the others but
they fear me. I notice the young braves, showing off to each
other throwing their spears at targets, grow silent even when
Clootie appears amongst them. Their shaman is terrified of the
cat. I am sure he has tried all his curses against me and Clootie
in vain, since the time when the daughter of the chief, Quheesquheenay, developed a terrible fever and was clearly going to
die. The shaman couldn't cure her, he could only make things
worse. The chief was desperate and asked if I could do anything.
They believe that those who are indifferent to death have great
power over life.

What makes John Knox tick? A question he sometimes asks
himself. He tells himself this story:

Once upon a time early in the sixteenth century, a little
Scottish boy lived on a farm near Edinburgh. He was a quick-
witted little boy, too smart by half for his schoolfellows, who
hated his guts. He possessed certain time-honoured schoolboy
traits: he liked to pluck the legs and wings from insects to see
their reactions. He possessed, too, certain other traits not so
time-honoured: with an axe, he enjoyed cutting the legs off live
rabbits and chickens. From time to time, he would take pleasure in dropping a dead mouse into his mother's stew. On such

occasions, he would play sick, and reap the double benefit of watching the others eat the stew, and of being himself considered rather delicate. This gained him additional attention. In short, that was the kind of boy he was. A practical joker.

He had many sisters, some of them quite attractive, and no brothers. His attitude toward his sisters was somewhat ambivalent. He hated their guts and would steal their makeup and pinch their arms quite cruelly. But, he liked to peep at them before bedtime through a crack in his bedroom wall, admiring the breasts and pudenda in their various stages of development. Yes, he found that rather a stimulating part of his day.

His father and mother, it should be noted, were honest-to-goodness farmers, and regular church-goers.

John Knox always likes the story to this point.

One of the practical jokes the boy liked to play concerned rats. He would capture rats in a wooden box. Then when no one was around, he would head on over to the pigsty, and call out the pigs. There was a small round hole through the wall beside the feed-troughs. The boy would chase the rats out of the box, into this hole, and right into the mouths of the pigs. The pigs had grown fond of such a regular treat. This was one prank the boy really enjoyed.

One thing leads to another. It happened that he was looking after his littlest sister, three months old, while his parents were making jams inside the house. As he wandered past the pigsty, carrying the baby, he wondered how the pigs would deal with a tiny pink infant rather than tiny pink rats. He gently laid the baby on the muddy floor of the sty, and called out the pigs.

Well, who knows what goes through a pig's mind? Did they even notice the different proportions, the different texture? Four huge porkers seized the baby's limbs, and ripped her to pieces, regardless of her screams, and swallowed her in great slobbering gobbets.

The howls of the baby and the snorting of the pigs attracted the attention of the honest father and mother, and they came running down from the farmhouse to see what was going on. What they saw horrified them. They saw the bloody mess on the sty floor. They saw their little boy looking at them apprehensively.

At that very moment, just then, quite as if by design, the boy found religion. As soon as he saw the genuine anguish on his parents' honest faces, he began to shout, as if by instinct, "O Jesus, O Jesus," and jumping in amongst the pigs, kicked and slapped at their snouts, shouting, "Begone, Satan, begone," an expression he had often heard from the preachers at the church to which his honest parents took him each Sunday. His father grabbed him by the coat and pulled him out of that sty. The boy said, "I was takin' the babby doon for a walk, when a great hairy black beastie wi' fire comin' oot o' its mooth and its ears pulled the bairnie oot o' ma airms and threw it ower the wa' to the piggies."

He could see that his parents already half-believed him, certain that no human child would be capable of feeding his baby sister to pigs. The boy understood then that all the quirks in himself he had misguidedly thought to be unnatural and perverse were really, if properly perceived, signs of a religious disposition. And so he decided that, as soon as he grew up, he would become a Reformer. And he did. His parents became, in due course, very proud of his achievements, though he sometimes thought he could see a skeptical glint in their eyes. But they all lived happily every after.

Such is the tale John Knox tells himself: he knows it doesn't cover all the bases, but it is generally quite pleasing. One thing still surprises him after all these years: when alone, religious matters never enter his head. He wonders if the other Reformers are the same, but hesitates to ask.

With my pussy-cat, Clootie, I went to her tepee. As we entered, a sweaty young man left, hitching up his loincloth. The tepee was all shadows and foul smells, the shaman's smoke. The girl lay on a frame bed of stretched skins, staring at the roof. She was naked, and she too was covered in sweat. Her legs were parted and her hand was at her crotch, fingers stroking. The chief, two of his councilors, and the shaman, stood beside the bed. He is a mouth shaman, and was leaning over her spitting some green mixture into her mouth. I saw her spit most of it right back in his face, and vomit up the rest. The shaman looked fierce with his red and white stripes but his eyes were anxious. He shook his rattles and howled, but they all knew and he knew, he had failed. The girl looked over at me and smiled, the shreds of vomit around her mouth. She lifted her hand from her crotch, and stretched it out to me, her fingers glistening.

She had sweated out her disease, her *furor uterinus* for days, and she would die soon, for they did not know how to save her. All they could think of was to supply her with men to satisfy her deadly appetite and to trust in the shaman's superstitious mumbo-jumbo.

"That hill, over there by the sacrificial stakes, would be a good spot for a church."

"Ah, yes."

"The longhouse would be all right as a temporary church, but they'd have to strip away those ornamental scalps and skulls."

"Indeed."

"If we burnt down the whole forest on the peninsula and ripped up the weeds and the flowers, and anything else alive, we could build a whole set of churches, one for every day of the week. Nothing fancy, no ornaments or any of that kind of thing, just plain seats and a stool for the preacher. Cats would be welcome. We'd have plain cemeteries with picket fences for each church."

"Interesting."

"How about a church under that waterfall? Made of fieldstone, very plain. You'd have to carry an umbrella for going in and out. A nice effect."

"Quite so."

I told them I must have absolute freedom in the treatment of the girl or I would do nothing. I ordered the shaman out with his barbarous cures. He mumbled at me, cursing me, no doubt, in his heathen way. I wouldn't let him away with that, but I replied moderately, damning him only according to the Scriptures. Clootie, as ever, snarling at him with hunched back, terrified him, and he hurried out of the tepee, along with the chief and the others. I called in two of the older sailors to help me begin this holy work.

First we forced her hands away from her groin. We lashed her hands and her feet to the sides of the crib to stop her thrashing about. She sweated even more and began screaming. I opened my Bible in my left hand, and, from under my coat, I unsheathed my whip, which I had brought with me on purpose.

Everything was ready. I ordered the sailors to stand outside the entrance of the tepee, and allow no one to enter. I began to read from the Book of Psalms in a loud voice, uncoiling my whip slowly before the patient's eyes. Clootie jumped onto the bed and rubbed himself against her.

"My wounds stink and are corrupt because of my foolishness.

"For my loins are filled with a loathsome disease and there is no soundness in my flesh.

"Thou shalt break them with a rod of iron.

"The heathen are sunk down in the pit that they made.

"Upon the wicked thou shalt rain snares, fire and brimstone, and a horrible tempest: this shall be the portion of their cup.

"Then did I beat them small as the dust before the wind.

"And I smote his enemies in the lower parts: I put them to a perpetual reproach."

I began to read the verses a second time, more loudly. By this time, after each verse, I lashed her naked body. She screamed as the skin lifted, the welts rose across her breasts. Then I aimed lower on her body, across the thighs and the open vulva. She stopped screaming. She gave great gasps and whimpers, and it was my turn to roar. I shouted the verses and lashed harder and harder. Her body convulsed, and, at last, the demon rushed out between her legs in a liquid gurgle. Clootie, who had been rubbing himself against her all through this, howled, and his hair stood on end. I myself was roused by that evil in her. To ensure it was completely gone, I lashed her several more times. Then I put my hand cautiously towards her groin, fearful of the bite of the beast. With my fingers I could feel nothing at the entrance, so I slid them into the round, moist cavern. Still, nothing to be afraid of. Unsatisfied, I inserted the long sweaty handle of my whip, turning it, moving it in and out, in and out, the sure way to scrape any remnants of the demon away. Her eyes glazed as she looked up at me, thankful for my precautions. I jerked the handle up and down rapidly, she convulsed again, sighed, and immediately fell asleep. I too was drained by my exorcism, but satisfied. I knew that all was well.

I sat for a moment to catch my breath, then I opened the tepee flap and let the chief and his men back in. I sensed their revulsion as they saw on her body the stripes of the lash. Yet she was in a deep, untroubled sleep and her fever was broken. I expected no thanks and received none. The shaman untied the ropes, and covered her sleeping body with skins. I told the chief that somebody must administer the same cure to her each time she fell into that fever. I told him, though I am not sure he understood, that he must build churches, churches, churches, in memory of her cure.

"You tell us we should not eat our enemies, yet the captain says that in France, he and his men eat Jehovah daily. Explain this."

"Filthy heathen, spare me your quibbles."

"Before original sin, did men still fart and shit after they ate?"

"Filthy heathen, you do not understand."

"What good is heaven if all our tribe do not go to heaven? What good is heaven if my wives and my sons and my dogs are not in heaven with me? What good is heaven if my enemies are not there so that we can all reminisce together in heaven about old battles?"

"Filthy heathen, cease your blasphemy."

"How can you hate the women and yet desire them so much at the same time?"

"Filthy lying heather. You are one of the damned."

How ugly the aliens are. Their skin is wormy white and marred by scabs. Boils sprout on them overnight like forest toadstools. Their clothing is clumsy and heavy. Their minds are a mystery. They adore their Book, a collection of dead words. We would have annihilated them long ago, but for their guns. We have never before faced enemies who were contemptible as men, yet could defeat us in battle because of their weapons.

Their shaman, the little man, Knox, is the living death. He has made a few converts amongst our people, even my own daughter. Pain was his gift to her. The captain, a simple man, admits that many like Knox will come to our hunting grounds in the future. Our own shaman has dreamed, for three nights, the end of the world.

"I am curious about the function of your shaman across the ocean. Here, our shaman prays for good luck, curses bad luck, sings songs and tells good stories at our feasts, blesses the penis and vagina of the newly-weds, teaches the children how to bind arrows well, how to be brave in battle. He defies the demons of darkness; in times of famine, he fasts and moves his tepee to the forest so that the rest of us may eat well and live in company in the village. He weeps for all the dead, he rejoices at births. He loves the river, the trout, the moose, the eagle, the pack-wolves, the muskrat, the morning sun, the snow in winter: He is the friend of our friends, he admires the ferocity of our enemies. Nothing that exists disgusts him."

"He is a filthy heathen fiend and is already damned."

Their stay amongst us has lasted only two moons. They must sail away before the winter storms. They have wiped out all game within six miles of the village – we will now face a hard winter. Some of our children have died of a cough we have never known. As a final gesture, the aliens say they will kill for us, with their guns, our enemies in a neighbouring village. I have thanked them and refused their offer. Our shaman is glad they are leaving, but he still whispers to me that he sees only death in his omens.

One night around midnight, while the village fires were still flickering, two huge marauding bears came barging out of the forest. Knox's cat, Clootie, fur on end, charged at them screeching from deep in his throat. The bears, startled, turned and ran. For days afterwards, Knox would wheeze with laughter at the memory. "Ach, Clootie," he would say, "ane wee Scottish cratur is mair than a match for a' the beasties in the New Warld."

Some thoughts on a brief code of behaviour to be followed by converts after I am gone.

A. *Sexual Matters*. Strict monogamy is a must, even bestiality is a lesser offence than adultery; sexual intercourse only for breeding; cover the flesh: shirts and trousers for men, underwear and breast bindings for women; absolutely no kissing, cuddling, or touching of the body of the other sex before marriage; the menstrual abomination to be dealt with in complete secrecy by the women.

B. *Other*. Hunting needs to be organized on a less seasonal basis to keep the men from being idle for lengthy spells; rites of passage for the boys should not be discouraged, the pain being a valuable disciple; likewise the practice of torturing enemies: it teaches contempt of the flesh (much of these heathens' behaviour may be turned to good account).

C. *Build churches, churches.*

The French captain (his wife was party to it) coaxed one of the older native women to be his mistress. She would then gossip with the other women about his fat paunch and his stinking breath. And about how, with his wife looking on, he always made love to her from behind like a dog. Whenever the captain appeared in the village afterwards, Knox would trot in front of him, barking as loudly as he could. All the village dogs would join the chorus. Some of the native women, inspired by this, would squat on the ground and urinate as the captain passed, their tongues dangling like those of hounds.

We will root out the shaman Knox's followers after he has gone. Even my own daughter. We will saw off their heads with the iron knife they gave me, then we will throw the bodies and the knife into the river. Nothing of him will remain. He longs to return to his homeland where his enemies are more like him. We are too innocent for his liking. This alone is certain: we are our only friends.

The day before they were due to sail, a native guide led a group of sailors through the forest and showed them a mound of earth in a clearing. Knox and his cat Clootie went with them, as always when there was the prospect of some hunting. The sailors began digging in the mound, hoping to find some of that elusive treasure. Instead, skulls. Hundreds upon hundreds of human skulls. They presumed they were in some kind of traditional tribal burial place. But the skulls, belonging to men, women, and children, all seemed recent. Perhaps some disease was responsible. Then, they noted that many of the skulls had been split, pierced with sharp objects. They saw, too, that the bone had not been picked clean by worms and ants. The guide told them the mound was the top of a shaft, hundreds of feet deep, and that it was the place where they had, for generations, buried the heads of enemies who had been decapitated. Their heads were boiled, he said, their brains eaten. In the last three moons before the sailors arrived, he said, Quheesquheenay's people had beheaded in this way at least one thousand enemies, and had filled the pit to overflowing. On the basis of that good omen, the arrival of the aliens had been welcomed. Some of the men were appalled, but Knox laughed heartily. They lacked faith, he said: it was clear from the Bible that Providence frequently operated by means of a timely massacre or two. Knox secretly suspected that Quheesquheenay had arranged the "discovery" to deter the Frenchmen from ever returning to the New World.

The outline of France looms in the distance. Knox alone, of those on deck, does not need to be there. He relishes the ferocious cold, the thin snow falling in a gusty wind. The coastal hills are dappled with it, like leprosy. Or is it, he smiles, heaven's vomit? Clootie would have purred at the idea. Clootie who is not with him. Clootie, who had to be left behind, prowling, he imagines, those forest thickets, terrifying man and beast for years yet, especially that old heathen shaman. Reminding them of something they would not easily destroy. He thinks of Clootie with fondness but with no regret. The New World was child's play. Now the battle will be among professionals, like himself. He breathes deeply, fills his lungs with the chill air sweeping over the water from all the chill regions of the Old World. His home.

YVES THÉRIAULT

ANGUISH OF GOD

A spring morning is like that when it is born in the mist and then comes to full life.

It has shaken off the white everywhere and emerged in golds and greens and you have loved it very much, because it was bright and beautiful.

It was just such a one that marks the first moment of this story.

Everything speaks here of Angoisse-de-Dieu – of his right name, David Coudois – who is a blacksmith and who also thinks.

So the morning was drowned in mist so hard and white that you have to open your eyes wide to see where you are going.

Great, oppressive white with sounds within, the voices of the cows as they are being led to pasture and of the men leading the cows.

Same thing in the blacksmith's shop where it is traditionally dark, there are shreds of mist which have come in by the big door and which hang near the ceiling.

David wanted to take hold of one, see what it's made of. But he laughed as he tried and the Judith, his own Judith, who is there, watched him do it and laughed also. Good springtime laughter, the rich sound feverish with memory and desires.

I'd like to get it.

So said the blacksmith.

Then no more. He did not say how the forge threw its fire which danced with long red tongues on the walls and that *la* Judith with her dark eyes and her soft bosom also, like the walls, had traces of fire playing on the pink of her skin. He did not say that he would have liked to catch the fringe of the mist and to offer it to her as a crazy jewel. That would have been words and even if a whole poem haunted him inside, David could not say it. It beat in him like a bellows and his heart which was going, too, but that only made a glowing in his eyes and no other words than:

"I'd like to get it."

"I'd really like for you to catch it."

And she also had confused images in her body as regards her heart and head. "Oh, look, I'd so much like to have the mist. Catch it and make me a shawl to adorn my neck. And then come closer, closer so that we touch." But she, too, had simply said, "I'd really like for you to catch it."

No, this morning in the low, rickety, ramshackle building, David and *la* Judith were thinking of things that they could not say.

The point is that they do have the right to think of things this way that would be guilty for others. *La* Judith is David's and she's very much his. And in the semidarkness of the shop they suddenly felt very close to each other. Near each other within, far more than skin deep. The inside where ideas are made.

And David who thinks and who wants to understand clearly all there is in life and in the world has great joy from these thoughts.

Then he said:

"*La* Judith, how long have you been with me?"

"Two years."

She had answered with a smile, which had seemed like a light in the dark nook.

"I'm very glad that you stay."

He had not said more this time than another. It was what was not said that was great and beautiful and that *la* Judith understood well. "Go..." Then she came a little closer, wishing that the distance, too, might not be so long if David were feeling any tender thoughts.

But Daumier entered just then.

Daumier, the joker, who must not see David and *la* Judith loving, since he would scoff at them in the hamlet and make those laugh who find the frolics of others ridiculous.

Then the game is broken off and the shop becomes dirty and damp and not very beautiful.

It becomes once more a black hole lighted by the fire in the forge and clouded by the whitish-grey mist from outside.

Daumier has done that, and he said:

"My horse, *le* David, needs shoes."

And David goes to the horse while *la* Judith goes out and goes to the house.

And perhaps despite Daumier's arrival, the Judith and *le* David have loved each other well this morning and that it is going to tie them still more strongly for the coming year.

And if she is singing very low in a voice muffled by the mist, it's because she feels in her man things that make her dream beautifully.

Daumier in the shop speaks to make David reply, for the blacksmith had become silent and awkward since Daumier had entered and *la* Judith had left and since that something had cropped up.

David goes toward the forge, and reaching it, he turns toward Daumier.

"Do you believe in God, you?"

"Yes and no. I believe in him because they say so. If I did not believe it, and if there is one, it would be bad and I would sin.

So I believe it. If there isn't one, I have all my trouble for nothing, and if there is one I gain on the exchange."

David remained dreamy, hammer in hand, for a moment reflecting carefully, then he turned toward the forge.

Since the year of the big crops, the last before the drought had interfered, David Coudois had had great doubts.

Not that he knew what caused the doubts, but it was like a disease.

He had said one time to the curé:

"I'm searching for God."

But that had been all. He had not been able to explain how and in what he was looking for God.

"I'm looking for God."

Inside him was a great muddy sea. You couldn't see inside; yet it's like waves are stirring.

Today the wave is strong; tomorrow it is still. But there is always the movement and the denseness. It moves and you can't tell what it hides.

He was saying to himself, "Is there a God?"

And he begins again, "But where is he?"

And that kept up for many years.

And from time to time, he spoke of it to the people in the hamlet.

To Lorgneau he said:

"I'm looking for God; I'd like to see how he is made."

Lorgneau, who believed nothing, had laughed.

And le Troublé, to whom David had spoken one day, because he had no person to speak to and because the wave was enormous and more muddy than ever, had shaken his head without a smile.

"God is a great fire far away, farther than the sun. When I sin it burns me in the guts. That's because it is fire, I tell you."

But David had not listened to him. "A big fire like your forge on market days. It is perhaps in this way that you have God in your hands."

David was lost in his confusion.

But if we are to speak of it, we must say that the hamlet knew of David's distress, and the mother Druseau, who knew how to put words together, had nicknamed him Angoisse-de-Dieu.

Ah, yes...

...she had said...

David Coudois, the man filled with the agony of God.

And it stuck.

They said "David" to him.

In front of him.

But behind, he had become Angoisse-de-Dieu.

When he had taken in *la* Judith, the name remained, but the doubt in David's insides blurred somewhat.

For a moment he believed that God was love like that he enjoyed with *la* Judith. But that wasn't so, for after a hard night, David still had the dark tide in his heart.

And as the months passed, the greater grew the tide.

One day le Troublé, who sometimes had the light of genius deep in his eyes, which made him feared by women, had said in the shop:

"David, you are very skillful with your hands; you make great things with your hammer, anvil, and soft iron. If you are looking for God and don't find him, invent him."

Which had made David smile.

Even whole days at a time, each time that le Troublé's words returned, "Invent him, manufacture him, make God, become more than God himself since you will have made him."

And David would stop to think. God is mover since we move, and he is joined since we move, and he thinks since we think and move.

But he found le Troublé's idea quite funny.

And this morning great sheets of slate had just been piled up in his mind. Like things that are built, they became an ordered pile. David had seen the shape of love close at hand.

He had wanted to seize a shred of mist and that had struck him. A shred of mist was love then? Trivial, fragile, colourless, lifeless but capable of muffling and covering so as to hinder ordinary things as they are.

And if love had come so close to revealing itself, wouldn't it be that God also only waited the moment to reveal himself?

"Eh, Daumier, God for you is what?"

Daumier thought carefully.

"It's something way up high that has no form, but that is very great and very powerful and that is going to punish us if we do bad deeds."

"But you don't see him in your idea."

"Yes, he is very great, I think, and very long with huge arms which can crush everything. If he gets angry, we will die as in the flood."

"I myself see him in a different way. It seems to me that it's all wheels and levers and that it's going all the time and if it gets angry it's going to burst and is going to perish."

Daumier wondered why there was such a flash in the depth of David's eyes. He saw it when David threw the glowing shoe on the ground which he should have put on the horse's hoof.

"I'm going to make your God for you... with my hands. I won't look for him any more. I'll have him and he'll be my own work."

Daumier wanted to know:

"My horse, are you going to shoe him?"

For David was already searching in the bottom of a big drawer trying to find something.

"Your horse? Take him to the big village. I'm not going to shoe him."

And from that day on he spent his every day making God.

He no longer went out, and the shop door stayed shut.

David Coudois, called Angoisse-de-Dieu, was making the God he had looked for. Only Judith saw him every evening when he returned to the house weary from the task that was wasting him. He had locked the main door and kept himself closed in the shop, refusing to open it to everyone, even to le Troublé.

And within it, the clear sounds of the anvil could be heard and the roaring of the forge.

In the hamlet they said that David was making God, and all shook their heads and looked at one another without saying what they thought.

Then one day, David rushed out and began to shout as he went along the three streets.

"I've made God! I've made God! I've invented him. Come and see him."

They went, and on the floor, there was David Coudois's God, which looked like a very complicated machine with its wheels and levers and which was polished and dark and full of the golden-brown gleams of well-oiled metal.

They were all there, and David made a quick move and set a wheel in motion.

But nothing happened. Then he looked around him and saw the mocking faces – four deep   which encircled the machine and filled the shop. There were even some children perched on the bellows of the forge.

David tried again... Nothing.

And again... Still nothing.

Then he wanted to smash the whole machine and shouted as he was struggling. But it was very plain that he had gone crazy, and he was taken away so that he might be shut up in the city.

In the deserted shop, Judith remained alone, resigned because she had for several weeks feared that *le* David might become mad and she had let him go his way.

They will cure him maybe in the city?

She stood in front of the machine and at first had stroked it because it was the dream of *le* David, whom she loved and it was precious.

Then the idea came to her that the machine was the reason that *le* David had become mad; so she spat on it and said:

"Damned machine!"

And the machine began to move and one of the levers wanted to snatch hold of Judith, and Judith ran outside shouting:

"God is real, David's God is real, David is not mad!"

And as she ran shouting, she heard a loud noise, and turning round she saw that David's shop was on fire and was going up into the air.

They did not believe her in the hamlet.

The shop had burned by itself. Someone had been negligent, and the fire had taken hold.

La Judith really cried for a long time, then she went away and they did not see her again.

MARGARET LAURENCE

A BIRD IN THE HOUSE

The parade would be almost over by now, and I had not gone.
My mother had said in a resigned voice, "All right, Vanessa, if
that's the way you feel," making me suffer twice as many jabs of
guilt as I would have done if she had lost her temper. She and
Grandmother MacLeod had gone off, my mother pulling the
low box-sleigh with Roddie all dolled up in his new red snow-
suit, just the sort of little kid anyone would want people to see.
I sat on the lowest branch of the birch tree in our yard, not
minding the snowy wind, even welcoming its punishment. I
went over my reasons for not going, trying to believe they were
good and sufficient, but in my heart I felt I was betraying my
father. This was the first time I had stayed away from the
Remembrance Day parade. I wondered if he would notice that
I was not there, standing on the sidewalk at the corner of River
and Main, while the parade passed, and then following to the
Court House grounds where the service was held.

I could see the whole thing in my mind. It was the same
every year. The Manawaka Civic Band always led the way.
They had never been able to afford full uniforms, but they had
peaked blue-navy caps and sky-blue chest ribbons. They were
joined on Remembrance Day by the Salvation Army band,
whose uniforms seemed too ordinary for a parade, for they
were the same ones the bandsmen wore every Saturday night
when they played "Nearer My God to Thee" at the foot of
River Street. The two bands never managed to practise quite

enough together, so they did not keep in time too well. The Salvation Army band invariably played faster, and afterwards my father would say irritably, "They play those marches just like they do hymns, blast them, as though they wouldn't get to heaven if they didn't hustle up." And my mother, who had great respect for the Salvation Army because of the good work they did, would respond chidingly, "Now, now, Ewen—" I vowed I would never say "Now, now" to my husband or children, not that I ever intended having the latter, for I had been put off by my brother Roderick, who was now two years old with wavy hair, and everyone said what a beautiful child. I was twelve, and no one in their right mind would have said what a beautiful child, for I was big-boned like my Grandfather Connor and had straight lanky black hair like a Blackfoot or Cree.

After the bands would come the veterans. Even thinking of them at this distance, in the white and withdrawn quiet of the birch tree, gave me a sense of painful embarrassment I might not have minded so much if my father had not been among them. How could he go? How could he not see how they all looked? It must have been a long time since they were soldiers, for they had forgotten how to march in step. They were old – that was the thing. My father was bad enough, being almost forty, but he wasn't a patch on Howard Tully from the drug-store, who was completely grey-haired and also fat, or Stewart MacMurchie, who was bald at the back of his head. They looked to me like imposters, plump or spindly caricatures of past warriors. I almost hated them for walking in that limping column down Main. At the Court House, everyone would sing *Lord God of Hosts, be with us yet, lest we forget, lest we forget.* Will Masterson would pick up his old Army bugle and blow "The Last Post." Then it would be over and everyone could start gabbing once more and go home.

I jumped down from the birch bough and ran to the house, yelling, making as much noise as I could.

I'm a poor lonesome cowboy
An' a long way from home—

I stepped inside the front hall and kicked off my snow boots. I slammed the door behind me, making the dark ruby and emerald glass shake in the small leaded panes. I slid purposely on the hall rug, causing it to bunch and crinkle on the slippery polished oak of the floor. I seized the newel post, round as a head, and spun myself to and fro on the bottom stair.

I ain't got no father
To buy the clothes I wear
I'm a poor lonesome—

At this moment my shoulders were firmly seized and shaken by a pair of hands, white and delicate and old, but strong as talons.

"Just what do you think you're doing, young lady?" Grandmother MacLeod enquired, in a voice like frost on a windowpane, infinitely cold and clearly etched.

I went limp and in a moment she took her hands away. If you struggled, she would always hold on longer.

"Gee, I never knew you were home yet."

"I would have thought that on a day like this you might have shown a little respect and consideration," Grandmother MacLeod said, "even if you couldn't make the effort to get cleaned up enough to go to the parade."

I realized with surprise that she imagined this to be my reason for not going. I did not try to correct her impression. My real reason would have been even less acceptable.

"I'm sorry," I said quickly.

In some families, *please* is described as the magic word. In our house, however, it was *sorry*.

"This isn't an easy day for any of us," she said.

Her younger son, my Uncle Roderick, had been killed in the Great War. When my father marched, and when the hymn was sung, and when that unbearably lonely tune was sounded by the one bugle and everyone forced themselves to keep absolutely still, it would be that boy of whom she was thinking. I felt the enormity of my own offence.

"Grandmother – I'm sorry."

"So you said."

I could not tell her I had not really said it before at all. I went into the den and found my father there. He was sitting in the leather-cushioned armchair beside the fireplace. He was not doing anything, just sitting and smoking. I stood beside him, wanting to touch the light-brown hairs on his forearm, but thinking he might laugh at me or pull his arm away if I did.

"I'm sorry," I said, meaning it.

"What for, honey?"

"For not going."

"Oh – that. What was the matter?"

I did not want him to know and yet I had to tell him, make him see.

"They look silly," I blurted out. "Marching like that."

For a minute I thought he was going to be angry. It would have been a relief to me if he had been. Instead, he drew his eyes away from mine and fixed them above the mantelpiece where the sword hung, the handsome and evil-looking crescent in its carved bronze sheath that some ancestor had once brought from the Northern Frontier of India.

"Is that the way it looks to you?" he said.

I felt in his voice some hurt, something that was my fault. I wanted to make everything all right between us, to convince him that I understood, even if I did not. I prayed that Grand-mother MacLeod would stay put in her room, and that my mother would take a long time in the kitchen, giving Roddie his lunch. I wanted my father to myself, so I could prove to him that I cared more about him than any of the others did. I wanted to speak in some way that would be more poignant and comprehending than anything of which my mother could possibly be capable of. But I did not know how.

"You were right there when Uncle Roderick got killed, weren't you?" I began uncertainly.

"Yes."

"How old was he, Dad?"

"Eighteen," my father said.

Unexpectedly, that day came into intense being for me. He had had to watch his own brother die, not in the antiseptic calm of some hospital, but out in the open, the stretches of mud I had seen in his snapshots. He would not have known what to do. He would just have had to stand there and look at it, whatever that might mean. I looked at my father with a kind of horrified awe, and then I began to cry. I had forgotten about impressing him with my perception. Now I needed him to console me for this unwanted glimpse of the pain he had once known.

"Hey, cut it out, honey," he said, embarrassed. "It was bad, but it wasn't all as bad as that part. There were a few other things."

"Like what?" I said, not believing him.

"Oh – I don't know," he replied evasively. "Most of us were pretty young, you know, I and the boys I joined up with. None of us had ever been away from Manawaka before. Those of us who came back mostly came back here, or else went no further away from town than Winnipeg. So when we were overseas – that was the only time most of us were ever a long way from home."

"Did you want to be?" I asked, shocked.

"Oh well—" my father said uncomfortably. "It was kind of interesting to see a few other places for a change, that's all."

Grandmother MacLeod was standing in the doorway.

"Beth's called you twice for lunch, Ewen. Are you deaf, you and Vanessa?"

"Sorry," my father and I said simultaneously.

Then we went upstairs to wash our hands.

That winter my mother returned to her old job as a nurse in my father's medical practice. She was able to do this only because of Noreen.

"Grandmother MacLeod says we're getting a maid," I said to my father, accusingly, one morning. "We're not, are we?"

"Believe you me, on what I'm going to be paying her," my father growled, "she couldn't be called anything as classy as a maid. Hired girl would be more like it."

"Now, now, Ewen," my mother put in, "it's not as if we were cheating her or anything. You know she wants to live in town, and I can certainly see why, stuck out there on the farm, and her father hardly ever letting her come in. What kind of life is that for a girl?"

"I don't like the idea of your going back to work, Beth," my father said. "I know you're fine now, but you're not exactly the robust type."

"You can't afford to hire a nurse any longer. It's all very well to say the Depression won't last forever – probably it won't, but what else can we do for now?"

"I'm damned if I know," my father admitted. "Beth—"

"Yes?"

They both seemed to have forgotten about me. It was at breakfast, which we always ate in the kitchen, and I sat rigidly on my chair, pretending to ignore and thus snub their withdrawal from me. I glared at the window, but it was so thickly plumed and scrolled with frost that I could not see out. I glanced back to my parents. My father had not replied, and my mother was looking at him in that anxious and half-frowning way she had recently developed.

"What is it, Ewen?" Her voice had the same nervous sharpness it bore sometimes when she would say to me, "For mercy's sake, Vanessa, what is it *now*?" as though whatever was the matter, it was bound to be the last straw.

My father spun his sterling silver serviette ring, engraved with his initials, slowly around on the table.

"I never thought things would turn out like this, did you?"

"Please—" my mother said in a low strained voice, "please, Ewen, let's not start all this again. I can't take it."

"All right," my father said. "Only—"

"The MacLeods used to have money and now they don't," my mother cried. "Well, they're not alone. Do you think all that matters to me, Ewen? What I can't bear is to see you forever reproaching yourself. As if it were your fault."

"I don't think it's the comedown," my father said. "If I were somewhere else, I don't suppose it would matter to me, either, except where you're concerned. But I suppose you'd work too hard wherever you were – it's bred into you. If you haven't got anything to slave away at, you'll sure as hell invent something."

"What do you think I should do, let the house go to wrack and ruin? That would go over well with your mother, wouldn't it?"

"That's just it," my father said. "It's the damned house all the time. I haven't only taken on my father's house, I've taken on everything that goes with it, apparently. Sometimes I really wonder—"

"Well, it's a good thing I've inherited some practicality even if you haven't," my mother said. "I'll say that for the Connors – they aren't given to brooding, thank the Lord. Do you want your egg poached or scrambled?"

"Scrambled," my father said. "All I hope is that this Noreen doesn't get married straightaway, that's all."

"She won't," my mother said. "Who's she going to meet who could afford to marry?"

"I marvel at you, Beth," my father said. "You look as though a puff of wind would blow you away. But underneath, by God, you're all hardwood."

"Don't talk stupidly," my mother said. "All I hope is that she doesn't object to taking your mother's breakfast up on a tray."

"That's right," my father said angrily. "Rub it in."

"Oh, Ewen, I'm sorry!" my mother cried, her face suddenly stricken. "I don't know why I say these things. I didn't mean to."

"I know," my father said. "Here, cut it out, honey. Just for God's sake please don't cry."

"I'm sorry," my mother repeated, blowing her nose.

"We're both sorry," my father said. "Not that that changes anything."

After my father had gone, I got down from my chair and went to my mother.

"I don't want you to go back to the office. I don't want a hired girl here. I'll hate her."

My mother sighed, making me feel that I was placing an intolerable burden on her, and yet making me resent having to feel this weight. She looked tired, as she often did these days. Her tiredness bored me, made me want to attack her for it.

"Catch me getting along with a dumb old hired girl," I threatened.

"Do what you like," my mother said abruptly. "What can I do about it?"

And then, of course, I felt bereft, not knowing which way to turn.

My father need not have worried about Noreen getting married. She was, as it turned out, interested not in boys but in God. My mother was relieved about the boys but alarmed about God.

"It isn't natural," she said, "for a girl of seventeen. Do you think she's all right mentally, Ewen?"

When my parents, along with Grandmother MacLeod, went to the United Church every Sunday, I was made to go to Sunday school in the church basement, where there were small red chairs which humiliatingly resembled kindergarten furniture, and pictures of Jesus wearing a white sheet and surrounded by a whole lot of well-dressed kids whose mothers obviously had not suffered them to come unto Him until every face and ear was properly scrubbed. Our religious observances also included grace at meals, when my father would mumble "For what we are about to receive the Lord make us truly thankful Amen," running the words together as though they were one long word. My mother approved of these rituals, which seemed decent and moderate to her. Noreen's religion, however, was a different matter. Noreen belonged to the Tabernacle of the Risen and Reborn, and she had got up to testify no less than seven times in the past two years, she told us. My mother, who could not imagine anyone voluntarily making a public spectacle of themselves, was profoundly shocked by this revelation.

"Don't worry," my father soothed her. "She's all right. She's just had kind of a dull life, that's all."

My mother shrugged and went on worrying and trying to help Noreen without hurting her feelings, by tactful remarks about the advisability of modulating one's voice when singing hymns, and the fact that there was plenty of hot water so Noreen really didn't need to hesitate about taking a bath. She even bought a razor and a packet of blades and whispered to Noreen that any girl who wore transparent blouses so much would probably like to shave under her arms. None of these suggestions had the slightest effect on Noreen. She did not cease belting out hymns at the top of her voice, she bathed once a fortnight, and the sorrel-coloured hair continued to bloom like a thicket of Indian paintbrush in her armpits.

Grandmother MacLeod refused to speak to Noreen. This caused Noreen a certain amount of bewilderment until she finally hit on an answer.

"Your poor grandma," she said. "She is deaf as a post. These things are sent to try us here on earth, Vanessa. But if she makes it into Heaven, I'll bet you anything she will hear clear as a bell."

Noreen and I talked about Heaven quite a lot, and also Hell. Noreen had an intimate and detailed knowledge of both places. She not only knew what they looked like – she even knew how big they were. Heaven was seventy-seven thousand miles square and it had four gates, each one made out of a different kind of precious jewel. The Pearl Gate, the Topaz Gate, the Amethyst Gate, the Ruby Gate – Noreen would reel them off, all the gates of Heaven. I told Noreen they sounded like poetry, but she was puzzled by my reaction and said I shouldn't talk that way. If you said poetry, it sounded like it was just made up and not really so, Noreen said.

Hell was larger than Heaven, and when I asked why, thinking of it as something of a comedown for God, Noreen said naturally it had to be bigger because there were a darn sight more people there than in Heaven. Hell was one hundred and ninety million miles deep and was in perpetual darkness, like a cave or under the sea. Even the flames (this was the awful thing) *did not give off any light*.

I did not actually believe in Noreen's doctrines, but the images which they conjured up began to inhabit my imagination. Noreen's fund of exotic knowledge was not limited to religion, although in a way it all seemed related. She could do many things which had a spooky tinge to them. Once when she was making a cake, she found we had run out of eggs. She went outside and gathered a bowl of fresh snow and used it instead. The cake rose like a charm, and I stared at Noreen as though she were a sorceress. In fact, I began to think of her as a sorceress, someone not quite of this earth. There was nothing unearthly about her broad shoulders and hips and her forest of dark red hair, but even these features took on a slightly sinister significance to me. I no longer saw her through the eyes of the expressed opinions of my mother and father, as a girl who had quit school at grade eight and whose life on the farm had been endlessly drab. I knew the truth – Noreen's life had not been drab at all, for she dwelt in a world of violent splendours, a world filled with angels whose wings of delicate light bore real feathers, and saints shining like the dawn, and prophets who spoke in ancient tongues, and the ecstatic souls of the saved, as well as denizens of the lower regions – mean-eyed imps and crooked cloven-hoofed monsters and beasts with the bodies of swine and the human heads of murderers, and lovely depraved jezebels torn by dogs through all eternity. The middle layer of Creation, our earth, was equally full of grotesque presences, for Noreen believed strongly in the visitation of ghosts and the communication with spirits. She could prove this with her Ouija board. We would both place our fingers lightly on the indicator, and it would skim across the board and spell out answers to our questions. I did not believe whole-heartedly in the Ouija board, either, but I was cautious about the kind of question I asked, in case the answer would turn out unfavourable and I would be unable to forget it.

One day Noreen told me she could also make a table talk. We used the small table in my bedroom, and sure enough, it lifted very slightly under our fingertips and tapped once for *Yes*, twice for *No*. Noreen asked if her Aunt Ruthie would get better from the kidney operation, and the table replied *No*. I withdrew my hands.

"I don't want to do it any more."

"Gee, what's the matter, Vanessa?" Noreen's plain placid face creased in a frown. "We only just begun."

"I have to do my homework."

My heart lurched as I said this. I was certain Noreen would know I was lying, and that she would know not by any ordinary perception, either. But her attention had been caught by something else, and I was thankful, at least until I saw what it was.

My bedroom window was not opened in the coldest weather. The storm window, which was fitted outside as an extra wall against the winter, had three small circular holes in its frame so that some fresh air could seep into the house. The sparrow must have been floundering in the new snow on the roof, for it had crawled in through one of these holes and was now caught between the two layers of glass. I could not bear the panic of the trapped bird, and before I realized what I was doing, I had thrown open the bedroom window. I was not releasing the sparrow into any better a situation, I soon saw, for instead of remaining quiet and allowing us to catch it in order to free it, it began flying blindly around the room, hitting the lampshade, brushing against the walls, its wings seeming to spin faster and faster.

I was petrified. I thought I would pass out if those palpitating wings touched me. There was something in the bird's senseless movements that revolted me. I also thought it was going to damage itself, break one of those thin wing-bones, perhaps, and then it would be lying on the floor, dying, like the pimpled and horribly featherless baby birds we saw sometimes on the sidewalks in the spring when they had fallen out of their nests. I was not any longer worried about the sparrow. I wanted only to avoid the sight of it lying broken on the floor. Viciously, I thought that if Noreen said, *God sees the little sparrow fall*, I would kick her in the shins. She did not, however, say this.

"A bird in the house means a death in the house," Noreen remarked.

Shaken, I pulled my glance away from the whirling wings and looked at Noreen.

"What?"

"That's what I've heard said, anyhow."

The sparrow had exhausted itself. It lay on the floor, spent and trembling. I could not bring myself to touch it. Noreen bent and picked it up. She cradled it with great gentleness between her cupped hands. Then we took it downstairs, and when I had opened the back door, Noreen set the bird free.

"Poor little scrap," she said, and I felt struck to the heart, knowing she had been concerned all along about the sparrow, while I perfidiously, in the chaos of the moment, had been concerned only about myself.

"Wanna do some with the Ouija board, Vanessa?" Noreen asked.

I shivered a little, perhaps only because of the blast of cold air which had come into the kitchen when the door was opened.

"No, thanks, Noreen. Like I said, I got my homework to do. But thanks all the same."

"That's okay," Noreen said in her guileless voice. "Any time."

But whenever she mentioned the Ouija board or the talking table after that, I always found some excuse not to consult these oracles.

"Do you want to come to church with me this evening, Vanessa?" my father asked.

"How come you're going to the evening service?" I enquired.

"Well, we didn't go this morning. We went snowshoeing instead, remember? I think your grandmother was a little bit put out about it. She went alone this morning. I guess it wouldn't hurt you and me to go now."

We walked through the dark, along the white streets, the snow squeaking dryly under our feet. The streetlights were placed at long intervals along the sidewalks, and around each pole the circle of flimsy light created glistening points of blue and crystal on the crusted snow. I would have liked to take my father's hand, as I used to do, but I was too old for that now. I walked beside him, taking long steps so he would not have to walk more slowly on my account.

The sermon bored me, and I began leafing through the Hymnary for entertainment. I must have drowsed, for the next thing I knew, my father was prodding me and we were on our feet for the closing hymn.

> *Near the Cross, near the Cross,*
> *Be my glory ever,*
> *Till my ransomed soul shall find*
> *Rest beyond the river.*

I knew the tune well, so I sang loudly for the first verse. But the music to that hymn is sombre, and all at once the words themselves seemed too dreadful to be sung. I stopped singing, my throat knotted. I thought I was going to cry, but I did not know why, except that the song recalled to me my Grandmother Connor who had been dead only a year now. I wondered why her soul needed to be ransomed. If God did not think she was good enough just as she was, then I did not have much use for His opinion. *Rest beyond the river* – was that what happened to her? She had believed in Heaven, but I did not think that rest beyond the river was quite what she had in mind.

To think of her in Noreen's flashy Heaven, though – that was even worse. Someplace where nobody ever got annoyed or had to be smoothed down and placated, someplace where there were never any family scenes – that would have suited my Grandmother Connor. Maybe she wouldn't have minded a certain amount of rest beyond the river at that.

When we had the silent prayer, I looked at my father. He sat with his head bowed and his eyes closed. He was frowning deeply, and I could see the pulse in his temple. I wondered then what he believed. I did not have any real idea what it might be. When he raised his head, he did not look uplifted or anything like that. He merely looked tired. Then Reverend McKee pronounced the benediction, and we could go home.

"What do you think about all that stuff, Dad?" I asked hesitantly, as we walked.

"What stuff, honey?"

"Oh, Heaven and Hell, and like that."

My father laughed. "Have you been listening to Noreen too much? Well, I don't know. I don't think they're actual places. Maybe they stand for something that happens all the time here, or else doesn't happen. It's kind of hard to explain. I guess I'm not so good at explanations."

Nothing seemed to have been made any clearer to me. I reached out and took his hand, not caring that he might think this a babyish gesture.

"I hate that hymn!"

"Good Lord," my father said in astonishment. "Why, Vanessa?"

But I did not know and so could not tell him.

Many people in Manawaka had the flu that winter, so my father and Dr. Cates were kept extremely busy. I had the flu myself, and spent a week in bed, vomiting only the first day and after that enjoying poor health, as my mother put it, with Noreen bringing me ginger ale and orange juice, and each evening my father putting a wooden tongue-depressor into my mouth and peering down my throat, then smiling and saying he thought I might live after all.

Then my father got sick himself, and had to stay at home and go to bed. This was such an unusual occurrence that it amused me.

"Doctors shouldn't get sick," I told him.

"You're right," he said. "That was pretty bad management."

"Run along now, dear," my mother said.

That night I woke and heard voices in the upstairs hall. When I went out, I found my mother and Grandmother MacLeod, both in their dressing gowns. With them was Dr. Cates. I did not go immediately to my mother, as I would have done only a year before. I stood in the doorway of my room, squinting against the sudden light.

"Mother – what is it?"

She turned, and momentarily I saw the look on her face before she erased it and put on a contrived calm.

"It's all right," she said. "Dr. Cates has just come to have a look at Daddy. You go on back to sleep."

The wind was high that night, and I lay and listened to it rattling the storm windows and making the dry and winter-stiffened vines of the Virginia creeper scratch like small persistent claws against the red brick. In the morning, my mother told me that my father had developed pneumonia.

Dr. Cates did not think it would be safe to move my father to the hospital. My mother began sleeping in the spare bedroom, and after she had been there for a few nights, I asked if I could sleep in there too. I thought she would be bound to ask me why, and I did not know what I would say, but she did not ask. She nodded, and in some way her easy agreement upset me.

That night Dr. Cates came again, bringing with him one of the nurses from the hospital. My mother stayed upstairs with them. I sat with Grandmother MacLeod in the living room. That was the last place in the world I wanted to be, but I thought she would be offended if I went off. She sat as straight and rigid as a totem pole, and embroidered away at the needle-point cushion cover she was doing. I perched on the edge of the chesterfield and kept my eyes fixed on *The White Company* by Conan Doyle, and from time to time I turned a page. I had already read it three times before, but luckily Grandmother MacLeod did not know that. At nine o'clock she looked at her gold brooch watch, which she always wore pinned to her dress, and told me to go to bed, so I did that.

I awakened in darkness. At first, it seemed to me that I was in my own bed, and everything was as usual, with my parents in their room, and Roddie curled up in the crib in his room, and Grandmother MacLeod sleeping with her mouth open in her enormous spool bed, surrounded by half a dozen framed photos of Uncle Roderick and only one of my father, and Noreen snoring fitfully in the room next to mine, with the dark flames of her hair spreading out across the pillow, and the pink and silver motto cards from the Tabernacle stuck with adhesive tape onto the wall beside her bed – *Lean on Him, Emmanuel Is My Refuge, Rock of Ages Cleft for Me.*

Then in the total night around me, I heard a sound. It was my mother, and she was crying, not loudly at all, but from somewhere very deep inside her. I sat up in bed. Everything seemed to have stopped, not only time but my own heart and blood as well. Then my mother noticed that I was awake.

I did not ask her, and she did not tell me anything. There was no need. She held me in her arms, or I held her, I am not certain which. And after a while the first mourning stopped, too, as everything does sooner or later, for when the limits of endurance have been reached, then people must sleep.

In the days following my father's death, I stayed close beside my mother, and this was only partly for my own consoling. I also had the feeling that she needed my protection. I did not know from what, nor what I could possibly do, but something held me there. Reverend McKee called, and I sat with my grandmother and my mother in the living room. My mother told me I did not need to stay unless I wanted to, but I refused to go. What I thought chiefly was that he would speak of the healing power of prayer, and all that, and it would be bound to make my mother cry again. And in fact, it happened in just that way, but when it actually came, I could not protect her from this assault. I could only sit there and pray my own prayer, which was that he would go away quickly.

My mother tried not to cry unless she was alone or with me. I also tried, but neither of us was entirely successful. Grandmother MacLeod, on the other hand, was never seen crying, not even the day of my father's funeral. But that day, when we had returned to the house and she had taken off her black velvet overshoes and her heavy sealskin coat with its black fur that was the softest thing I had ever touched, she stood in the hallway and for the first time she looked unsteady. When I reached out instinctively towards her, she sighed.

"That's right," she said. "You might just take my arm while I go upstairs, Vanessa."

That was the most my Grandmother MacLeod ever gave in, to anyone's sight. I left her in her bedroom, sitting on the straight chair beside her bed and looking at the picture of my father that had been taken when he graduated from medical college. Maybe she was very sorry now that she had only the one photograph of him, but whatever she felt, she did not say.

I went down into the kitchen. I had scarcely spoken to Noreen since my father's death. This had not been done on purpose. I simply had not seen her. I had not really seen anyone except my mother. Looking at Noreen now, I suddenly recalled the sparrow. I felt physically sick, remembering the fearful darting and plunging of those wings, and the fact that it was I who had opened the window and let it in. Then an inexplicable fury took hold of me, some terrifying need to hurt, burn, destroy. Absolutely without warning, either to her or to myself, I hit Noreen as hard as I could. When she swung around, appalled, I hit out at her once more, my arms and legs flailing. Her hands snatched at my wrists, and she held me, but still I continued to struggle, fighting blindly, my eyes tightly closed, as though she were a prison all around me and I was battling to get out. Finally, too shocked at myself to go on, I went limp in her grasp and she let me drop to the floor.

"Vanessa! I never done one single solitary thing to you, and here you go hitting and scratching me like that! What in the world has got into you?"

I began to say I was sorry, which was certainly true, but I did not say it. I could not say anything.

"You're not yourself, what with your dad and everything," she excused me. "I been praying every night that your dad is with God, Vanessa. I know he wasn't actually saved in the regular way, but still and all—"

"Shut up," I said.

Something in my voice made her stop talking. I rose from the floor and stood in the kitchen doorway.

"He didn't need to be saved," I went on coldly, distinctly. "And he is not in Heaven, because there is no Heaven. And it doesn't matter, see? *It doesn't matter!*"

Noreen's face looked peculiarly vulnerable now, her high wide cheekbones and puzzled childish eyes, and the thick russet tangle of her hair. I had not hurt her much before, when I hit her. But I had hurt her now, hurt her in some inexcusable way. Yet I sensed, too, that already she was gaining some satisfaction out of feeling sorrowful about my disbelief.

I went upstairs to my room. Momentarily I felt a sense of calm, almost of acceptance. *Rest beyond the river.* I knew now what that meant. It meant Nothing. It meant only silence, forever.

Then I lay down on my bed and spent the last of my tears, or what seemed then to be the last. Because despite what I had said to Noreen, it did matter. It mattered, but there was no help for it.

Everything changed after my father's death. The MacLeod house could not be kept up any longer. My mother sold it to a local merchant who subsequently covered the deep red of the brick over with yellow stucco. Something about the house had always made me uneasy – that tower room where Grandmother MacLeod's potted plants drooped in a lethargic and lime-green confusion, those long stairways and hidden places, the attic which I had always imagined to be dwelt in by the spirits of the family dead, that gigantic portrait of the Duke of Wellington at the top of the stairs. It was never an endearing house. And yet when it was no longer ours, and when the Virginia creep had been torn down and the dark walls turned to a light marigold, I went out of my way to avoid walking past, for it seemed to me that the house had lost the stern dignity that was its very heart.

Noreen went back to the farm. My mother and brother and myself moved into Grandmother Connor's house. Grandmother MacLeod went to live with Aunt Morag in Winnipeg. It was harder for her than for anyone, because so much of her life was bound up with the MacLeod house. She was fond of Aunt Morag, but that hardly counted. Her men were gone, her husband and her sons, and a family whose men are gone is no family at all. The day she left, my mother and I did not know what to say. Grandmother MacLeod looked even smaller than usual in her fur coat and her black velvet toque. She became extremely agitated about trivialities, and fussed about the possibility of the taxi not arriving on time. She had forbidden us to accompany her to the station. About my father, or the house, or anything important, she did not say a word. Then, when the taxi had finally arrived, she turned to my mother.

"Roddie will have Ewen's seal ring, of course, with the MacLeod crest on it," she said. "But there is another seal as well, don't forget, the larger one with the crest and motto. It's meant to be worn on a watch chain. I keep it in my jewel box. It was Roderick's. Roddie's to have that, too, when I die. Don't let Morag talk you out of it."

During the Second World War, when I was seventeen and in love with an airman who did not love me, and desperately anxious to get away from Manawaka and from my grandfather's house, I happened one day to be going through the old mahogany desk that had belonged to my father. It had a number of small drawers inside, and I accidentally pulled one of these all the way out. Behind it there was another drawer, one I had not known about. Curiously, I opened it. Inside there was a letter written on almost transparent paper in a cramped angular handwriting. It began – *Cher Monsieur Ewen* – That was all I could make out, for the writing was nearly impossible to read and my French was not good. It was dated 1919. With it, there was a picture of a girl, looking absurdly old-fashioned to my eyes, like the faces on long-discarded calendars or chocolate boxes. But beneath the dated quality of the photograph, she seemed neither expensive or cheap. She looked like what she probably had been – an ordinary middle-class girl, but in another country. She wore her hair in long ringlets, and her mouth was shaped into a sweetly sad posed smile like Mary Pickford's. That was all. There was nothing else in the drawer.

I looked for a long time at the girl, and hoped she had meant some momentary and unexpected freedom. I remembered what he had said to me, after I hadn't gone to the Remembrance Day parade.

"What are you doing, Vanessa?" my mother called from the kitchen.

"Nothing," I replied.

I took the letter and picture outside and burned them. That was all I could do for him. Now that we might have talked together, it was many years too late. Perhaps it would not have been possible anyway. I did not know.

As I watched the smile of the girl turn into scorched paper, I grieved for my father as though he had just died now.

JACQUES FERRON

THE ROPE AND THE HEIFER

Translated by Betty Bednarski

Father Godfrey did not stir, curled up in a ball, snug in the belly
of the night. It was the servant who had to rouse him. In she
rushed, her great bony hand like a spider at the end of her arm,
clutched his shoulder, wouldn't let go. He struggled; she held
on. Then he had no choice but to pull himself up as far as his
eyes, reassemble ears, nose and mouth, and putting his hand to
his chin, his face still awry, say: "What is it, Marguerite?"

"The bell, *Monsieur le curé.*"

"Uh, go see who's there."

"No, the bell in the belfry."

The bell in the belfry – but that was for the Lord! He, poor
priest, had quite enough trouble as it was, already obliged to get
up in the night, dress, and go out whenever, to his misfortune,
someone came to his door. "It's the wind, Marguerite, it's the
wind." And he let himself sink back down.

"*Monsieur le curé! Monsieur le curé!*"

"Eh? What?"

"There is no wind."

So he was obliged to sit himself up, this time with more dignity, his face now all of a piece, and announce that he knew,
since it wasn't the wind... "Are you sure of that, Marguerite?"
"Sure as I'm a Christian."... just what it was about. He knew
above all that a priest has to have an answer for everything: "Ah,
yes, it's the souls in purgatory." "God a mercy!" said the servant.
Whereupon he pronounced a few words in Latin, finishing off

with three amens, which old Marguerite repeated before tiptoe-
ing out.

The next morning the angelus bell was late. From his window the priest saw the verger go by with a stepladder on his
shoulder. Shortly afterwards the bell rang out. The morning was
radiant. At the sound of the angelus the most pious fishermen
bowed their heads in prayerful contemplation; the others said to
themselves, more trivially, that the time was now six o'clock,
and as a just punishment for their lack of faith they were a full
ten minutes out. The grass had collapsed under the dew. On the
thin mist that covered the sea the boats were set out like dishes
on a tablecloth. The priest emerged from the presbytery and, as
usual, began to recite his breviary while waiting for mass. The
sun, full and round over the mountain tops, gazed down in
wonder at the familiar landscape. The day was called morning
and longed to keep its name.

Then it was Marguerite's turn to come out. With her shrill
voice she called to her hens and put an end to all this compla-
cency. The hens came running, their eyes fixed to their beaks,
empty-headed as hunger. The sun remembered its own appetite
and set to work; it drank the dew, even ate the tablecloth, then
climbed high in the sky to digest this frugal breakfast. The
magic of the morning evaporated. The fishermen had jumped
from their porcelain vessels into old wooden boats. The wind
gusted in from all quarters and gathered around the steeple to
ask the weathercock the way. The cock spun three times in one
direction, then three times in the other, and made up its mind:
"That-a-way!" But the seagulls came wheeling in and disagreed.
The weathercock creaked, they squealed. They would never
have settled the matter if Father Godfrey had not lifted his head,
one hand on his biretta, and reminded the wind that it alone
had the right to decide what its course should be.

"Just go whichever way you like!"

Then the cock turned to face the gulls, who let themselves be carried away, and it stopped still. Meanwhile, old Marguerite the servant, dark and gnarled, scattered her grain with a cautious hand for fear it would fall into the sea. When she had finished, she counted her flock: all were there. She also counted the boats: one was missing. Far out at sea, over seven miles from shore, just beyond the reach of the law, Captain Bove's schooner, favoured by the weather, was lying undisturbed in the spot it had occupied for a full week now. Old Marguerite turned away; she preferred not to think of her nephew Wellie, whose boat was missing, and who might at that very moment be anchored off the smuggler's ship, with no protection but that of the great Saint Pierre of Miquelon. She went back inside. Noises from the kitchen alerted Father Godfrey that it was time to say his mass.

He was approaching the sacristy when at the far end of the building he spied a rare parishioner, not known for his piety during the week, diving into the church. Curiosity got the better of his hunger. He changed course and veered away from the sacristy. This parishioner was Bezeau the merchant, his nose to the wind like a frantic hound, who, not finding what he was looking for, headed straight for the verger now, and – what the deuce? – was surprised to find him at the top of a ladder.

"Just looking for the end of our rope, Monsieur Bezeau."

"Has the belfry moved up?"

"No, the rope's been cut with a knife."

"A knife! That's no joke."

"There was no joke meant, Monsieur Bezeau."

Of this the merchant was well aware.

"Say, verger, you wouldn't have seen my heifer by any chance? I've lost her."

"Your heifer? Not that I know of."

"A devout little heifer, quite capable of coming to mass."

"Yes indeed, a fine reputation she had."

"And appetizing! Verger, you would have gotten a piece of her in due course."

"You're too kind, Monsieur Bezeau."

With that, Father Godfrey arrived on the scene.

"Well now, merchant Bezeau, have you come to serve my mass?"

"You can't be serious, Father Godfrey! That would take years off me and be dangerous for my salvation. You'd never stop confessing me. And you know how I hate to trouble you."

Merchant Bezeau spoke like a man who knows that his flour is every bit as useful to an isolated village as God's grace. Father Godfrey did not reply, feeling suddenly peeved. To have come out of his way just to be spoken to like this! There was nothing he could do: to him egalitarianism smacked of arrogance. But he managed not to appear ruffled. This Bezeau fellow hadn't an ounce of shame: did he even give a damn about his salvation, the old serpent? And what respect did he really have for his age, more dangerous himself than all the young lads of the village put together, an inveterate chaser of skirts, pulling them up with a rare dexterity, never missing a shot. He was worse than a Protestant, and yet he was as French-Canadian as anybody, born like everyone else of parents who'd hailed from Montmagny – a cousin one could have done quite nicely without! It was simple: he even made Father Godfrey look kindly on the Jersey merchants, who never paid a cent in tithes to anyone, but at least had the decency to be foreigners.

"Monsieur Bezeau has lost his heifer," announced the verger.

Father Godfrey, surprised at hearing a stepladder speak, raised his eyes, fearing some machination. He saw his sorry-faced verger, who showed him the rope, cut off at the height of a man's arm.

"Burned by a fiery hand?"

"No, cut with a knife."

"Dear souls in purgatory! But this is a sacrilege."

"A sacrilege? That's just what I was a thinking myself."

"I think I might know who the culprit is," said Father God-frey.

"And might you know the thief who stole my heifer too?" asked the merchant.

The priest stopped himself just in time from saying, "They're one and the same."

"Your heifer?"

"Yes, she disappeared last night."

"No idea."

"Oh, come now. Just stop and think. A fine devout creature, a regular little Child of Mary.[1] It wouldn't surprise me if she'd come to mass."

"Enough talk of this heifer," said the priest angrily. "Devout creature, indeed! And you? I know all about your devotions, merchant Bezeau!"

He knew all about them, for sure, but small good it had done him, since he'd learned everything at the confessional.

"The flesh is weak, Father Godfrey. I don't mind telling you, she made my mouth water, that creature of God – well fed, appetizing."

"Monsieur Bezeau would have given us a cut."

"A piece of the tail?"

"No, the rump of your choice."

"That would have been something new: I've never had any-thing from you but your leftovers, merchant Bezeau."

Merchant Bezeau was not a man to let an opportunity pass; chasing the ladies had at least taught him that. He retorted at once:

---

[1] Child of Mary (in French, *enfant de Marie*). A member of the international Catholic organization, or sodality, the Children of Mary (*les enfants de Marie*), which was founded in France and flourished in Quebec in the mid-twentieth century.

"You have to admit, Father Godfrey, that there are some mighty juicy scraps in those leftovers of mine, and you'd have a hard time getting by without them."

The verger, high on his perch, decided that the meeting had gone on long enough. It was not in his interests to let things become acrimonious. Indebted, like everyone else, to God and to the devil, he intended to stay on good terms with their representatives.

"With your permission, *Monsieur le curé*, we'll ring the bell so that merchant Bezeau can get his heifer back."

The priest muttered a response in Latin, or perhaps it was in Hebrew, but in any case the verger hadn't bothered to wait: the bell was already ringing. The merchant left the church and set off again for his store. A great rustling of cassock swept in the opposite direction, filling the nave. The priest entered the sacristy all black and re-emerged all white and gold. Mass began.

On his way, Bezeau, still sniffing the wind, came to a sudden stop, having picked up the sound of an engine that gave off something quite unlike the roar associated with a good day's catch. It came from farther out, a dull, wet, almost woozy throb. He looked out to sea to where the schooner lay, and observed a smaller boat heading in from the same spot; the closer it drew, the sharper and drier the noise became. It stopped in the midst of the fishing boats, just long enough to pull on some drums and cod, setting off again with the honest bluster of an Acadia engine leaving off work early for the day. It was old Marguerite's nephew returning home after an eventful night that was destined to go down in memory. "Confounded Wellie!" said the merchant. It was not so much that he was angry; he was doing his best to keep from laughing – after all, he had been robbed! However, his loss seemed to be more than compensated by Father Godfrey's mortification, in which he took a sincere but disproportionate delight, for he believed the priest to be nearer

to God than he really was, just as the priest overestimated the
extent of his own exchanges with the devil. In these troubling
matters the opposing parties always edify themselves each at the
other's expense and carry on a combat which, when all is said
and done, is indispensable to religion.

All the same, for Father Godfrey it was a difficult mass to
say, and this precisely because of God, whose anger he was
unable to assuage. Canon law has all the drawbacks of colonial
law. The celestial home country does not see things quite the
way they are seen to be in the Gaspé. "*Seigneur*," said Father
Godfrey, "our money is good; if you accept it you won't be out
of pocket. Just think about it: a little piece of rope for a fine
heifer, and rope is worth nothing in these parts, any fisherman
can boast far more length than you, whereas a horned animal is
a rare and precious commodity. Come now, *Seigneur*! If I were
in your shoes, I'd just forget this whole affair." But God turned
a deaf ear, a sign that he intended to stick to the letter of his law,
which is quite explicit on the chapter of sacred objects – article
four: to touch is to desecrate.[1] There was nothing to be done:
canon law was against the Gaspé in general and the said Wellie
in particular. He would have to denounce him from the pulpit;
there would be no avoiding it. The priest returned from his
mass, sullen.

He ate breakfast like an archpriest of the Church of
England, receptive to bacon, closed to questions, his eyes pale,
impenetrable. He was frightening to see. Under this phlegm,
was divine wrath smouldering? Old Marguerite wondered.
Divine wrath explodes in the pulpit on Sunday. The threat was
terrible. Her nephew Wellie was in danger of being denounced
before the whole parish; such a dishonour would have to be pre-
vented. But how? By falling sick? When it came to treatment,

---

[1] Canon law includes rules that govern the touching of liturgical objects – more
specifically, holy vessels.

Father Godfrey believed in the virtues of iodine and she could
not bear the smell or the substance of iodine. Besides, he would
be quite capable of using this sickness as an excuse to hire a
helper for her; there were plenty of candidates for the job, even
some who were young and shapely. Ah, sweet Jesus, that was
more of a danger than iodine! Clearly, another way would have
to be found.

All day long the servant thought about this business of hers.
After supper she went to sit a while with her sister, Wellie's
mother, whom prolonged widowhood and poverty and a linger-
ing beauty had accustomed to resolving with little fuss, but sen-
sibly, the great problems of life. The visit was helpful. She set
out again, her hump lightened, tripping along like a young girl.
In the gathering dusk the spiders were drawing out the first
threads of the night. The western light was fading; already the
church and the surrounding houses stood out against the sky
like silhouettes in a shadow play. As she passed in front of the
store, she gave a start. "Where are you trotting off to like this,
fair Marguerite?" she heard the merchant call.

"So, you're not in bed yet, you old mackerel!"

"I was waiting for you."

She replied: "Bezeau, I'm off to put my priest to bed."

"Tell me: how is the dear fellow?"

"There's a rope in his gullet, hanging from his brains and
making him gag. Are you satisfied?"

The merchant was not displeased. He raised a finger and
waved her on. She continued along the road. Back at the presbytery the priest was waiting for her. He said nothing at first,
and nor did she. He was sitting in his rocking chair in the
kitchen. She laid the table for breakfast, then prepared to go
upstairs. Father Godfrey said to her: "Where have you been,
Marguerite?"

"You know very well where I've been."

"Who did you speak to on your way back?"

"You know that too, but you didn't see the man himself: quite out of sorts he was. He put me in mind of a big cow who's lost its calf."

The rocking movements had gradually become shorter. "So it was our friend Bezeau?" "It was, indeed, himself and none other." With a kick of his heel the priest set the rocking chair back in motion. Marguerite took this opportunity to come closer. Her little eyes had begun to flicker in an attempt to hide the curiosity her sharp gaze might have revealed. "Beware!" said Father Godfrey to himself. Marguerite was a housekeeper he could not manage without; he had grown too accustomed to her. Because of her age and her hump she could bring him no discredit at the bishop's palace, where purple sashes are woven.[1] But she had her nephew Wellie's eyes, and those eyes, especially when they began to flicker, made Father Godfrey suspicious.

"Your nephew Wellie, now... you have to admit!"

"What about my nephew Wellie?"

"He's going a bit too far."

"He's a sailor, Father Godfrey."

"He sails a bit too close to the schooner."

"He sails as best he can; his mother needs him."

"Where was he last night?"

"Last night, Father Godfrey, my nephew Wellie conducted himself like a true Catholic and a good *Gaspésien*."

"You don't say, Marguerite, you don't say!"

She came and stood in front of him, drawing herself up around her hump.

"And that's not all: you won't be mentioning his name in your sermon next Sunday."

The priest brought his chair to a standstill.

"A sacrilege is a sacrilege, Marguerite."

---

[1] The purple sash of a Canon.

"A sacrilege! Ask merchant Bezeau what he thinks of that, or Captain Bove!"

"I don't know the Captain, but Bezeau is certainly no great theologian."

"He's the devil's henchman, and Bove... Bove could even be Satan himself. You don't know him – consider yourself lucky! His neck is twisted, his shoulders hunch, his head jerks to one side, and his eyes are all shot with blood; put a ring in his nose and you'd have a bull."

"But he has no ring and he's Captain Bove, the boss of the schooner, a smuggler and your nephew Wellie's friend."

"His friend? For the love of Jesus! He only keeps company with the man because it'll be him or one of his kind who'll give him a job once his poor mother is well again."

"He could go out fishing like everyone else."

"You're forgetting that he has his engineer's diploma, second class. On Sundays, aren't you proud to have him there at mass in his fine uniform? He's a credit to the parish."

"But he cut my rope."

"Listen, *Monsieur le curé*: Captain Bove said to him: 'Wellie, I'm going to be needing a nice little heifer tonight'."

"And he stole merchant Bezeau's heifer and tied her up with the..."

"Do you know what that really meant, 'a nice little heifer'? He's a bull, is Captain Bove – I warned you he was. 'Heifer' meant..."

"No, Marguerite, that's impossible."

"Impossible? To every monster his female. Heifers for Captain Bove, why, they're to be found in every parish in the Gaspé."

"But I would know."

"You don't know: you give these girls their absolution without ever asking where it was they sinned."

"On the schooner?"

"Bove never leaves it. If he came ashore he'd be hanged."

Father Godfrey was devastated. The sea had always been good to him. It pervaded his spirituality. He believed that with its restless fluidity it could bring about exchanges between the eternal and the temporal, between God and his own parish. Many a time he had seen shadows glide over its surface among the morning mists or the mirages of evening and shield the arrival or the departure of a soul, the imminence of a joy or a misfortune, which he had then predicted, unfailingly. And now, on this vast magic mirror, resting against the sky and tilted toward the land, on this mirror where he had learned to read, he was being shown a hideous blot.

"Is it possible?"

"You're too good, you are. The wickedness of the world escapes you, but you couldn't help but understand my poor Wellie. Just think, *Monsieur le curé*: what a fool he must have looked when he came back to the schooner with his specimen. Think how they must have laughed at him! But he didn't care, because there had been no offence to God."

Father Godfrey remained thoughtful. He had heard a great many confessions but he realized now that there was still much he hadn't learned. There were also some gaps in his knowledge of the scriptures.

"I had better reread the Apocalypse. Perhaps he's in there in the guise of a black bull."

"You're not talking about Wellie?"

"No, Marguerite, your nephew is a true Catholic and a good *Gaspésien*. I was thinking of this Captain Bove... But I can't quite remember, even though it's the word of God. I'm slipping. Yes, slipping I am."

And he was overcome with dismay. Marguerite said no more; she went upstairs to bed and slept well. Father Godfrey, on the other hand, stayed awake. He went far into the night, farther than he had ever been, with the monsters of the Apocalypse for company, in an eerie calm that caused him to apprehend the trumpets and the din of the battle of Armageddon. To the raptures of the Prophet he added his own nightmares, so that by morning he was more confused than ever on the subject of Bove and the diabolical bull. He had a bad day, then a night that was better than the previous one. The following day was Saturday. Father Godfrey regained his composure. When the winds gathered around the church tower to ask their way, he didn't wait for the weathercock to creak three times or for the gulls to intervene; he shouted:

"Make for the schooner!"

With the result that before the day was out Captain Bove was obliged to weigh anchor and hightail over the horizon. "God prevails, Marguerite." "Yes, *Monsieur le curé*, especially when he is well represented." Sunday dawned as usual. It was different from other Sundays, however, because of the sermon, which was a sermon on monsters. This was a genre Father Godfrey was trying out for the very first time. He shouted loudly, and through his nose. It was always the same: when he raised his voice, it refused to come out through his mouth. "There has been in our midst a black bull. A black bull, I say. And when I say 'a black bull,' I know full well what that means..."

The parishioners, for their part, hadn't the faintest idea what it meant. Everyone on the Shore knew that Captain Bove was a gentleman. Marguerite was the only one to grasp the allusion. After mass Wellie was invited to dine at the presbytery. That same evening he had supper with merchant Bezeau. Until that day people had judged him rather severely because of his drinking. But doesn't everyone have their little weaknesses? From that moment on he was seen as a true Catholic and a good *Gaspésien*, to be sure, but above all as a skilful navigator.

MORLEY CALLAGHAN

A SICK CALL

Sometimes Father Macdowell mumbled out loud and took a deep wheezy breath as he walked up and down and read his office. He was a bulky priest, white-headed except for a shiny baby-pink bald spot on the top of his head, and he was a bit deaf in one ear. His florid face had many red interlacing veins. For hours he had been hearing confessions and he was tired, for he always had to hear more confessions than any other priest at the cathedral; young girls who were in trouble, and wild but at times repentant young men, always wanted to tell their confessions to Father Macdowell, because nothing seemed to shock or excite him, or make him really angry, and he was even tender with those who thought they were most guilty.

While he was mumbling and reading and trying to keep his glasses on his nose, the house girl knocked on the door and said, "There's a young lady here to see you, Father. I think it's about a sick call."

"Did she ask for me especially?" he said in a deep but slightly cracked voice.

"Indeed she did, Father. She wanted Father Macdowell and nobody else."

So he went out to the waiting room, where a girl about thirty years of age, with fine brown eyes, fine cheekbones, and rather square shoulders, was sitting daubing her eyes with a handkerchief. She was wearing a dark coat with a gray wolf collar. "Good evening, Father," she said. "My sister is sick. I wanted you to come and see her. We think she's dying."

"Be easy, child; what's the matter with her? Speak louder. I can hardly hear you."

"My sister's had pneumonia. The doctor's coming back to see her in an hour. I wanted you to anoint her, Father."

"I see, I see. But she's not lost yet. I'll not give her extreme unction now. That may not be necessary. I'll go with you and hear her confession."

"Father, I ought to let you know, maybe. Her husband won't want to let you see her. He's not a Catholic, and my sister hasn't been to church in a long time."

"Oh, don't mind that. He'll let me see her," Father Macdowell said, and he left the room to put on his hat and coat.

When he returned, the girl explained that her name was Jane Stanhope, and her sister lived only a few blocks away. "We'll walk and you tell me about your sister," he said. He put his black hat square on his head, and pieces of white hair stuck out at the sides. They went to the avenue together.

The night was mild and clear. Miss Stanhope began to walk slowly, because Father Macdowell's rolling gait didn't get him along the street very quickly. He walked as if his feet hurt him, though he wore a pair of large, soft, specially constructed shapeless shoes. "Now, my child, you go ahead and tell me about your sister," he said, breathing with difficulty, yet giving the impression that nothing could have happened to the sister which would make him feel indignant.

There wasn't much to say, Miss Stanhope replied. Her sister had married John Williams two years ago, and he was a good, hard-working fellow, only he was very bigoted and hated all church people. "My family wouldn't have anything to do with Elsa after she married him, though I kept going to see

her," she said. She was talking in a loud voice to Father Macdowell so that he could hear her.

"Is she happy with her husband?"

"She's been very happy, Father. I must say that."

"Where is he now?"

"He was sitting beside her bed. I ran out because I thought
he was going to cry. He said if I brought a priest near the place
he'd break the priest's head."

"My goodness. Never mind, though. Does your sister want
to see me?"

"She asked me to go and get a priest, but she doesn't want
John to know she did it."

Turning into a side street, they stopped at the first apartment house, and the old priest followed Miss Stanhope up the
stairs. His breath came with great difficulty. "Oh dear, I'm not
getting any younger, not one day younger. It's a caution how a
man's legs go back on him," he said. As Miss Stanhope rapped
on the door, she looked pleadingly at the old priest, trying to ask
him not to be offended at anything that might happen, but he
was smiling and looking huge in the narrow hallway. He wiped
his head with his handkerchief.

The door was opened by a young man in a white shirt with
no collar, with a head of thick, black, wavy hair. At first he
looked dazed, then his eyes got bright with excitement when he
saw the priest, as though he were glad to see someone he could
destroy with pent-up energy. "What do you mean, Jane?" he
said. "I told you not to bring a priest around here. My wife
doesn't want to see a priest."

"What's that you're saying, young man?"

"No one wants you here."

"Speak up. Don't be afraid. I'm a bit hard of hearing,"
Father Macdowell smiled rosily. John Williams was confused by
the unexpected deafness in the priest, but he stood blocking the

door with sullen resolution as if waiting for the priest to try to launch a curse at him.

"Speak to him, Father," Miss Stanhope said, but the priest didn't seem to hear her; he was still smiling as he pushed past the young man, saying, "I'll go in and sit down, if you don't mind, son. I'm here on God's errand, but I don't mind saying I'm all out of breath from climbing those stairs."

John was dreadfully uneasy to see he had been brushed aside, and he followed the priest into the apartment and said loudly, "I don't want you here."

Father Macdowell said, "Eh, eh?" Then he smiled sadly, "Don't be angry with me, son. I'm too old to try and be fierce and threatening." Looking around, he said, "Where's your wife?" and he started to walk along the hall, looking for the bedroom.

John followed him and took hold of his arm. "There's no sense in your wasting your time talking to my wife, do you hear?" he said angrily.

Miss Stanhope called out suddenly, "Don't be rude, John."

"It's he that's being rude. You mind your business," John said.

"For the love of God let me sit down a moment with her, anyway. I'm tired," the priest said.

"What do you want to say to her? Say it to me, why don't you?"

Then they both heard someone moan softly in the adjoining room, as if the sick woman had heard them. Father Macdowell, forgetting that the young man had a hold of his arm, said, "I'll go in and see her for a moment, if you don't mind," and he began to open the door.

"You're not going to be alone with her, that's all," John said, following him into the bedroom.

Lying on the bed was a white-faced, fair girl, whose skin was so delicate that her cheekbones stood out sharply. She was feverish, but her eyes rolled toward the door, and she watched them coming in. Father Macdowell took off his coat, and as he mumbled to himself he looked around the room, at the mauve silk bed-light and the wallpaper with the tiny birds in flight. It looked like a little girl's room. "Good evening, Father," Mrs. Williams whispered. She looked scared. She didn't glance at her husband. The notion of dying had made her afraid. She loved her husband and wanted to die loving him, but she was afraid, and she looked up at the priest.

"You're going to get well, child," Father Macdowell said, smiling and patting her hand gently.

John, who was standing stiffly at the door, suddenly moved around the big priest, and then bent down over the bed and took his wife's hand and began to caress her forehead.

"Now, if you don't mind, my son, I'll hear your wife's confession," the priest said.

"No, you won't," John said abruptly. "Her people didn't want her, and they left us together, and they're not going to separate us now. She's satisfied with me." He kept looking down at her face as if he could not bear to turn away.

Father Macdowell nodded his head up and down and sighed. "Poor boy," he said. "God bless you." Then he looked at Mrs. Williams, who had closed her eyes, and he saw a faint tear on her cheek. "Be sensible my boy," he said. "You'll have to let me hear your wife's confession. Leave us alone for a while."

"I'm going to stay right here," John said, and he sat down on the end of the bed. He was working himself up and staring savagely at the priest. All of a sudden he noticed the tears on his wife's cheeks, and he muttered as though bewildered, "What's the matter, Elsa? What's the matter, darling? Are we bothering you? Just open your eyes and we'll go out of the room and leave you alone till the doctor comes." Then he turned and said to the priest, "I'm not going to leave you here with her, can't you see that? Why don't you go?"

"I could revile you, my son. I could threaten you; but I ask you, for the peace of your wife's soul, leave us alone." Father Macdowell spoke with patient tenderness. He looked very big and solid and immovable as he stood by the bed. "I liked your face as soon as I saw you," he said to John. "You're a good fellow."

John still held his wife's wrist, but he rubbed his other hand through his thick hair and said angrily, "You don't get the point, sir. My wife and I were always left alone, and we merely want to be left alone now. Nothing is going to separate us. She's been content with me. I'm sorry sir; you'll have to speak to her with me here, or you'll have to go."

"No; you'll have to go for a while," the priest said patiently.

Then Mrs. Williams moved her head on the pillow and said, "Pray for me, Father."

The old priest knelt down by the bed, and with a sweet unruffled expression on his florid face he began to pray. At times his breath came with a whistling noise as though a rumbling were inside him, and at other times he sighed and was full of sorrow. He was praying that young Mrs. Williams might get better, and while he prayed he knew that her husband was more afraid of losing her to the Church than losing her to death.

All the time Father Macdowell was on his knees, with his heavy prayer book in his two hands, John kept staring at him. John couldn't understand the old priest's patience and tolerance. He wanted to quarrel with him, but he kept on watching the light from overhead shining on the one baby-pink bald spot on the smooth, white head, and at last he burst out, "You don't understand, sir! We've been very happy together. Neither you nor her people came near her when she was in good health, so why should you bother her now? I don't want anything to separate us now; neither does she. She came with me. You see you'd be separating us, don't you?" He was trying to talk like a reasonable man who had no prejudices.

Father Macdowell got up clumsily. His knees hurt him, for the floor was hard. He said to Mrs. Williams in quite a loud voice, "Did you really intend to give up everything for this young fellow?" and he bent down close to her so he could hear.

"Yes, Father," she whispered.

"In Heaven's name, child, you couldn't have known what you were doing."

"We loved each other, Father. We've been very happy."

"All right. Supposing you were. What now? What about all eternity, child?"

"Oh, Father, I'm very sick and I'm afraid." She looked up to try to show him how scared she was, and how much she wanted him to give her peace.

He sighed and seemed distressed, and at last he said to John, "Were you married in the church?"

"No, we weren't. Look here, we're talking pretty loud and it upsets her."

"Ah, it's a crime that I'm hard of hearing, I know. Never mind. I'll go." Picking up his coat, he put it over his arm; then he sighed as if he were tired, and he said, "I wonder if you'd fetch me a glass of water. I'd thank you for it."

John hesitated, glancing at the tired old priest, who looked so pink and white and almost cherubic in his utter lack of guile.

"What's the matter?" Father Macdowell said.

John was ashamed of himself at appearing so sullen, so he said hastily, "Nothing's the matter. Just a moment. I won't be a moment." He hurried out of the room.

The old priest looked down at the floor and shook his head; and then, sighing and feeling uneasy, he bent over Mrs. Williams, with his good ear down to her, and he said, "I'll just ask you a few questions in a hurry, my child. You answer them quickly and I'll give you absolution." He made the sign of the cross over her and asked if she repented for having strayed from the Church, and if she had often been angry, and whether she had always been faithful, and if she had ever lied or stolen – all so casually and quickly as if it had not occurred to him that such a young woman could have serious sins. In the same breath he muttered, "Say a good act of contrition to yourself and that will be all, my dear." He had hardly taken a minute.

When John returned to the room with the glass of water in his hand, he saw the old priest making the sign of the cross. Father Macdowell went on praying without looking up at John. When he had finished, he turned and said, "Oh, there you are. Thanks for the water. I needed it. Well, my boy, I'm sorry if I worried you."

John looked at his wife, who had closed her eyes, and he sat down on the end of the bed. He was too disappointed to speak.

Father Macdowell, who was expecting trouble, said, "Don't be harsh, lad."

"I'm not harsh," he said mildly, looking up at the priest. "But you weren't quite fair. And it's as though she turned away from me at the last moment. I didn't think she needed you."

"God bless you, bless the both of you. She'll get better," Father Macdowell said. But he felt ill at ease as he put on his coat, and he couldn't look directly at John.

Going along the hall, he spoke to Miss Stanhope, who wanted to apologize for her brother-in-law's attitude. "I'm sorry if it was unpleasant for you, Father," she said.

"It wasn't unpleasant," he said. "I was glad to meet John. He's a fine fellow. It's a great pity he isn't Catholic. I don't know as I played fair with him."

As he went down the stairs, puffing and sighing, he pondered the question of whether he had played fair with the young

man. But by the time he reached the street he was rejoicing amiably to think he had so successfully ministered to one who had
strayed from the faith and had called out to him at the last
moment. Walking along with the rolling motion as if his feet
hurt him, he muttered, "Of course they were happy as they
were... in a worldly way. I wonder if I did come between them?"

He shuffled along, feeling very tired, and couldn't help
thinking, "What beauty there was to his staunch love for her!"
Then he added quickly, "But it was just a pagan beauty, of
course."

As he began to wonder about the nature of this beauty, for
some reason he felt inexpressibly sad.

ALICE MUNRO

WILD SWANS

Flo said to watch out for White Slavers. She said this was how they operated: an old woman, a motherly or grandmotherly sort, made friends while riding beside you on a bus or train. She offered you candy, which was drugged. Pretty soon you began to droop and mumble, were in no condition to speak for yourself. Oh, Help, the woman said, my daughter (granddaughter) is sick, please somebody help me get her off so that she can recover in the fresh air. Up stepped a polite gentleman, pretending to be a stranger, offering assistance. Together, at the next stop, they hustled you off the train or bus, and that was the last the ordinary world ever saw of you. They kept you a prisoner in the White Slave place (to which you had been transported drugged and bound so you wouldn't even know where you were), until such time as you were thoroughly degraded and in despair, your mind destroyed by drugs, your hair and teeth fallen out. It took about three years, for you to get to this state. You wouldn't want to go home, then, maybe couldn't remember home, or find your way if you did. So they let you out on the streets.

Flo took ten dollars and put it in a little cloth bag which she sewed to the strap of Rose's slip. Another thing likely to happen was that Rose would get her purse stolen.

Watch out, Flo said as well, for people dressed up as ministers. They were the worst. That disguise was commonly adopted by White Slavers, as well as those after your money.

Rose said she didn't see how she could tell which ones were disguised.

Flo had worked in Toronto once. She had worked as a waitress in a coffee shop in Union Station. That was how she knew all she knew. She never saw sunlight, in those days, except on her days off. But she saw plenty else. She saw a man cut another man's stomach with a knife, just pull out his shirt and do a tidy cut, as if it was a watermelon not a stomach. The stomach's owner just sat looking down surprised, with no time to protest. Flo implied that that was nothing, in Toronto. She saw two bad women (that was what Flo called whores, running the two words together, like badminton) get into a fight, and a man laughed at them, other men stopped and laughed and egged them on, and they had their fists full of each other's hair. At last the police came and took them away, still howling and yelping.

She saw a child die of a fit, too. Its face was black as ink.

"Well, I'm not scared," said Rose provokingly. "There's the police, anyway."

"Oh, them! They'd be the first ones to diddle you!"

She did not believe anything Flo said on the subject of sex. Consider the undertaker.

A little bald man, very neatly dressed, would come into the store sometimes and speak to Flo with a placating expression.

"I only wanted a bag of candy. And maybe a few packages of gum. And one or two chocolate bars. Could you go to the trouble of wrapping them?"

Flo in her mock-deferential tone would assure him that she could. She wrapped them in heavy-duty white paper, so they were something like presents. He took his time with the selection, humming and chatting, then dawdled for a while. He might ask how Flo was feeling. And how Rose was, if she was there.

"You look pale. Young girls need fresh air." To Flo he would say, "You work too hard. You've worked hard all your life."

"No rest for the wicked," Flo would say agreeably.

When he went out she hurried to the window. There it was – the old black hearse with its purple curtains.

"He'll be after them today!" Flo would say as the hearse rolled away at a gentle pace, almost a funeral pace. The little man had been an undertaker, but he was retired now. The hearse was retired too. His sons had taken over the undertaking and bought a new one. He drove the old hearse all over the country, looking for women. So Flo said. Rose could not believe it. Flo said he gave them the gum and the candy. Rose said he probably ate them himself. Flo said he had been seen, he had been heard. In mild weather he drove with the windows down, singing, to himself or to somebody out of sight in the back:

> *Her brow is like the snowdrift*
> *Her throat is like the swan*

Flo imitated him singing. Gently overtaking some woman walking on a back road, or resting at a country crossroads. All compliments and courtesy and chocolate bars, offering a ride. Of course every woman who reported being asked said she had turned him down. He never pestered anybody, drove politely on. He called in at houses, and if the husband was home he seemed to like just as well as anything to sit and chat. Wives said that was all he ever did anyway but Flo did not believe it.

"Some women are taken in," she said. "A number." She liked to speculate on what the hearse was like inside. Plush. Plush on the walls and the roof and the floor. Soft purple, the colour of the curtains, the colour of dark lilacs.

All nonsense, Rose thought. Who could believe it, of a man that age?

Rose was going to Toronto on the train for the first time by herself. She had been once before, but that was with Flo, long before her father died. They took along their own sandwiches and bought milk from the vendor on the train. It was sour. Sour chocolate milk. Rose kept taking tiny sips, unwilling to admit that something so much desired could fail her. Flo sniffed it, then hunted up and down the train until she found the old man in his red jacket, with no teeth and the tray hanging around his neck. She invited him to sample the chocolate milk. She invited people nearby to smell it. He let her have some ginger ale for nothing. It was slightly warm.

"I let him know," Flo said looking around after he had left. "You have to let them know."

A woman agreed with her but most people looked out the window. Rose drank the warm ginger ale. Either that, or the scene with the vendor, or the conversation Flo and the agreeing woman now got into about where they came from, why they were going to Toronto, and Rose's morning constipation which was why she was lacking colour, or the small amount of chocolate milk she had got inside her, caused her to throw up in the train toilet. All day long she was afraid people in Toronto could smell vomit on her coat.

This time Flo started the trip off by saying, "Keep an eye on her, she's never been away from home before!" to the conductor, then looking around and laughing to show that was jokingly meant. Then she had to get off. It seemed the conductor had no more need for jokes than Rose had, and no intention of keeping an eye on anybody. He never spoke to Rose except to ask for her ticket. She had a window seat, and was soon extraordinarily happy. She felt Flo receding, West Hanratty flying away from her, her own wearying self discarded as easily as everything else. She loved the towns less and less known. A woman was standing at her back door in her nightgown, not caring if everybody on the train saw her. They were travelling south, out of the snow belt, into an earlier spring, a tenderer sort of landscape. People could grow peach trees in their backyards.

Rose reflected in her mind the things she had to look for in Toronto. First, things for Flo. Special stockings for her varicose veins. A special kind of cement for sticking handles on pots. And a full set of dominoes.

For herself Rose wanted to buy hair-remover to put on her arms and legs, and if possible an arrangement of inflatable cushions, supposed to reduce your hips and thighs. She thought they probably had hair-remover in the drugstore in Hanratty, but the woman in there was a friend of Flo's and told everything. She told Flo who bought hair dye and slimming medicine and French safes. As for the cushion business, you could send away for it but there was sure to be comment at the Post Office, and Flo knew people there as well. She also hoped to buy some bangles, and an angora sweater. She had great hopes of silver bangles and powder-blue angora. She thought they could transform her, make her calm and slender and take the frizz out of her hair, dry her underarms and turn her complexion to a pearl.

The money for these things, as well as the money for the trip, came from a prize Rose had won, for writing an essay called "Art and Science in the World of Tomorrow." To her surprise, Flo asked if she could read it, and while she was reading it, she remarked that they must have thought they had to give Rose the prize for swallowing the dictionary. Then she said shyly, "It's very interesting."

She would have to spend the night at Cela McKinney's. Cela McKinney was her father's cousin. She had married a hotel manager and thought she had gone up in the world. But the hotel manager came home one day and sat down on the dining room floor between two chairs and said, "I am never going to leave this house again." Nothing unusual had happened, he had just decided not to go out of the house again, and he didn't, until he died. That had made Cela McKinney odd and nervous. She locked her doors at eight o'clock. She was also very stingy. Supper was usually oatmeal porridge, with raisins. Her house was dark and narrow and smelled like a bank.

The train was filling up. At Brantford a man asked if she would mind if he sat down beside her.

'It's cooler out than you'd think," he said. He offered her part of his newspaper. She said no thanks.

Then lest he think her rude she said it really was cooler. She went on looking out the window at the spring morning. There was no snow left, down here. The trees and bushes seemed to have a paler bark than they did at home. Even the sunlight looked different. It was as different from home, here, as the coast of the Mediterranean would be, or the valleys of California.

"Filthy windows, you'd think they'd take more care," the man said. "Do you travel much by train?"

She said no.

Water was lying in the fields. He nodded at it and said there was a lot this year.

"Heavy snows."

She noticed his saying *snows*, a poetic-sounding word. Anyone at home would have said *snow*.

"I had an unusual experience the other day. I was driving out in the country. In fact I was on my way to see one of my parishioners, a lady with a heart condition—"

She looked quickly at his collar. He was wearing an ordinary shirt and tie and a dark blue suit.

"Oh, yes," he said. "I'm a United Church minister. But I don't always wear my uniform. I wear it for preaching in. I'm off duty today.

"Well, as I said, I was driving through the country and I saw some Canada Geese down on a pond, and I took another look, and there were some swans down with them. A whole great flock of swans. What a lovely sight they were. They would be on their spring migration, I expect, heading up north. What a spectacle. I never saw anything like it."

Rose was unable to think appreciatively of the wild swans because she was afraid he was going to lead the conversation from them to Nature in general and then to God, the way a minister would feel obliged to do. But he did not, he stopped with the swans.

"A very fine sight. You would have enjoyed them."

He was between fifty and sixty years old, Rose thought. He was short, and energetic-looking, with a square ruddy face and bright waves of grey hair combed straight up from his forehead. When she realized he was not going to mention God she felt she ought to show her gratitude.

She said they must have been lovely.

"It wasn't even a regular pond, it was just some water lying in a field. It was just by luck the water was lying there and I had to drive by there. And they came down and I came driving by at the right time. Just by luck. They come in at the east end of Lake Erie, I think. But I never was lucky enough to see them before."

She turned by degrees to the window, and he returned to his paper. She remained slightly smiling, so as not to seem rude, not to seem to be rejecting conversation altogether. The morning really was cool, and she had taken down her coat off the hook where she put it when she first got on the train, she had spread it over herself, like a lap robe. She had set her purse on the floor when the minister sat down, to give him room. He took the sections of the paper apart, shaking and rustling them in a leisurely, rather showy, way. He seemed to her just the sort of person who does everything in a showy way. A ministerial way. He brushed aside the sections he didn't want at the moment. A corner of newspaper touched her leg, just at the edge of her coat.

She thought for some time that it was the paper. Then she said to herself, what if it is a hand? That was the kind of thing she could imagine. She would sometimes look at men's hands, at the fuzz on their forearms, their concentrating profiles. She would think about everything they could do. Even the stupid ones. For instance the driver-salesman who brought the bread to Flo's store. The ripeness and confidence of manner, the settled mixture of ease and alertness, with which he handled the bread truck. A fold of mature belly over the belt did not displease her. Another time she had her eye on the French teacher at school. Not a Frenchman at all, really, his name was McLaren, but Rose thought teaching French had rubbed off on him, made him look like one. Quick and sallow; sharp shoulders; hooked nose and sad eyes. She saw him lapping and coiling his way through slow pleasures, a perfect autocrat of indulgences. She had a considerable longing to be somebody's object. Pounded, pleasured, reduced, exhausted.

But what if it was a hand? What if it really was a hand? She shifted slightly, moved as much as she could towards the window. Her imagination seemed to have created this reality, a reality she was not prepared for at all. She found it alarming. She was concentrating on that leg, that bit of skin with the stocking over it. She could not bring herself to look. Was there a pressure, or was there not? She shifted again. Her legs had been, and remained, tightly closed. It was. It was a hand. It was a hand's pressure.

Please don't. That was what she tried to say. She shaped the words in her mind, tried them out, then couldn't get them past her lips. Why was that? The embarrassment, was it, the fear that people might hear? People were all around them, the seats were full.

It was not only that.

She did manage to look at him, not raising her head but turning it cautiously. He had tilted his seat back and closed his eyes. There was his dark blue suit sleeve, disappearing under the newspaper. He had arranged the paper so that it overlapped Rose's coat. His hand was underneath, simply resting, as if flung out in sleep.

Now, Rose could have shifted the newspaper and removed her coat. If he was not asleep, he would have been obliged to draw back his hand. If he was asleep, if he did not draw it back, she could have whispered, *Excuse me*, and set his hand firmly on his own knee. This solution, so obvious and foolproof, did not occur to her. And she would have to wonder, why not? The minister's hand was not, or not yet, at all welcome to her. It made her feel uncomfortable, resentful, slightly disgusted, trapped and wary. But she could not take charge of it to reject it. She could not insist that it was there, when he seemed to be insisting that it was not. How could she declare him responsible, when he lay there so harmless and trusting, resting himself before his busy day, with such a pleased and healthy face? A man older than her father would be, if he were living, a man used to deference, an appreciator of Nature, delighter in wild swans. If she did say *Please don't* she was sure he would ignore her, as if overlooking some silliness or impoliteness on her part. She knew that as soon as she said it she would hope he had not heard.

But there was more to it than that. Curiosity. More constant, more imperious, than any lust. A lust in itself, that will make you draw back and wait, wait too long, risk almost anything, just to see what will happen. *To see what will happen.*

The hand began, over the next several miles, the most delicate, the most timid, pressures and investigations. Not asleep. Or if he was, his hand wasn't. She did feel disgust. She felt a faint, wandering nausea. She thought of flesh: lumps of flesh, pink snouts, fat tongues, blunt fingers, all on their way trotting and creeping and lolling and rubbing, looking for their comfort. She thought of cats in heat rubbing themselves along the top of board fences, yowling with their miserable complaint. It was pitiful, infantile, this itching and shoving and squeezing. Spongy tissues, inflamed membranes, tormented nerve-ends, shameful smells; humiliation.

All that was starting. His hand, that she wouldn't ever have wanted to hold, that she wouldn't have squeezed back, his stubborn patient hand was able, after all, to get the ferns to rustle and the streams to flow, to waken a sly luxuriance.

Nevertheless, she would rather not. She would still rather not. Please remove this, she said out the window. Stop it, please, she said to the stumps and barns. The hand moved up her leg past the top of her stocking to her bare skin, had moved higher, under her suspender, reached her underpants and the lower part of her belly. Her legs were still crossed, pinched together. While her legs stayed crossed she could lay claim to innocence, she had not admitted anything. She could still believe that she would stop this in a minute. Nothing was going to happen, nothing more. Her legs were never going to open.

But they were. They were. As the train crossed the Niagara Escarpment above Dundas, as they looked down at the preglacial valley, the silver-wooded rubble of little hills, as they came sliding down to the shores of Lake Ontario, she would make this slow, and silent, and definite, declaration, perhaps disappointing as much as satisfying the hand's owner. He would not lift his eyelids, his face would not alter, his fingers would not hesitate, but would go powerfully and discreetly to work. Invasion, and welcome, and sunlight flashing far and wide on the lake water; miles of bare orchards stirring round Burlington.

This was disgrace, this was beggary. But what harm in that, we say to ourselves at such moments, what harm in anything, the worse the better, as we ride the cold wave of greed, of greedy assent. A stranger's hand, or root vegetables or humble kitchen tools that people tell jokes about; the world is tumbling with innocent-seeming objects ready to declare themselves, slippery and obliging. She was careful of her breathing. She could not believe this. Victim and accomplice she was borne past Glassco's Jams and Marmalades, past the big pulsating pipes of oil refineries. They glided into suburbs where bedsheets, and towels used to wipe up intimate stains flapped leeringly on the clotheslines, where even the children seemed to be frolicking lewdly in the schoolyards, and the very truck drivers stopped at the railway crossings must be thrusting their thumbs gleefully into curled hands. Such cunning antics now, such popular visions. The gates and towers of the Exhibition Grounds came to view, the painted domes and pillars floated marvellously against her eyelids' rosy sky. Then flew apart in celebration. You could have had such a flock of birds, wild swans, even, wakened under one big dome together, exploding from it, taking to the sky.

She bit the edge of her tongue. Very soon the conductor passed through the train, to stir the travellers, warn them back to life.

In the darkness under the station the United Church minister, refreshed, opened his eyes and got his paper folded together, then asked if she would like some help with her coat. His gallantry was self-satisfied, dismissive. No, said Rose, with a sore tongue. He hurried out of the train ahead of her. She did not see him in the station. She never saw him again in her life. But he remained on call, so to speak, for years and years, ready to slip into place at a critical moment, without even any regard, later on, for husband or lovers. What recommended him? She could never understand it. His simplicity, his arrogance, his perversely appealing lack of handsomeness, even of ordinary grown-up masculinity? When he stood up she saw that he was shorter even than she had thought, that his face was pink and shiny, that there was something crude and pushy and childish about him.

Was he a minister, really, or was that only what he said? Flo had mentioned people who were not ministers, dressed up as if they were. Not real ministers dressed as if they were not. Or, stranger still, men who were not real ministers pretending to be real but dressed as if they were not. But that she had come as close as she had, to what could happen, was an unwelcome thing. Rose walked through Union Station feeling the little bag with the ten dollars rubbing at her, knew she would feel it all day long, rubbing its reminder against her skin.

She couldn't stop getting Flo's messages, even with that. She remembered, because she was in Union Station, that there was a girl named Mavis working here, in the Gift Shop, when Flo was working in the coffee shop. Mavis had warts on her eyelids that looked like they were going to turn into sties but they didn't, they went away. Maybe she had them removed, Flo didn't ask. She was very good-looking, without them. There was a movie star in those days she looked a lot like. The movie star's name was Frances Farmer.

Frances Farmer. Rose had never heard of her.

That was the name. And Mavis went and bought herself a big hat that dipped over one eye and a dress entirely made of lace. She went off for the weekend to Georgian Bay, to a resort up there. She booked herself in under the name of Florence Farmer. To give everybody the idea she was really the other one, Frances Farmer, but calling herself Florence because she was on holidays and didn't want to be recognized. She had a little cigarette holder that was black and mother-of-pearl She could have been arrested, Flo said. For the *nerve*.

Rose almost went over to the Gift Shop, to see if Mavis was still there and if she could recognize her. She thought it would be an especially fine thing, to manage a transformation like that. To dare it; to get away with it, to enter on preposterous adventures in your own, but newly named, skin.

NOTES ON THE AUTHORS

AMPRIMOZ, ALEXANDRE (b. 1948 in Rome, Italy) He is a renowned multilingual scholar, critic, translator, writer, and poet, and has published widely in literary and scholarly journals in English, French, Italian, and Spanish. He teaches Modern Languages, Literatures and Cultures at Brock University, St. Catharines, Ontario. His books include: *A Season For Birds: Selected poems by Pierre Morency; Nostalgies de l'ange,* (1990) and *Too Many Popes* (1990). Amprimoz has a distinctive voice, and is a teller of short tales unlike any other in this country. Wild flights of surrealistic vision are rooted in a sometimes grim reality, a sometimes whimsical abandon.

BLAIS, MARIE-CLAIRE (b. 1939 in Quebec City, Quebec) She has lived in Montreal, France, and the United States, where she now resides, in Key West. Her novels in English translation include *Mad Shadows* (1960), *A Season in the Life of Emmanuel* (1966), *The Manuscripts of Pauline Archange* (1969), *The Wolf* (1974), *Deaf to the City* (1980), *Pierre* (1991), *These Festive Nights* (1997), and *Augustino and the Choir of Destruction* (2007). Her collections of poetry were published in English as *Veiled Countries/Lives* (1994), her plays in *wintersleep* (1999), and her articles for *Le Devoir* in *American Notebooks: A Writer's Journey* (1996). Much of Blais' writing has been in the form of social commentary, with intermixed elements of good and evil in settings part real and part fantasy.

CALLAGHAN, BARRY (b. 1937 in Toronto, Ontario) is the well-known novelist, poet, and man of letters, whose fiction and poetry have been translated into seven languages. He was a war correspondent in the Middle East and Africa in the 70s, and at the same time began the internationally celebrated literary quarterly *Exile*, and from that evolved the publishing house Exile Editions. Callaghan was a professor of contemporary literature at York University in Toronto, and is now Professor Emeritus and Distinguished Scholar at that institution. His works include *The Black Queen Stories* (1982), *The Way the Angel Spreads Her Wings* (1989), *A Kiss Is Still a Kiss* (1995), *Barrelhouse*

Kings (1998), *Between Trains* (2007), and *Beside Still Waters* (2009). He was the recipient of the inaugural W. O. Mitchell Award given to an individual who has produced a substantial body of work and has acted as a mentor to new writers, as well as receiving more than a dozen National Magazine Awards, and the Pushcart Prize.

CALLAGHAN, MORLEY (1903-1990) was born in Toronto, Ontario. A novelist and short story writer, he studied law at Osgoode Hall and was called to the bar, but never practiced law. His novels include *Such Is My Beloved* (1934), *More Joy in Heaven* (1937), and *The Loved and the Lost,* which won the Governor General's Award in 1951, as well as publishing numerous collections such as *Now That April's Here* (1936) and *Morley Callaghan's Stories* (1959), the children's story *Luke Baldwin's Vow* (1948), and *That Summer in Paris* (1963), a memoir about his youthful literary adventures abroad. Many of Morley's other books have been reprinted by Exile Editions as part of *The Exile Classics Series.* He was made a Companion of the Order of Canada in 1982.

CARRIER, ROCH (b. 1937 in Sainte-Justine-de-Dorchester, Quebec) He is a celebrated French-Canadian novelist and author of "contes" – a very brief form of the short story – of which "The Hockey Sweater" is the best known; an excerpt from it is reprinted on the back of the Canadian $5 bill (the story also appears in *The Exile Book of Canadian Sports Stories,* 2009). He has been secretary-general of the Théâtre du Nouveau Monde, Montreal, taught at the Collège Militaire St-Jean, served a term, ending in 1997, as director of the Canada Council, and was National Librarian of Canada. He is also a successful lecturer in both French and English. His works include *La guerre, yes sir!* (1968), *Floralie, où es-tu?* (1969; *Floralie, where are you?,* 1971); and *Il est par là le soleil* (1970; *Is it the sun, Philibert?* 1972).

COADY, MARY FRANCES was born in Saskatchewan and raised in Alberta. She attended the University of Alberta, and has worked as a freelance journalist for a number of religious publications. She is the author of the children's novel, *Lucy, Maud and Me* (1999) and numerous biographies, most recently, *With Bound Hands: A Jesuit in Nazi Germany: The Life and Selected Prison Letters of Alfred Delp (2003). The Practice of Perfection* (2009)is her first collection of short stories. Her short fiction has been published in several literary journals. She has taught professional writing at Ryerson University and has conducted writing workshops at the University of Toronto School of Continuing Studies and St. Michael's College Continuing Education, as well as other venues in the Toronto area.

FERRON, JACQUES (1921-1985) was born in Louiseville (Maskinongé), Québec. He graduated from Laval University with a medical degree and practiced family medicine most of his life. But this was only one part of the amazingly multifaceted career of this true Renaissance man, who wrote novels, plays, poetry, political pamphlets, medical texts, letters to newspapers, the list goes on... Sometimes compared to Rabelais and Chekhov, Ferron has also been called the "Voltaire of Quebec." Confessing his lack of inventiveness as a storyteller, he reworks universal myths in *Le Ciel de Québec* (1969), *Papa Boss* (1966), and *L'Amélanchier* (1970). *Le Salut de l'Irlande* (1970) tilts at the notion of the racial purity of the Québécois. The Parti Rhinocéros, which he founded, aimed at a similar ironic treatment of Canadian federal politics.

GARNER, HUGH (1913-1979), one of Canada's best-known novelists and short story writers, was born in Yorkshire, England, and grew up in Toronto's Cabbagetown. During the Depression, he rode freight trains across Canada and the US, working at every conceivable job. Garner is regarded as one of the major exponents of realism in Canadian fiction. His early life in Cabbagetown, a run-down inner city district of Toronto, was the basis for *Cabbagetown* (1950), which initially appeared in a heavily edited version; only when the full text was published in 1968 did it receive critical acclaim as one of Canada's finest social novels. Garner's other novels include *The Storm Below* (1949), *The Silence on the Shore* (1962), *The Legs of the Lame* (1967), and *The Intruders* (1975). He won the Governor General's Award for fiction for his 1963 short story collection *Hugh Garner's Best Stories*.

HOOD, HUGH (1928-2000), born in Toronto, Ontario, was a novelist, short story writer, essayist and university professor. Hood wrote 32 books: 17 novels including the 12-volume New Age novel sequence (influenced by Marcel Proust and Anthony Powell), several volumes of short fiction, and 5 of nonfiction. He taught English literature at the Université de Montréal. In the early 1970s he and fellow authors Clark Blaise, Raymond Fraser, John Metcalf, and Ray Smith formed the well-known Montreal Story Tellers Fiction Performance Group, which popularized the public reading of fiction in Canada. In 1988, he was made an Officer of the Order of Canada. His books include *Flying a Red Kite* (1962) and *Be Sure to Close Your Eyes* (1993).

KEATING, DIANE (b. 1943) comes from Winnipeg, Manitoba, and has lived in Toronto for the past thirty years. She has writen four books of poetry. Her second volume, *No Birds or Flowers,* was nominated for the Governor General's Award in 1982. Her poetic fictions, "The Salem Diary" and "The Salem Letters" were shortlisted for The Journey Prize in 1989 and 1991.

LAURENCE, MARGARET (1926-1987) was born in Neepawa, Manitoba, and wrote many novels and stories about Africa and Canada. The five Manawaka novels feature strongly etched heroines and won international acclaim. She lived in Africa with her engineer husband in the 1950s; her experiences there provided material for her early works. She is best known for depicting the lives of women struggling for self-realization in the male-dominated world of western Canada. Her works include the novels *The Stone Angel* (1964), *A Jest of God* (1966), *The Fire-Dwellers* (1969), the stories collected in *A Bird in the House* (1970), and *The Diviners* (1974). In the 1970s she turned to writing children's books.

M^CCORMACK, ERIC P. (b. 1938) is Scottish-born and lives and writes in Kingston, Ontario. In 1966 he left Scotland to embark on his doctoral studies at the University of Manitoba in Winnipeg, Canada, and wrote his PhD on *Burton's Anatomy of Melancholy*. In

1970 McCormack moved to take up a teaching post in the English Department of St. Jerome's College at the University of Waterloo. His areas of specialization are seventeenth-century literature and contemporary literature. Novels and short stories, which have won international awards, include *The Paradise Motel* (1989), *The Mysterium* (1993*)*, *First Blast of the Trumpet Against the Monstrous Regiment of Women* (1998), and *The Dutch Wife* (2002)

MUNRO, ALICE (b. 1931 in Wingham, Ontario) is a short story writer, winner of the 2009 Man Booker International Prize for her lifetime body of work, and a three-time winner of Canada's Governor General's Award for fiction. Generally regarded to be one of the world's foremost writers of fiction, her stories focus on the human condition and relationships seen through the lens of daily life. Her theme has often been the dilemmas of the adolescent girl coming to terms with family and small town. Her more recent work, such as *Hateship, Friendship, Courtship, Loveship, Marriage* (2001) and *Runaway* (2004), has addressed the problems of middle age, of women alone, and of the elderly. While the locus of Munro's fiction is Southwestern Ontario, her reputation as a short story writer is international.

NOWLAN, ALDEN (1933-1983) born in Windsor, Nova Scotia, left school early, and during his adolescent years worked at a variety of jobs, all of them menial, manual, or both. Primarily self-educated, he later went on to work as a newspaperman, and published poetry, plays, short stories, and novels. He is widely recognized as one of the most important poets to appear in Canada in the last thirty years. His poetry collection *Bread, Wine and Salt* won the Governor's General award in 1967. Much of his work reflects his regional roots and an affection for ordinary people.

ROOKE, LEON (b. 1934 in Roanoke Rapids, North Carolina) is a short story writer, novelist, and playwright. Rooke has been writer-in-residence at two US colleges and taught creative writing at University of Victoria and elsewhere in Canada since 1969. An energetic story-teller, his writing is characterized by inventive language, experimental form, and an extreme range of offbeat characters with distinctive voices. He has produced numerous collections of short stories, including *Sing Me No Love Songs I'll Say You No Prayers: Selected Stories* (1984), and his novels have received critical acclaim: *Fat Woman* (1980), *Shakespeare's Dog* (1983 Governor General's Award winner), and *A Good Baby* (1989). Rooke received the Canada-Australia Literary Prize in 1981.

SAWAI, GLORIA (b. 1932 in Minneapolis, Minnesota) is a short story writer, dramatist, and editor currently based in Edmonton. In early childhood, she moved with her family to Saskatchewan, then in her youth to Alberta. Her most famous short story, "The Day I Sat With Jesus On The Sun Deck and a Wind Came Up and Blew My Kimono Open and He Saw My Breasts," has appeared in a dozen anthologies and literary journals. *A Song for Nettie Johnson* (2001) is her first book-length publication. She has also had her drama scripts produced by Alberta Theatre Projects and Lunchbox Theatre in Calgary, and at the Edmonton Fringe Festival.

THÉRIAULT, YVES (1915-1983) born in Quebec City, Quebec, is one of the most prolific writers in Canada, with some 1,300 radio and television scripts and some 50 books to his credit. He was hailed as a literary genius after the publication of *Agaguk* (1958), a poignant tale about an Inuit (Eskimo) family faced with the white man's code of law. It received the Prix de la Province de Québec in 1958 and the Prix France-Canada in 1961, and has been translated into six languages. Other works include *Aaron* (1954) and *Ashini* (1961), which received the Governor General's Award for French Language Fiction.

VIRGO, SEÁN (b. 1940, Malta) grew up in South Africa, Malaya, Ireland, and the U.K., and became a Canadian citizen in 1972. Poet, essayist, novelist, and conservationist, Virgo had been a sheep farmer, a logger, and a well witcher. Along the way, he has written about

Northwest Coast native cultures and artists. His books include *Selakhi* (1987), *Selected Poems* (1989), *A Traveller Came By: Stories About Dying* (2000), *Through the Eyes of a Cat* (2001), and *Begging Questions* (2007). His work has won various awards, including the CBC Competition (first prize for fiction, 1979); the BBC3 Short Story Competition (first prize, 1980); and National Magazine Awards (first prizes for both poetry (1979) and fiction(1990).

PERMISSIONS

ALEXANDRE AMPRIMOZ "Too Many Popes" is reprinted by permission of the author. MARIE-CLAIRE BLAIS "The New Schoolmistress" is reprinted by permission of the author. BARRY CALLAGHAN "Dog Days of Love" and "Third Pew to the Left" are reprinted by permission of the author. MORLEY CALLAGHAN "Sister Bernadette" and "A Sick Call" are reprinted by permission of the Estate of Morley Callaghan. ROCH CARRIER "The Wedding" is reprinted by permission of the author. MARY FRANCES COADY "Practice of Perfection" is from the collection *Practice of Perfection*, published by Coteau Books, and is reprinted by permission of the publisher. JACQUES FERRON "Mélie and the Bull" and "The Rope and the Heifer" is from the *Tales from the Uncertain Country and Other Stories*, published by McLelland & Stewart and is reprinted by permission of the publisher. HUGH GARNER "The Conversion of Willie Heaps" is reprinted by permission of the authr's estate. HUGH HOOD "Brother André, Pere Lamarche and My Grandmother Eugénie Blagdon" is reprinted by permission of the Estate of Hugh Hood. DIANE KEATING "The Salem Letters" is reprinted by permission of the author. MARGARET LAURENCE "A BIRD IN THE HOUSE" is reprinted by permission of the Estate of Margaret Laurence. ERIC MᶜCORMACK "Knox Abroad" is reprinted by permission of the author. ALICE MUNRO "Wild Swans" is reprinted by permission of the author. ALDEN NOWLAN "Miracle At Indian River" is reprinted by permission of the author's estate. LEON ROOKE "The Heart Must From Its Breaking" is reprinted by permission of the author. GLORIA SAWAI "The Day I Sat with Jesus on the Sundeck and a Wind Came Up and Blew My Kimono Open and He Saw My Breasts" is from *A Song for Mother Johnson, published by Coteau Books, and is reprinted by permission* of the publisher. YVES THÉRIAULT "Anguish" is reprinted by permission of the author's estate. SEÁN VIRGO "The Castaway" is reprinted by permission of the author.